ALSO BY REEVE LINDBERGH

*The View from the Kingdom*
*Moving to the Country*


FOR CHILDREN:

*View from the Air*
*Benjamin's Barn*
*The Midnight Farm*
*The Day the Goose Got Loose*
*Johnny Appleseed*

# The
# NAMES
## *of the*
# MOUNTAINS

A Novel *by*

# REEVE LINDBERGH

SIMON & SCHUSTER
New York   London   Toronto   Sydney   Tokyo

SIMON & SCHUSTER
Simon & Schuster Building
Rockefeller Center
1230 Avenue of the Americas
New York, New York 10020

SIMON & SCHUSTER and colophon are
registered trademarks of Simon & Schuster Inc.

Designed by Caroline Cunningham

Manufactured in the United States of America

5   7   9   10   8   6   4

Library of Congress Cataloging-in-Publication Data
Lindbergh, Reeve.
The names of the mountains : a novel / by Reeve Lindbergh.
p.   cm.
I. Title.
PS3552.R6975N3   1992
813'.54—dc20           92-22949
CIP
ISBN: 0-671-73148-3

FOR ANSY

*with love and pockets*

# The
# NAMES
*of the*
# MOUNTAINS

# Chapter

## 1

MOTHERS, like elephants, must always remember. Most important, they must always remember *us,* their children—who we are and where we are at any point in our lives. Mothers hold us in their memories as in their arms: affirming our existence, upholding our importance to ourselves, and making the world safe. We assume for all our lives that they will do this job without faltering, forever.

I am well along into a telephone conversation with my own mother, Alicia Linley, one morning in early March, before I realize that she does not know who is at the other end of the line.

"I'm so sorry—I don't hear well . . . *who* is this?"

I am caught off guard, and almost cannot remember who I am myself. An interviewer? I am calling to remind her about an upcoming television interview, though I haven't mentioned it yet. A newspaper reporter? There have been many of them over the eight decades of her life. An admirer? These, too. Or one of Alicia's former private secretaries? They are also her daughters, in a sense, and they all still telephone her from the four corners of the earth. It has been a long time since the last one, regretfully, moved on. Alicia's life has been less interesting to the public in the fifteen years following her husband's death, and the volume of mail has decreased proportionately, all those letters and requests and messages that used to pile up every day on the Chinese chest by the front door.

Now it is different. The pile is still there, but it is half as high. There are no longer two famous Linleys to keep track of, just this one quiet widow, bereft of the controversial, reclusive former hero to whom she was married for over forty years. These days Alicia manages most secretarial tasks by herself, or with the help of her neighbor, Martha Elsen, a woman about my age.

"It's *me,* Mother," I say. "It's Cress, your daughter Cressida."

"Oh, yes, dear. And where are you now?"

At home. On the farm in Vermont, with my husband and the children. Exactly where I was yesterday, when you and I spoke on the telephone together.

"It's *Cress,* Mother. I'm at home. At my house. With Joe and the girls. And Nicholas."

"Dear Nicholas!"

Dear Nicholas. My three-year-old son, her grandson. What a relief to hear him, fully recognized, in her voice. I should not be so alarmed. I scold myself. Alicia is just absentminded and forgetful this morning, as any woman of eighty-two might be.

"Dear Nicholas. How is that young man?" Her voice is rich with amusement now, and she is thoroughly aware.

"He's fine, Mother," I answer in a louder voice. "They're so *funny* at this age!" I go on to tell her what Nicky has been saying and doing this morning. She laughs, asks questions, and we talk lightly for a while.

To tell the truth, Alicia has always had a tendency to escape into her own thoughts during conversations, but she has such good manners that it is hard to spot. I suspect that she began to be elusive in this way early on in her marriage as a way of protecting herself from the relentless eloquence of her husband, my father, Calvin Linley, the most exhausting talker I have ever known. At family dinners during our childhood in the old house on Long Island Sound, or walking in the deep hardwood forests in Switzerland, or sitting under the maple trees here in Vermont or on the black-sand beaches of his last home, in Hawaii, Cal could hold forth on any subject, without stopping, for hours at a time. He talked about his profession, aviation: "The controls of an airplane, Matt, Luke—are you listening?—are just like the steering mechanism of a bobsled"; about his travels: "That aboriginal tribe has lived in the same set of caves for over a thousand years, and let me tell you, Helen, there isn't a scratch on the walls of those caves (my sister tended to keep a messy room)"; about Europe: "Your Italian driver is a flashy risk taker, Mark, while your German driver is reliable but stubborn"; or politics: "Cress, I know you're at college now, but intellect is no substitute for instinct. Left-wing theories are not practical." As a child I used to try to see whether he would pause for breath as he talked, or just take one big gulp of air at the beginning and another at the end. I never did figure that out.

Cal's talking was most intense when he returned from a trip. He was rarely gone for less than a month, frequently for

three months or more. When he was away, his five children
went wild one way or the other: staying out late and then
scrambling up the drainpipes of the old house at midnight;
smuggling stray and filthy animals into our rooms; and once
Matthew, the oldest of my three brothers, took the boat all the
way across Long Island Sound. The nurses hired to take care
of us—poor souls—fretted and feared he had drowned, but we
knew this was a ridiculous notion. Water is Matt's natural element, as air was Cal's. Matt was as safe in the sound as any
fish.

In Cal's absence our mother became silent and distracted,
not noticing our behavior. If one looked for her in her writing
room or in the garden, she was always attentive and kind, and
she smelled like lily of the valley. Still, our house held within
its stone walls at these times an odd, mixed atmosphere of
freedom and emptiness, and we were always glad, if apprehensive, when Cal returned again. Our life was then normal—for
us—even with its characteristic undercurrent: the ceaseless insistent rumble of our father's words.

I had the feeling that Cal wandered the outside world without communicating with its citizens, like some itinerant and
fanatical monk, bound by an oath of silence. But then he would
break into tremendous bouts of talking as soon as he returned
to Alicia. I thought it a tribute to female power that Alicia had
this effect upon her husband, but as I got older I wondered if
he even knew, in his verbal self-absorption, how often she
escaped right out from under the blaze of words and into the
shadowy protected realms of her inner self.

My father was so difficult to escape. Even at the end of his
life, a mellower man than in middle age, he would batter us all
with excited, interminable descriptions of airline meetings in
Beirut, or his work with the game wardens in East Africa, or
the latest chapter in his autobiography. And his children sub-
mitted to these onslaughts from infancy to adulthood with a

glum forbearance in which respect and resentment and love and ridicule were mingled in a heady emotional soup.

Once, for instance, he returned from Kenya and trained us in the proper method of avoiding a charging rhinoceros: "There's no way to outrun a rhino—remember that! Too many damn fool tourists don't understand that, and get in real trouble. But a rhino can't turn easily. And when he charges, he's got his head down, so he can't see you. All you have to do is step aside and lie down in the tall grass . . . Did I tell you about the tall, waving grass of the African savannah?" He had told us, of course, but he told us again. Shortly after this, exhausted by travel and verbosity, our father fell asleep on the living room sofa, and we brazenly mimicked his instructions, whispering and giggling. "Luke—you be the rhinoceros and Mark can be the tourist. Cressy—you and I are the tall waving grasses of the African savannah!" (My sister Helen produced these satirical pieces, brilliantly and with malice.) In the excitement of the moment someone balanced a ginger ale can, half full, on Cal's stomach so it followed the rise and fall of our father's barrel-chested breath—"And when he was in the army they called him 'Slim'!" we jeered, watching him—a great beached whale, an oblivious rhinoceros, belly up.

Throughout the time we shared our lives with him, we thought our father all-powerful, long-winded, poignant, and absurd. He in his turn claimed, with a resonant sigh preceding each lecture, that his children never listened to him. He seemed surprised and even amused when he said this, as if our attitude was unique in his experience, as perhaps it was. He complained many times that he was casting pearls of wisdom before swine. ("Your father is casting pearls again," he would begin, with the resigned, benign look of a Buddha, and we knew we were in for it.)

But Alicia listened to him, or appeared to. And she smiled, and commented, and seemed able to absorb without flinching the steady single-minded invasion of words that characterized a "talk" with our father. Still, when she felt the pressure of her husband's personality too strongly, she would simply disappear into herself as we watched.

Widowed, she is still skillful at this. Alicia can vanish during conversations in her own living room at teatime, and virtually nobody except the family notices she has gone. People will talk to one another in the usual way, while Alicia sits quietly with a look on her face that tells me she has sailed away again, slipped anchor and traveled swiftly off on the wind of an idea, an image, a memory. She sails on a tack all her own, briefly achieving some free, far reach of private imagination before courtesy and kindness bring her back to her present company.

Today, with dignity, she has returned to harbor in our telephone conversation. I think of a great ship slowly changing course. "The Queen Alicia," as my husband Joe once affectionately referred to her, and it was apt. Though my mother is what people call a "tiny" woman, certainly not built to suggest an ocean liner, still her small barque is solidly afloat, abundantly seaworthy, and significant. Whatever mysterious waters buoy Alicia Linley, her place upon them is assured, unsinkable, her vessel worth far more than anything it displaces.

Alicia and I talk on about the family, and she asks me what my two teenaged daughters are doing at school, and when Joe's two sons will come to the farm for spring vacation. She wants to know about the farm animals, too. Is there any news about the sheep yet? She knows they are about to have lambs. Any day now, I tell her.

Next Alicia fills me in on her own life. She tells me that a cardinal has been coming to her feeder in Connecticut, and that her terrier, Felix, has been driven to distraction by a red squirrel.

This conversation would reassure me except that Alicia and I have already had it, yesterday afternoon. She is saying all the same things she said twenty-four hours ago, right down to the red squirrel. She does not seem to remember yesterday's telephone call at all.

Alicia is not ill—I know that. She takes good care of herself, as she has always done. She eats well, exercises daily, and has regular medical checkups. Her health, according to the jovial experts, is excellent, remarkable for her age. But I have noticed these sudden blank places lately, times just like this when pieces of her memory seem to be erased without warning. Helen has noticed it too, and we have begun to talk together.

For me it began with the names of the mountains. While driving Alicia north six months ago for an autumn weekend in the country, I was surprised that she asked me to identify one of the peaks we saw rising near us, off Interstate 91.

"Is that Ascutney?" she asked, pointing out the window.

"Ascutney? Maybe so," I hazarded, my eyes flickering at a road sign. "I'm not sure." Later she asked me the same question, when another mountain appeared, blue and dreamlike off to our left. Again I could not answer, and cursed my ignorance. I tried to think of what might be visible from this section of the highway. Mt. Washington? Or Mansfield? No, they were too far to the east and west, respectively. I had to admit that I had no idea which mountains these were, and we drove along in silence after that. Alicia's hands were resting in her lap, unperturbed, but my mind was agitated.

Cal and Alicia always, always knew the names of the mountains. It was the kind of thing we could take for granted. Wherever we lived or traveled as a family, anywhere in the world, our parents could name the mountains around us, and the stars over our heads.

Their knowledge was natural enough, because the stars had been important in their early years together as pilots. In the first flying days, like ship captains, most of the pioneer aviators knew how to navigate celestially; it was important for a pilot to be familiar with the stars. Knowing the names of the mountains may have started early too, and then later it became idiosyncratic, just something they liked to pin down about a locale, like the native birds and flowers. Or maybe, I sometimes think, our parents lived so completely in their own world that they had their own geography. Cal and Alicia chose to identify themselves not with the towns and the cities of the earth, but with the mountains and the stars.

Whatever the reason, in Switzerland our parents would point out to us the greater and lesser Alps: Mont Blanc, Dent du Midi, Dent de Morcles, Dent de Jaman, Col des Mosses. In Hawaii they knew the volcanos: Haleakala, Mauna Loa, Mauna Kea. In New England, Alicia could always list with accuracy every peak of the Presidential Range. Why, then, was she asking me which mountain was Ascutney?

Helen has her own questions. Helen and I have been neighbors for three years, ever since she packed up her family after a divorce and moved north to the same dirt road Joe and I live on, giving up city life forever. Helen says that Alicia never seems to be sure where she, Helen, *is*.

"She can't place me, Cress," Helen told me not long ago, and her words are sharply in my thoughts this morning. "It's happened four or five times lately. When I talk to her she always asks where I'm living. I remember her being confused when we first moved up here, but everybody else was confused, too. We lived with you, and then rented, and finally bought a place—it was crazy. But we've been settled so long now! For Alicia to keep asking where I am . . . it seems so odd!"

"Maybe she just doesn't have your *marital* living arrangements straight in her head," I suggested. Helen was remarried recently to local writer and professor Eben Stone, but they have kept both her home and his rather than combining households. This way she and Eben and their various children can go from the college to the country, and vice versa, whenever they wish, and no child has to surrender territory to a stepsibling.

"Maybe," said Helen, unconvinced. I was not convinced myself.

We have not yet shared our concern about Alicia with our three brothers. Helen and I refer to them collectively as The Brothers, or sometimes, The Gospel Makers, because of their names: Matthew, Mark, and Luke. When we asked Alicia to explain the choice of names, she said it was a compromise. She had always liked biblical names, but Cal had maintained that a child should be given a name that had few syllables and was easy to spell. There had been another son, called Cal after our father, but he had died before any of the rest of us were born, taken in the night from his crib and found dead in the woods a month later. He had nothing to do with us, we thought. We did not speak of him.

Helen and I were given not biblical, but classical names. Helen's name followed Cal's line of reasoning, but mine, five years later, definitely did not. For a long time I hated my name. "Cressida," I thought, sounded like a green vegetable, in Latin. Having famous parents was bad enough without a name that embarrassed me in suburban Connecticut in the 1950s. My friends had names like "Trish" or "Peggy," and these to me were enviable, as was "Helen." "How can you say that?" my sister would ask, amazed. Helen at that time was reading Shakespeare and Sir Walter Scott. " 'Cressida' is so romantic! 'Helen' is just boring." "Cress as in salad," was my depressed reply, "Helen as in Troy."

Our brothers live far from both of us, and from Alicia. Matthew is an aquaculture consultant in Washington State, Luke a former cattle rancher teaching resource management in Montana, and Mark works with endangered species around the world. For a long time he studied primates in Central America, and now he serves on an international team that studies the long-term effects of the Valdez oil spill up in Alaska.

My children and Helen's refer to our three brothers as "the fish uncle," "the cow uncle," and "the monkey uncle." Our children do not see these uncles often, and tend to mix them up. This makes me sad, because the Linley family, individually and collectively, has been the treasure and bulwark of my own life. I will never forget the initial shock of longing disbelief I felt, as the youngest, when the first one of them—Matt—grew up and left home. After him, astonishingly, one by one the rest of them went away too. Away they went—to go to college, to be a rancher, to get married, to go to war. How could they do that? How could they leave me behind? It never occurred to me that this was their job: to grow up and leave the family they had been born into. It was a long time before it occurred to me, and perhaps I will never completely believe it, that this was my job too.

No, I don't believe it. I am marked by the perpetual indignation of the abandoned youngest child. And as the youngest I am still convinced, with the tenacious driving self-centeredness of the "baby" of any family, that I am the family's ultimate owner. Mother, father, brothers and sister, the house and sound, are all rightfully mine.

Matthew was the oldest brother, except for the first, lost baby whom none of the rest of us ever knew. Shy, silent, and thin, Matt was a master fisherman, navigating the sound with the ease of a boy on his backyard pond. I remember him splashing heavily out of the water in tall boots and a pea-green slicker smelly with fish scales, waving as we ran to help him haul his boat to shore. He was more than ten years older—the help must have been a nuisance but he never said so. I can see him tip the faded Evinrude outboard motor up onto the stern seat, and hear the hiss of the sea grass under the keel as we pulled, the slap of Matt's boots in the mussel-riddled mud of our cove at low tide. And he would grin when we were done, and lift me up on his fishy shoulders and take me back to the house.

Luke, four years younger than Matthew, was from birth heftier, and appeared more confident. Since childhood Luke wanted to raise cattle out West. Since adolescence he has worn blue jeans and Western boots, and I think he was born to walk with a bowlegged cowboy stride. Luke invented the cattle brand back in elementary school in Connecticut that he later used as a rancher in Montana. The brand is a splayed-out, upside-down letter W that sandwiches his middle initial, M, between two tilted L's. Luke would grind this into his school notebooks with a ballpoint pen while his friends were inscribing jet fighters, Confederate flags, and Yankee pennants.

Luke was the least shy of the Linley children and the most popular in school. He taught me to dance. ("Just move to the music, Cressy. Here, I'll show you.") Right out of college he married Emma, a dark-haired, bright-eyed artist who had come from a big family herself. From the minute Emma came into our house, with a Zuni necklace and a warm laugh and silver bracelets jingling all down one arm, I knew that the Linley family had a bridge to the real world. She and Luke moved to Montana and raised their two children there. People who meet Luke now find it hard to believe he has ever lived anywhere else.

Mark, the youngest of the brothers, was dreamy and forgetful. Alicia said he was like her father, sweet natured and forever wandering in an intellectual mist. But Mark could drive our own methodical, meticulous father into a frenzy. Mark once forgot to pick up an elderly uncle of Cal's, who waited bewildered and in vain for hours at the railroad station. Some years after Matthew had left his boat to him and gone off to join the Navy, Mark went out for a whole day, taking with him both Cal's and Alicia's car keys and the duplicate keys as well. He immobilized the household, and upon his return was not able to explain why. He just stood silent by the front door, weathering Cal's thunder until it passed. Mark invariably chose to bow his head and ride out Cal's storms. I used to think it was masochistic, but now I see it as a kind of respect.

Matthew, Mark, Luke, Helen, and Cress. Five children, Alicia, and later your grandchildren. All yours. Are we still with you? Are we all still there?

"You know, dear. I have that nice picture of Nicky you sent, right up here in front of me as I'm talking," says my mother. I do know, because she told me yesterday. It is in the kitchen, on the refrigerator, where all the grandchildren's pictures are fastened with magnets. When she speaks to her sons and daughters on the telephone she can see their children's faces. I am wondering now if she can remember all the names. I feverishly plan a series of name tags to go under the photographs: my children: Sarah, Megan, Nicky (and Joe's two, Jed and Nathan); Helen's: Michael and Melissa; Matthew and his wife Gwen's grown daughter Penelope and her husband Jake, who live near Alicia, and Penelope's five younger siblings at home on the west coast: Kristin, Peter, Toby, Max, and Benjamin. Finally, Luke's pair, Eli and his sister Lauren, in Montana. Mark has no children.

Maybe we could order personalized magnets with all the grandchildren's names on them. Somebody must make such things. I'll look in a catalog. I should be able to find them somewhere between the Imari coffee mugs and the "country floral" place mats. Alicia and her sister Violet have stacks of catalogs like this in their homes. When I visit either one of them, I often take a pile of these to bed with me at night, leafing through the pages and taking comfort from the items pictured: a visual litany of quiet living.

I picture Alicia in her kitchen, and realize that she must have been standing up all this time if she is in front of the refrigerator. There is nothing to sit down on in that part of the room except for a very rickety step stool that she will not replace, probably because it came from the old house and Cal bought it for her hoping she would stop standing on the arms of chairs to fetch things from high shelves, or to change light bulbs, when he was away. He bought the stool as a safety measure, and would have replaced it long ago for the same reason, were he still living. She, however, replaces nothing if she can help it. I think it is a matter of affection: For Alicia the things she lives with, like the people she loves, are irreplaceable. If they are a little unsteady, it's simply how they are.

"I have this one more thing . . ." I plunge in, finally, with the original reason for my call, "about the Japanese television people, Mother." And then, a nervous venture, "Remember . . . ?"

"Yes, of course. They were here just the other day, and for quite some time, too."

She sounds irritated, perhaps at them, for staying so long—she has spoken of their lingering before this—perhaps at me, for reminding her of it. The interview took place only three days ago. But early this morning the producer called me from New York, insisting that they had originally scheduled a second session in order to accommodate a senior executive of the company, who will be flying in from Kyoto next week to talk with Alicia himself. And yet Alicia yesterday told the assistant who called to confirm the second date that she was very sorry, but she had decided to give no more interviews. Ever.

I thought the Japanese producer was remarkably polite in explaining this, considering how disturbing Alicia's response must have been. I tend to be surprised by politeness from newspaper and television people, not because I've known anything else but because I am still influenced by Cal's stories of an earlier era, and the constant lingering cloud of fear and distrust over all his dealings with newspaper people, magazine people, and television people, whom he suspiciously and bitterly re-

ferred to as "The Press." In fact, when Cal decided to build a
fallout shelter in the backyard of the stone house at the height
of the cold war, we were sure that he imagined hiding there,
not from Joseph Stalin, but from Walter Cronkite and Edward
R. Murrow. Other children grew up in the fifties afraid of the
Russians, but not us. We feared instead the *New York Herald
Tribune, The Washington Post, Time, Life,* and *Newsweek.* (We
subscribed to *The New York Times,* the one shining exception. I
have never heard either of my parents say a word against it.)

I told the woman from the Japanese TV affiliate in New
York that I'd check again with my mother. I was sure it was
just a misunderstanding. To Alicia herself I've decided to offer
an inversion of the truth.

"Well, I hate to tell you this, but they forgot to do one
crucial segment of the interview that day. They were too embarrassed to tell you, so they called here. They need to come
back or it's a . . . loss of face."

"Oh, dear! What a pity." Alicia sighs. "Well, of course, if
that's it, we mustn't make difficulties. They are such a consid-
erate people. I suppose that poor man is frantic."

What poor man? I talked with a woman, and in the first
interview so did my mother. But Alicia goes on to describe the
cameraman who had accompanied the first interviewer: his
gentlemanly behavior, his evident, excessive anxiety that he
tried so hard to hide and that turned out to come from his fear
of dogs. Felix, ancient and amiable Norwich terrier that he is,
has a fierce bark in protection of his mistress, but his bite,
owing to temperament and toothlessness, is nonexistent.

"I coaxed him into the kitchen, and closed the door. It took
a whole package of chipped beef, but frankly, it was worth it to
have him comfortable."

"Felix?"

"Well, both of them. Mr. Takahashi was simply under the
wrong impression, but Felix's feelings were hurt. You know

how people usually love him—he comes right over, and they make a fuss over him, with that cunning little face and those whiskers, and then he puts his paws up . . . Really the only explanation I can think of is that he had been watching too much television."

I long to say "Felix?" again, but know better. Mr. Takahashi. How can Alicia so easily recall the nervous cameraman's name when she has forgotten the plan for the second interview entirely? There were letters and telephone calls for weeks establishing the schedule in everyone's mind. She does not remember. We talked on the phone yesterday and she mentioned it. She does not remember. But she remembers Mr. Takahashi.

"It's all that nonsense about pit bulls, I expect. So much in the news. When you were children the stories were the same, only it was German shepherds, poor things. Do you remember Hamilton, dear? Such a noble creature, and we had to be so careful because everybody was afraid of him. And finally we did have to give him away, of course."

"Oh, God, yes, Hamilton. That was so sad. We cried and cried. I thought Helen would never stop crying, or forgive anybody, ever."

"I wish I were the *shoemaker's* daughter!" Helen had sobbed, over and over. "Who cares about Cal's stupid publicity. I want *Hamilton.*"

Hamilton was a dark shepherd with mournful, innocent eyes. He had been bought to protect us from celebrity seekers, kidnappers, and, perhaps, "The Press," though like Felix only his bark was ferocious. He was with the family for five years, until a hysterical jogger called the police and claimed that he had been threatened and chased by the Linley's "Attack Dog." He insisted he had been forced to hail a passing patrol car in order to have the dog taken away. Nobody in the family believed the jogger, and the neighborhood policeman who showed up with Hamilton later apologized to Alicia. "Look, I *know* this dog; this dog is no problem," he had said to Alicia, "but the guy was going bananas. He was scared out of his skin, yelling like a maniac. I took the dog away for his own protection. Who knows what a guy like that would do next?"

What the guy did next was to bring suit against Cal and Alicia, who decided as always to settle out of court in order to avoid publicity (as they did when the woman cut her finger on a knife in our kitchen and sued us because the knives were too sharp; as they did when Mark's girlfriend sat sideways in her seat and bumped her head on the windshield of his car at a stoplight, and her parents sued for mental anguish). My parents always paid, always traded justice for privacy, every time. Hamilton went to a family in the country, and the Linley children's hearts were broken. We bitterly blamed our parents, assuming their own hearts, being adult, were hard and unmoved. We did not care about privacy. We were on the side of the dog.

Today, if Alicia had not mentioned Hamilton's name, I would have had trouble recalling it. Too much time has passed and too many greater heartbreaks have been sustained since then. The loss of a kind German shepherd is an old muffled hurt by now, gentled by more vivid losses that have accumulated over the past thirty years of the family's life like so many succeeding snowfalls, altering the landscape until one forgets the look of underlying ground.

"After we gave him away I dreamt about him for weeks, night after night, you know," my mother is saying. I did not know.

"Oh, Mother—I'm so sorry," I begin, but she cuts me off.

"Dear old Hamilton. In my dream he was always running home, right down the middle of that grassy median strip on the Merritt Parkway, just running along—not fast, really, just loping along the way he did, so good-natured and friendly, not scared of the cars, enjoying the outdoors and enjoying the

exercise, just happily running home. I would wake up afterwards and the tears wouldn't stop. I was so angry and upset. I
felt just like Helen. Dreams are crazy things," she finishes.
"I don't think so," I say. "I think they're important. Hamilton was important to you. I know those dreams."

I remember my dreams after Jason, my first son, died at the
age of two. It was so sudden, so unexpected, despite his fragile
health and the doctors' warnings for months ahead of time. In
my dreams following the death he was always alive and well—
it was all a mistake—and my job was simply to persuade everyone else—my first husband, Garrett, and the family doctor—
that Jason was not dead at all. These dreams were not crazy.
They represented what *should* be true, sane and true. It was
reality, not the dream, that was crazy. It was Jason's real death
five years ago that presented me with an unacceptable, unreal
craziness I would have to live with for the rest of my life. You
do not find your baby dead in the morning and believe afterwards that life is sane and dreams are crazy. From that moment
on parents know that the opposite is true.

"Yes, I know those dreams," says Alicia quietly. In the
silence that follows there is not only our old dog Hamilton, not
only my son Jason, but also Alicia's own lost child, the brother
born and dead before even Matthew arrived, the child whose
name I never heard Calvin Linley speak once in all my life with
him. Sometimes, though, Alicia would talk of the child, not by
name but in a shy, embarrassed way as "my first baby." It
chilled me to hear the way she said those words, until Jason.

When Jason died, and Alicia came to comfort me, she said
very little, only, "A part of you dies also, Cressida. That's what
happens now. A part of you simply dies with him." And when
I looked up at my mother I said with a harshness that came of
the difficulty in using my voice at all, "But not enough, I bet."
Alicia winced, then nodded her head. We have not spoken to
each other in quite this way at any other time in our lives.

I have dreams and images moving around one another in my mind now; one, two, three layers, in and around, over and under: Hamilton and Jason and a little faraway photograph of a curly-haired baby in an old-fashioned romper suit, frowning down at something invisible on the chair by which he stood. The lost child, the first one.

"Tell me, dear," my mother says, "do you still have those awful nightmares, or is that over for you now?"

"Over, pretty much. Thank God." There was a period of bad dreams for me, after the disbelieving ones. And in these dreams it seemed as if all the laws and conditions of nature were suspended—gravity, friction, centrifugal force—so that when I tried to put Jason down in his crib he floated upwards instead, and away from me, and then the ceiling itself dissolved, and he floated higher, and higher, and I could not reach him because I myself had no body, no weight, no force, no will. There was nothing in Jason's mother that worked anymore. In another dream my car would not hold to the road. It was both insubstantial and disobedient, so that when I drove around a curve it simply flew off the road sideways, slowly but inexorably refusing to function, as if it knew that no law applied to me, not even the laws of physics, and nothing would hold me steady.

"Thank God for Nicholas," I say to my mother, seeking steadiness now. "It's not the same—it doesn't make everything all better—but it does make life *worth it.*"

"I know it does. It makes life worth it to me, too, to have him."

Nicholas, cheerful and healthy—a miracle baby, born into my new life with Joe, after the divorce from Garrett who was the father of the girls, and Jason.

The divorce happened just the way all the "bereaved parents" studies showed. There seemed to be no way to stop it from happening, a growing detachment from one another. It was a separateness of grief, yes, but also of exhaustion. No blame—anyone in our situation knows too much after experiencing the merciless illness and loss of a child to place blame, but Garrett and I were nonetheless unable to comfort one another, unable to help one another, and finally unable to be together at all.

"The cure for loneliness is solitude," Alicia wrote in her best-loved book of all. But for me it was not true. For me solitude was unbearable. For me the cure for loneliness was love. Joe, and then Nicholas, and finally I could be myself again.

"Grandchildren are the love affair of old age," says Alicia now, sighing. She has said this before. For Nicky, it is certainly true. He runs to his grandmother whenever he sees her, and he is getting so big now that I am afraid he will throw Alicia off balance, but he never does. They seem to understand each other's strengths and weaknesses, and to work easily around them. Nicky knows when his grandmother wants to hold his hand—going downstairs, for instance—and she in turn understands that he likes to walk without assistance to the mailbox.

"Someone said that this relationship may be so wonderful, between grandparents and grandchildren, I mean, because little children have just come from the infinite, and we who are old are approaching it. And somehow there is a kind of recognition."

I can appreciate what she is saying, but don't like it very much. "I suppose, somehow, maybe. I think he just *loves* you, Mother. You're familiar, you're obviously family, but you're still not the same as Joe and I. He can't quite figure it out, and it's like a wonderful puzzle, a treat for him."

"Mmm . . . I don't know. There's something else, I think."

I hate it when my mother talks about the infinite. What is she saying, really? That Nicholas loves her because they have something in common—he is newly alive and she is almost dead? What a creepy idea! I can hear myself protesting to Helen: Why does she *say* these things?

"You know, Nicky thinks he's been here forever—you can tell by the way he walks around, as if he owns the world. And Mother, you'll live to be at least a hundred. We all know that."

"Oh, no! That would be dreadful! So inconvenient for everybody, and so uncomfortable for me. I feel sorry for people who live too long. But that reminds me, dear. I have finally decided what I want done with my ashes."

"*Mother!*"

"No, I mean it, Cressida. I've been trying to think it out, and it's quite difficult. I've lived in so many places, and I've loved them all—they're all part of me—and I might want to be part of them, too. But still, no matter what your Aunt Violet says about the Buddhists, I don't like the idea of being scattered in a lot of different places. It's not peaceful. And as a matter of fact, I don't want to be scattered over your father's grave either, in case anyone suggests that: It's too disorganized; he'd hate it. I never was happy in that climate, anyway. But what about right here in Connecticut, under the big copper beech tree? Isn't that a good idea?"

"If you say so. It's up to you entirely, Mother."

How long will she go on talking this way? I begin to fidget like one of my own children.

"It's such a lovely spot and I've known it for so many years, all the time you children were growing up. It seems a very pleasant solution. And besides," Alicia concludes, on a little upward lilt of her voice, "it would be *so* good for the lilies of the valley!"

When I repeat this to Joe during lunch he says, "But she's absolutely right, you know," smiling at my exasperation. "It would. Your mother, as always, knows exactly what she's doing."

# Chapter

# 2

THE month of March is always hazardous for driving, I find. This is not just because of the mud and slush and deep ruts that remain half-frozen on our Vermont roads after winter, but also because where I grew up, in southern Connecticut, March meant spring, and I attach to that month the same eager hope here in Vermont, where we have another four to six weeks before the season changes. I see signs of spring everywhere in March, a sign not so much of myopia as misplaced optimism. Every object, animate or inanimate, takes on new life in my eyes. I think that branches in the wind are deer about to leap dangerously in front of my windshield, that piles of icy grit in the middle of the road are colonies of migrating birds on their

return flight north, and that every lump of slush by the highway
is a turtle trying to cross. Always one to anticipate the future
more than is necessary or even wise, I rush the season every
year, and slam on my brakes with an "Oh, look!" whenever I
think I catch a glimpse of spring's arrival. I am nearly always
mistaken.

My daughters, Sarah who is seventeen and Megan thirteen,
are sleek teenagers born and raised right here in Vermont, and
fully accustomed to its climate. Used to living in the country,
they are annoyed by my enthusiasms.

"No, it was *not* a scarlet tanager, Mom. Anyway, they don't
come this far north in March. It's just a piece of old cloth. I saw
it in exactly the same place yesterday."

"Mother! Please—it's scary when you stop like that . . ."

"Hey! Mom! You tell *me* to drive carefully on the back
roads . . ." Sarah has a learner's permit, and will have her driver's license before long.

Today the drive to school is even more confusing than usual
because the road is overcast in places with a fine mist that
emanates at this time of year from the retreating snowbanks
and sodden hayfields bordering our route. Still, I am dreaming
of April and May as I drive along, so the mist and the moistness
everywhere are magical, full of promise.

In the backseat Sarah rolls her window down and takes a
deep, appreciative breath.

"It smells like Hawaii!"

This is an old cry, from years ago when, as little girls, Sarah
and Megan visited the islands, traveling with their mother and
grandmother not long after Cal's death to that odd, dreamlike
hothouse of a state he came to know only at the end of his life.
When he first saw it, stopping to visit an old friend there on his
way home from a trip to the Philippines, he immediately, in-
explicably, loved Hawaii beyond all other places he had known.
He bought land and had a house built there for himself and

Alicia, then when he was diagnosed with a fatal illness shortly after the house was completed, he chose to die there and to be buried nearby, alone in one corner of an old missionary church-yard by the sea, far from the colder inspirations of New England and his Minnesota youth.

It was hard for any of us to understand this at first, with all his professed love for altitude and the wind-chill factor. But when I walked for the first time through that house in Minnesota where he had grown up, and stood with other tourists in the room he had slept in as a child, I saw a whole shelf of books that made me think differently. I saw *Robinson Crusoe, Treasure Island,* and half a dozen others whose titles promised the same elements: Pacific islands, solitary adventures, boys alone and fully competent with tropical jungles, empty beaches, and warm seas.

"Let me smell—wait a minute—" says Megan. "You're right, it does smell like Hawaii, but not exactly. It's a smell that's sort of like Hawaii, but even more like something else." Megan frowns, considering. She, the younger sister, is imaginative and maddeningly unfocused in her practical life, but precise in her art, which is ballet. She is also flawlessly accurate about the sensual minutiae of nostalgia. "I know, Sarah! I've got it! It's like the smell in Alicia's bathroom, right after she fills the tub in the morning."

"Hmm . . . maybe," Sarah sniffs again and agrees. "I love that smell—eau de cologne and silk blouses."

"And dust," Megan adds.

"Mmmm . . . yes."

"Dust?" I have to question this. I don't want to think my mother's house is dusty.

"She has that little electric heater, and it sort of collects dust inside, on the heating coils or something. When she turns it on the dust heats up. You can smell it. It's a nice smell," Sarah reassures me.

"And there's that smell on the stairs, too," says Megan. "In Connecticut, I mean. The stairs that go down to the cellar."

"Wood smoke . . . and . . . wet cattails! Right?"

"Right!"

They are off in mutual reminiscence, lost in experiences that took place while I was present, but that I cannot share. They have their own sisterly and generational perspective, just as Helen and I do. I can't even smell what they smell, I realize. I can't love the hot dust in my mother's bathroom; I can only fret about it.

"Is the heater on when she's in the tub?" I ask.

The girls are laughing over memories of childhood mischief at their grandmother's house, and do not hear the question. Before I repeat it I watch them in the rearview mirror, and I marvel. Exquisite, my girls. I think them exquisite. I love them passionately, overprotectively, with, among other things, a gentle physical obsession that I had previously reserved—during my childhood—for my very own body. I remember secretly, guiltily cherishing the warm, salty, familiar taste of it as I licked the sudden sting of a scrape or mosquito bite off my arm after swimming in Long Island Sound in the summer, privately admiring the strangely transparent freckled Scandinavian skin that in the girls differs just enough from mine to protect them better from the sun—thanks to Garrett's role in their creation. I treasure their fine, light-bodied hair, one blond head of it and one brown, smoothly waving down to their shoulders. I love to feel the girls' hair under my hand, its winter silkiness next to the collars of their down parkas in December, its warm, lank, summer-dirt smell in July. I love these children the way any mother animal loves her young, all the time and in all conditions: clean or dirty, wet or dry, older or younger. I love every millimeter of them: heads, bodies, knees, elbows, chins, cheeks, noses, and bottoms. I even love their fingernails: baby clean and almost invisible at three days old, grubby with

tricycle riding at three years, polished pink and opalescent at
fifteen. I love the flesh and bone of my own children with an
intensity that awes but does not distress me, familiar as I am
with the wildly atavistic instincts of motherhood by now, and
also with the narcissistic, self-protective family passions of the
Linleys.

What is new for me, these last few years, is the beginning
of an understanding that in the Linley family—as in other
families of this type, no doubt, and maybe even in all families
—there is the strong, nearly incestuous and always overriding
lifelong kinship that exists among people who feel they are
bound together because they are set apart from everyone else
in the world. This exists despite geographical or emotional
distance, despite circumstance, despite time. And while they
may not be sure whether this means they are shut *out* all together or shut *in* all together, the members of such a family at
least recognize, depend upon, and ultimately love best among
all human beings those they know to be with them.

"Have you ever noticed the heater on when Alicia's actually
in the tub?" I ask the girls again.

They stop talking at once, and I realize how loud my voice
sounds. The girls look at one another with raised eyebrows—I
can see the exchange in the mirror.

"Of course not! You could get electrocuted that way,"
Sarah says. "She just has it on to warm up the room while she
runs the bath."

"And afterwards," says Megan. "I mean, after it's over and
she's busy in the bathroom, you know, rummaging around like
a little mouse, with all the creams and pieces of cotton and
stuff."

I laugh at the image. Alicia, a sweet-smelling after-the-bath
mouse, busy with all the things she has always gathered around
herself—yes, cotton balls and face cream, and eau de cologne
and silky blouses, and rinsed-out stockings and very small pink

bedroom slippers paired neatly under her white wooden bathroom bureau. And on top of the bureau a pin cushion, and in the cushion, as well as pins, there is perhaps a feather, and next to that, on the bureau itself, a smooth stone or an empty shell.

"I'm glad you two know your grandmother so well," I say as Sarah prepares to get out of the car at the high school.

"We are too!" Sarah kisses me quickly—too fast to be seen and embarrassed in front of her fellow students—and then hops out with her pocketbook and her striped Mexican straw bag, full to straining with heavy textbooks, and flapping with loose notebook paper. The high school girls all walk with their shoulders drooping under the weight of these bags, but I've only heard Sarah complain once, and that was because the straw had made a run in her stocking when she put the bag down on the floor in chemistry class.

"See you later Mom. Bye Meg . . ."

A red pickup truck roars up behind us, slowing down past the school to honk at the group of girls congregating around Sarah on the sidewalk. Some of the girls laugh and wave back. Some, including Sarah, hunch their shoulders over their books and ignore the attention. The driver of the truck is wearing a red cap with a visor, his companion is bareheaded. I hate them both. These aren't boys, they're men! What do they think they're doing honking at high school girls at eight o'clock in the morning? I decide I will just wait here by the curb until the bell rings, for just a minute, to make sure the two ruffians move on.

The pickup makes a screeching turn into the school parking lot. A boy in a sweatshirt with school colors yells across the street, "Hey, Travis! Hold it!" and lopes off after the truck. High school boys, not men, after all. Sarah turns and waves at one of the boys, not at me. I pull away from the curb.

Next Megan is dropped off at the junior high in her usual cheerful fog—she has to walk back to the car once for her jacket and once again for lunch money. Then I drive away in the direction of Helen's house—she has suggested that we discuss Alicia and the Japanese interview over coffee this morning. Driving, I brood about teenagers, budding sexuality, and the endless possibilities for parental anguish.

My hovering adoration of my daughters may be just another result of having lost Jason, I suppose. To lose one child may make all other, living children perfect, simply by virtue of the fact that they are still here. And why not? Being here has become my idea of perfection. Just life, that's all, with its mess and clutter, bloody noses and tears, the fights, jokes, and turmoil, and that sprawling satisfied slumber at the end of the day. That's it, as far as I'm concerned. Perfection.

This is not everyone's idea of perfection, of course. I remember how greatly Garrett and I differed on this very subject, and how it affected everything we did together. This happened even toward the end, even on the day we went to choose a gravestone for Jason. We thought we could find a small and simple stone, a little slab of granite to hold his name and the dates of his short life, to be placed on the plot of ground where he was buried, in the old churchyard on top of a green hill above our town. Jason took such a small amount of our time, with his two years, and he occupied such a small space in his final plot of earth. I was surprised to know that he would fit into a two-foot neatly edged oblong, to be surrounded by soil and covered over with grass. It was no bigger than the little space behind the backseat of our compact car, the place where I stacked the grocery bags.

To find a stone for Jason, Garrett and I had gone to a granite factory near our town, and at first while he talked to the owner I wandered among the stones displayed there, noticing especially the ones for children. There were lambs and rosebuds, cherubs and even teddy bears carved in the stones. It reminded me all at once of the little village graveyards I used to see in the hill towns between Switzerland and Italy—the plastic flowers, the framed photographs of the dead, the "phoniness" I thought I saw there. It all seemed repellant and strange.

I heard Garrett trying to make himself clear to the factory owner, who listened attentively to his customer, and tried his best to understand what he wanted in a stone. Garrett was having trouble, and I went over to help.

What Garrett wanted, and what I wanted too, was a stone without carving of any kind except for Jason's name and his dates. Something very simple. Yes, of course it could be done that way, the man agreed.

But also, the thing was, Garrett said earnestly, almost pleading, that the stone had to be of a particular thickness too, and a certain width. It could not be a fat and shiny modern stone, the kind other families used nowadays, the kind (we were tactful, not wanting to give offense) displayed here. It was important that it be older, purer, smaller, thinner, a stone like ones the first settlers in the town had used for their dead children two hundred years ago. We had seen these in the little overgrown graveyard in the back. It was a soothing place to walk, with its great towering maple trees, its simple old stones, and the feeling of lives long ago laid to rest.

At that moment, catching the man's bewilderment, Garrett turned to me, "Don't you see?" he asked. "It has to be historically accurate!"

I saw at once and supported this vision because in Garrett's mind it was perfect, and beautiful, and it was right that these two qualities should be represented now, Garrett Trainor's gifts to his son. But even as I stood there with him, seconding his wish, I shivered inside and grew cold at the thought of the long-dead New England settlers, at their modestly marked, beautifully proportioned children's gravestones, centuries removed from my own child. I suddenly understood the lambs and the cherubs, and the fat ugly shiny stones and the plastic flowers, and the unseemly photographs of the dead in the little Italian churchyards, in the hill towns of southern Switzerland, where Cal and Alicia once had their home.

Later it was Garrett's turn to support me, after the stone had been cut according to his wishes, carved simply with the names and dates, and put in the ground beside the grave. But when Garrett and I went together to look at it, I observed with horror that Jason's middle name, Linley, had been carved in unmistakably larger letters than his first name or his last, as if in tribute to his famous ancestor. I raged and wept at the unfairness, at this final assault upon our child's own identity and existence. I was inconsolable and unrelenting, and Garrett, who hated making any kind of fuss, went home and telephoned the stone carvers. They came and took the stone out of the ground. The next time I visited the grave the stone was back, with all the letters exactly the same size. That first summer I would trace their contours with my finger, going from top to bottom: Jason Linley Trainor, born January 24, 1983, died January 8, 1985. Often I took flowers: a half dozen narcissus, a branch of wild cherry blossom, or a fistful of dandelions that Sarah and Megan had picked from our lawn and stuffed into a pickle jar.

I am thinking about death and about love, about the idea of perfection and the imperfect surprises of my life, and finally about the living children now moving along, just as we did, toward the sexual awareness that will keep life going on. Where is Planned Parenthood, anyway, I wonder, as I pull into my sister's driveway.

"They've moved," Helen tells me. "They're over on Bank Street now, in new offices. Somebody asked me to come help paint them. I said no thanks, I'm already fixed—my plans are over. Why, Cress? You're *not* pregnant again—you promised!" (Nicholas's birth, though joyfully anticipated, turned out to be complicated and it was decided that it should be my last.) I shake my head, smiling at her. She looks like a little girl, my big sister, standing in her blue jeans and a soft blue flannel shirt, fair haired and barefoot in the sunny open doorway of her home. The house is a kind of expanded log cabin in a clearing, surrounded by woods and, in the summer, by wild birds seen nowhere else in the area. People who have lived here a long time comment with disbelief on the birds they see at Helen's house. An indigo bunting? Can it be? A pair of Blackburnian warblers? But we haven't had those on this road for years!

I myself am not surprised at all. Megan, who is like her, said to me not long ago and with simple certainty, "Helen is magic." I have always thought so. She seems able to live in several worlds at once and attracts exotic birds, shy children, and brilliant, difficult men. Helen can find a dozen four-leaf clovers in a meadow in five minutes just by walking through it on her way somewhere, though the rest of us may have combed the area for a whole afternoon and found none at all.

"It's not me," I tell Helen, "It's the girls. No, don't look like that—they aren't pregnant either—or not to my knowledge. I was just thinking about sex and our children."

"Better not to think!" Helen warns me. "Do you want coffee? I'll get some."

Over coffee we talk about sex education, first our children's and then our own. The children are casually well informed at this age and we were well informed too. Cal was oppressively thorough on this topic, sitting me down at the age of twelve or thirteen and outlining every possible biological detail about the meeting of egg and sperm. I remember and remind Helen that he finished by impressing upon me over and over what at the time seemed like just another of Cal's boring facts: the exact moment in her menstrual cycle when a woman is most likely to conceive should she have intercourse. Helen and I burst out laughing.

"The rhythm method!" Helen crows, "Cal was trying to teach us the rhythm method!"

"Oh, my God. You're right! Remember what they used to say? 'What do you call people who use the rhythm method?' "

" 'Parents,' of course! How could I forget? Do you think anybody ever uses it anymore?"

"Parents," I say.

Helen asks speculatively, "Do you think ours did?"

"I'm not sure they had to use anything; Cal was away too much."

"Was he really gone as much as I think? Months at a time?" Helen asks me now.

"I think so—it certainly seemed like it."

Then he would come back in his pinstriped suit, or in his military uniform, and the house would be full of him—his voice, his wound-tight, shivering energy in the daytime, the sound of his feet springing him up the stairs two at a time, up and down, all day long. When he walked at night, though, the sound was slow and heavy and even, like the footsteps of a benevolent sailor walking out his midnight watch on the deck of a moving ship—the ship of the old stone house, the ship of Cal's family. I could hear him from my bed at night and loved the protective rhythm of that sound. But in the daytime he was bounding, leaping, almost directly from his first-floor office to the big second-floor bedroom he shared with Alicia, excited with a new idea or angry over a phone call, eager to reach his wife and let go of his thoughts before they burned him. "The man is impossible! He's like a . . . a soft burr—you can't shake him loose!" he would shout angrily, and then laugh at Alicia's moderating response. "But it's true, and you know it!" Or "Our civilization *is* headed for a major breakdown, I tell you. Look at this package I picked up at the supermarket. Read this label! Pure horsefeathers!"

When he went up the stairs he also hummed a dolefully tuneless noise that Helen finally named "The Minnesota Funeral Dirge," because its somber pace and tone contradicted Cal's exuberant, never-ending motion. While he was home in good weather he had his children swimming; when it was cold, chopping up firewood or shooting at targets in the great gray barn of a garage. Sometimes he would burst into some kind of mad practical joke, getting up from the dining-room table without any warning at all to pour a pitcher of water over somebody (usually Luke), which sent all of us shrieking and giggling to find our own water pitchers, washcloths, and other defensive weapons in a raging wet battle that would last half an hour.

"How *awful!*" one woman friend exclaimed, outraged, when I told her of this.

"No, it was wonderful . . ." I smiled. Why? Because then I could join in, I could become part of the whirlwind—a sudden diatribe about something I was too young to understand ("Our Civilization is *what?*"), a sudden attack upon the person (usually Mark) who had left the rake out in the rain—not just watch it and try to stand clear of the dangers.

To watch that much force—to witness such relentless energy searching for a guilty family member and then finding that person and then focusing that force, like the blinding light of truth, upon one vulnerable brother or sister—to observe that was so frightening that more than once during my childhood I confessed to household crimes I had not committed (and still do not know who did) just to ease the tension I felt.

Helen tells me that a year ago her daughter Melissa asked permission to investigate methods of birth control.

"What did you say?"

"What could I say? I told her it was a good idea, go ahead."

Melissa is Sarah's age. Better not to think. On the other hand, maybe Melissa could talk to Sarah. Not a bad idea. Maybe she already has. I feel a little better.

Helen and I talk about our sons now, who are younger than the girls and safely in the grubby realms of boyhood still. Helen's Michael is twelve, nine years older than Nicky, but affectionate and patient with his baby cousin, another of the unexpected blessings of Helen's move to Vermont. Finally I mention our mother's forgetting all about her television interview.

"From sex to Japanese TV," is Helen's first comment.

"Well, Cress, you've got to admit, it's all pretty weird."

"You mean Alicia? Alicia's being weird?" I want to probe as lightly as possible, because Helen and I talk best lightly, but I also want to find out what she thinks. She is my adult companion and friend, but first and always in my eyes she is the sister who has gone ahead of me and who knows things I don't yet know. If I run as fast as I can, she will still be waiting for me, always, with her head bent down as it is when she concentrates, with her hair pulled back by a gold clip so that it does not fall in her eyes, which maddens her; but even when held back there are escaping wisps of hair that still curl at the back of her neck and below her left ear. To me she looks the way she did at fifteen, and will look when we are both in our nineties and beyond. These things don't change in a family, whatever else does.

Helen waves my question away absently, as if it were an irrelevant species of gnat, too small to have a name.

"No, that's not what I mean—just us, the way we are, the things we think and talk about. Sometimes it seems . . . weird, you know?"

I nod. "Yes, of course I do. Well, here's an example of weird, if you want. It's something that crossed my mind not long ago, and I wonder about it every so often: Helen, did Cal ever hit you? Really hit, not just spank?"

Spanking. It was a known hazard, though not a frequent factor, in living with Cal. We were spanked for property dam-

age—breaking a sibling's toy wantonly, destroying valuable
tools—for physical cruelty to a brother or sister or an animal;
or for recklessness—walking on the seawall by the water before you could swim, running out in the road. Once Helen and
I started a campfire on a neighbor's beach, hoping to cook
breakfast there early one morning. The fire was too small for
the neighbor to notice from his house, set majestically on a hill
far back from the water in the Fairfield County manner. It was
a dry day, and we had hidden ourselves among the dry sea
grasses so that nobody else would notice either. We should
have known better. Cal, ever vigilant, saw the faint plume of
smoke drifting up into the October air over the cove, and his
wrath when he found its source was fierce indeed. We were
sent to our separate rooms to await punishment, and duly received it—the usual evenly administered half-dozen sharp slaps
on the rear, more humiliating than painful, intended to teach.
The worst part was the waiting.

Helen was once spanked for filing some cookies under "C"
in Cal's alphabetically ordered filing cabinet one day. She
thought it would be funny, and after the spanking he gave her
when he discovered the mess, she told Cal blandly that she *still*
thought it was funny, and for that she was spanked again.
Helen has a way of sabotaging self-control.

I was convinced that these spankings were barbaric and
unfair every time. Theoretically, I still believe that. But when
my children do something that I feel is dangerous, or witlessly
cruel to a sibling or friend, and I have to intervene, then I must
face and control my own temper, and find it harder than I would
have imagined years ago. And I think of Cal with his intensity
and his anger, and I think of the five children he fathered, all of
us carrying our own intensities along with a few of his and
Alicia's. I think of the five of us running wild among the woods
and marshes of Connecticut, with Cal coming and going and

still trying to be at the controls. And I wonder how hard that was for him, and I wish I could ask him.

Helen is looking at me very directly, frowning. Maybe I have gone too far.

"No, he didn't. Cal never hit me. I keep thinking—but anyway, no. He didn't. Ever. Except for spankings. I got a few of those. We all did. What makes you ask, anyway?"

"What do you keep thinking?" I press her, and she sighs, reminding me instantly, vividly, of our mother. I think Helen looks very much like Alicia anyway, though she is blond where our mother is dark. They are both beautiful women, with the same delicate, finely drawn features, nose and mouth, and the same look in the eyes—deep blue in Alicia's face, but lighter, like a summer ocean, in Helen's.

My face is different, though there is certainly a family resemblance. On the whole I think I may look more like Cal's side of the family, as Luke does. A little fuzzier featured, a little more all-American. Beyond that I cannot really describe it. My chief trouble with my face was that I had trouble recalling what it looked like unless I was standing directly in front of a mirror. In college I used to do this so often that my roommate would laugh at me, at the sheer vanity of it. But when we knew each other better, she watched once and said, "It's not just vanity, is it, Cress? You really have to keep making sure there's somebody in there, looking back. Poor boundaries, honey. You'll make some shrink rich sooner or later." I laughed at her, an overeager psychology major, and told her I just never could decide whether to wear makeup or not. But she made me uneasy, all the same.

"Okay," Helen tells me. "I just keep thinking that it *should* be true. Not that he should have hit us, of course—abused us, whatever you want to call it. What I'm saying is that the effect he had on us, the effect they *both* had on us—though it's absurd to think of Alicia lifting a finger to hurt anybody—is so enormous, you'd think there must be some explanation of that kind. Do you know what I mean?"

"Yes, of course. Our parents were too important to us."

Helen laughs at this. "Cress! Come on! All parents are too important to their kids. That's the way it is. You grow up, you get some perspective from the world, and you get away from them. Parents get less important. It balances out."

"But not for us," I insist. "For us it doesn't ever balance out. Our parents weren't just too important to us, they were too important to everybody else, too. They still are. So we don't get perspective from the world."

"Well, no, I suppose we don't." Helen looks thoughtful. "Or at least not in the same way."

"What on earth *do* we get from the world, then?" I ask, with an exasperation that is only partly serious.

"Craziness!" she replies, only partly joking.

"But whose craziness?" I ask, standing up to go. "Is it theirs or ours?"

I stare at her, and abruptly we start to laugh again, then I move toward the door. I have to get home to Nicky, and Helen is revising a children's book for a June deadline at her publisher's. It is a story of fantasy and adventure, the latest of a score of books in this genre.

"So shall we go check out Alicia and the Japanese?" I ask my sister when I am halfway out the door, "and find out what's going on, if anything?"

"If anything, yes." Helen is cautious. "But let's not get carried away. We don't want to scare her. One of us could go down for a weekend with the kids, the way we've always done. That way we might get . . . a feel for the situation." This was a favorite expression of Cal's, getting "a feel for the situation." I wonder if Helen is aware of it.

"Sure, why not," I say, relieved. "If only to reassure ourselves. After all, she did agree to do the second interview when she was reminded. And I called the Japanese producer *immediately* after that. I'm sure they followed up with Alicia right away. So what's to worry about, really, if you think about it?"

Helen moves with the two empty coffee cups toward the sink.

"Better not to think. Don't you think?" She calls back over her shoulder.

"Definitely! I'm so glad I came over." I have a lifted feeling, a feeling of lightness, just from being with my sister. All the same, in spite of her advice, I am still thinking. I can't help it. I am thinking all the way home.

# Chapter
## 3

O F all the homes I have known since the stone house of my Connecticut childhood, this farm where I live with Joe is my favorite. The house itself is an early New England cape, built about 1830. It was originally white, like so many old farmhouses in our region. The summer after Nicky was born, Joe and I hired a friend and his two daughters to paint it light gray. We liked the looks of the one or two other gray houses we'd seen, serene and Quaker-neat, with an off-white trim around the windows. Our painter friend was enthusiastic, but then to our surprise suggested a red roof.

"I know it sounds gaudy, but it isn't," he said. "I've done this with gray houses before. And you'll be amazed at how much brighter the whole place will seem in the winter. People forget that paint is for all seasons. That gray-and-white look is nice now, with the fields all green and the wildflowers blooming, but it's a lot different in February."

He convinced us, and when I saw the final result I felt a profound, bone-deep satisfaction. I could not think why, but when I flew west later that year to visit my father's boyhood home for the second time, I observed with delight that the farmhouse where Cal had lived as a boy, a building I had remembered from my visit a decade ago as being white, was now light gray, with an off-white trim and a red roof.

The old home is a museum now, with visiting hours and a curator, whom I sought out and questioned. When had the place been repainted? Why had these particular colors been chosen? The man gave me a curious look.

"It hasn't been repainted. This is a historic site. These are the original colors. Linley homes were always painted this way: gray, white trim, red roof. It must have been a custom the family brought over from the old country."

I suppose I had been told this once by my father in one of his stories about his boyhood and the family past. But like most children, I was not interested in my ancestors, and didn't listen carefully. Now in middle age I am obsessed by them all: Cal and Alicia, their families of origin, their adventures separately and together as young people, and the overdocumented glories and tragedies of their marriage—stories that are often more familiar to other people than to the family, stories that have yet to be presented in a way that seems real to me except, at times, in the writings of Cal and Alicia themselves.

This sense of unreality may be a tribute to our parents' success in keeping their children isolated from public life and from the past. Still, however protected we were as children, our celebrity background did exist, made us uncomfortable, and was attended by a kind of lofty confusion. We knew there was glory to be claimed—Luke once answered a classmate at kindergarten, who had asked if his father was really the one who flew over the ocean, by saying "Yes, of course—that was how he discovered America!" On the other hand, Cal's behavior especially pointed another, more troubling, way: If we stayed at a motel or went out for dinner and some customer approached him unexpectedly, our father would respond by standing up and telling the whole family to put down their forks, pick up their belongings, and leave—Cal Linley had been recognized. The grim look on his face when this happened was terrible to behold, and we would slink away with our faces red and our hearts pounding, not in glory but in shame.

I am haunted now by the memory of this, and by the dazzling, bewildering burden of fame that my parents' marriage seemed to have borne from beginning to end. I have never come to terms with it, was born too late to feel the shock of its first impact upon the family's life, and have judged it differently at different times in my own coming of age. I have judged it compassionately, as utterly realistic and unutterably painful; condescendingly, as largely imaginary or delusional—a family neurosis, a kind of paranoia acquired during admittedly terrible times; skeptically, as a theatrical performance—overdramatic, self-important; and finally, I have judged it a bit more objectively, as a case of misperception on all sides, intensified by the nature of American culture, and by my parents' chosen isolation.

But in middle age I realize that I am still in the dark after all these years, and I look to the "burden" itself for illumination. I see this whole business of Cal and Alicia—public selves and private selves—as a shimmering skeleton hidden away in every closet in our family, waiting for its chance to come out and light the way through every family house, gray or white, in the city or in the country, rattling its shiny bones under every Linley's red roof.

This morning, my own farmhouse nestles down in its valley in a colorful, welcoming squat, looking as comfortable there as a red-capped hen settled on her nest, and as ample as an ark. When I pull up by the big maple tree near the driveway the door opens (also red, to keep the roof company) and my husband comes out to stand within its frame. He carries Nicholas, wiggling and grinning, in his arms.

"Boy, am I glad to see you!" says Joe. "This guy is much too full of beans. And he's got honey in his hair."

"Beans and honey, is it?" I smile at Nicky.

"Honey-bunny," murmurs Nicholas, smiling back. He does look sticky. A glowing, sticky boy, round faced and still dimpled with babyhood, but large of limb and strong of torso. He will be very big, too soon. I feast my eyes on him.

"I stopped at Helen's. I'm sorry. I didn't realize I had stayed so long."

I get out of the car and reach for Nicky, who laughs and snuggles into my neck as we walk into the kitchen, Joe following.

"The Japanese film people want to talk to you again," he says. "They just called. About the date for Alicia's second interview."

"They're changing it?" I turn back to him. "Oh, no! We finally got it all arranged yesterday afternoon. She's all *set* for the twenty-first." We are inside now, and Joe leans against the counter by the sink, crossing his arms. He is wearing jeans and what the girls call his "army shirt"—frayed olive drab with epaulets on top of the shoulders, and an ink stain on the chest pocket where he keeps his pens and forgets to put the tops on them. Joe owns three of these shirts, each stained in the same place.

"Well, that's just it. They're not so sure she's set, I guess." I stand still. Joe shrugs. "There's a bit of a problem with that, from what this woman said."

I sit down at the kitchen table keeping Nicholas in my arms but also trying to stay free of the stickiness on his hair and fingers. This is not possible, I quickly discover, so I hug him, regardless. Finally I look up, my cheek just touching the sticky patch on Nicky's head. My husband is watching the two of us, wife and son.

Joe and I have been married for five years. He is such a source of peace for me that if I wake at night troubled by a thought or a memory, one of those phantoms that plague us in the dark, I can soothe myself completely just by recalling where I am—lying near this man as he sleeps, close enough to feel his breath on my own skin, like the rhythmic patter of rain on the red roof, and to feel his steady, even heartbeat all night long. I have found him to be benign, deliberate, deeply trust-worthy as a partner, and someone who can almost always make me laugh. He is also moody, preoccupied, obsessed by his own dreams and his own sorrows: illness and loss in his family, incommunicable memories of war. Once he told me about crawling under fire through an abandoned vegetable garden in Vietnam, admiring "some of the best cabbages I've ever seen." He was a platoon leader, an officer much loved by his men, who learned that the most important thing to him in battle was to keep these men alive. He came home decorated for his lead-ership, but he told me that he never was able to stop thinking about the farmer who had grown those magnificent cabbages: what his secret was, whether he was still alive, what he was finding to eat while Joe and the soldiers went through his gar-den like nightmare locusts. After the war Joe moved from New York to the country, determined to grow enough food to feed an army—anyone's army. He has also told me many times that if he has anything to say about it, none of his three sons will ever go to war.

"What is it?" I ask him now about the Japanese producers. "What did they tell you?"

"It looks as though Alicia has forgotten that she's all set for the twenty-first. In fact, she seems to have forgotten the second interview entirely . . . again." He finishes the sentence on a low note, picked up somewhere in his search for gentleness. Twenty-four hours, and she forgot . . . again.

I can feel something in my stomach. I think it is called the pit. The pit of my stomach, and I understand for the first time what the pit of my stomach is. Not a gravel pit, not a hole of any kind, but a *pit*—like a peach pit, something you had not intended to swallow, now lodged in an indigestible place. I try to speak around it.

"I don't understand."

Nicky plays with the buttons on my shirt, then with my collar, then walks his honeyed fingers across my neck.

"Tickee, tickee tee!" He laughs, seductive.

I take his hand in mine and bring it to my mouth to kiss. Quickly, he wiggles his fingers free and thrusts them between my lips.

"Tickee!"

"I don't get it," I say thickly to Joe, mouthing Nicky's knuckles. The fingers feel like little pebbles.

"Maybe it's something about that second interview . . . It just doesn't sit right with your mother. It isn't acceptable to her in some way." Joe puts his hand on my shoulder now. I look out the window at the bird feeder, fixed firmly on a post in the snow. A nuthatch is moving down one side of the little house-shaped box that holds the birdseed, head first and upside down. Somebody always has to be different.

"It was acceptable *yesterday!*" I say. "Nicky, don't do that with your fingers—nostrils are yucky. Yesterday it was fine. Everything was well organized and lucid and agreed upon, and—and there was Felix! It was her idea! Felix was going to spend the day next door, with Martha. You remember Martha Elsen?"

Joe smiles at me, but closes his eyes for an instant and slowly shakes his head. "It's okay, Cress. It's natural. You don't have to take it so hard."

"Oh, come on, Joe! She's the tall one—quiet, nice, with that low laugh. She takes Alicia to the movies, remember? *"Out of Africa? Hope and Glory?"*

"Cress . . ."

*"Room with a View?"*

"Cress," Joe says, and now both of his hands are on my shoulders. "Of course I remember Martha. It's not me with the memory loss. And it's normal for your mother to begin having it now. Many older people have trouble with short-term memory. This is exactly how it works, I think: Long-ago events are still vivid—sometimes more vivid than ever—at least it was that way for my grandmother; things that happened yesterday are much harder to hang on to."

He leans over and puts his arms around us. I bend over Nicky and rock him from side to side, and he giggles in the place his parents have made for him, the boat of mother and father, rocking first to port and then to starboard over the side of the kitchen chair.

"What if she has a brain tumor?" I ask Joe.

"Not likely. She just had a checkup, didn't you tell me? At Columbia Presbyterian, no less. Alicia doesn't mess around. I think they would have picked up on a brain tumor, don't you?"

"Then what makes it happen?"

"I'm trying to remember. I think it's circulatory, but I'm not sure how. Maybe tiny little strokes that can't be detected—there's a name for them, TIA, I think. Anyway it's just part of the aging process."

"Part of the process! I hate it when people say that. What do you really mean, Joe? That she's getting senile?" I know this is petulant, childish. There is no reason to pick a fight. Joe does not fight back.

"That's not what I said, Cress. You know it isn't. She's just forgetting some things, sometimes. It happens."

"Great. It happens. What am I supposed to do when it happens? What am I supposed to do about this interview?"

Nicky is restless now, and eager to be free. I release him as Joe straightens up and considers my question.

"Mmm . . . How about . . . cancel it if it troubles her so much?"

But later on when I consult Helen, she does not think the interview should be cancelled. "She doesn't forget all the time, just once in a while. Sooner or later she'd know we'd done it if we cancel and rearrange things. We'd be running her life behind her back. She'd hate that! Wouldn't you?"

I am sitting with my sister and both of our husbands in front of the fire in our farmhouse living room after dinner. It is a cold evening. Tonight March is wintery, despite my wishful thinking and the photographs of thawing streams and dripping sap buckets on the local calendars. The fire is welcome; it spits a shower of sparks and Joe moves to attend to it.

"Somebody confused my woodpiles," he complains. "That's cherry. I always put cherry out by the wood stove."

"Why?" Helen asks.

"It's a wood that pops in the fire, as you see," Eben answers for Joe. "It's fine in the wood stove, because that's an enclosed space." The two men have become friends since marrying Linley women, and have more than that in common. They are both writers, old soldiers (for Eben it was Korea), and men who cut wood in the fall and struggle with secondhand farm machinery in the spring and summer.

They compare woodcutting experiences while Helen and I try to plan out the time between now and Alicia's interview, should it take place.

"I'll go down this weekend, then," I say, "and take the kids, if you still think that's a good idea."

"I think it is for now. Be careful about how much you disturb her about this, though, Cress," Helen warns me. "It may not be too serious."

I am stung. "Disturb her! I don't disturb her! I *support* her. I always have. Everyone else is disturbed about it. What have we just been talking about?"

"Don't get too upset, that's all. It will complicate her life unnecessarily and make *you* feel terrible. Of course we're all concerned. That's not what I mean."

I bristle at Helen's tone. Calm down, little sister. Don't get hysterical. Of course we're all concerned.

I turn to Joe for support, but he is not looking at me. The men have broken off their own conversation and are both staring at the fire. They have heard the last exchange between Helen and me, and their fear that we will fight hangs like smoke in the air over the hearth.

"Okay. I'll try to take it easy," I say to Helen. "I have another idea, though. What if we call Luke, just to see what he thinks?"

"Brother Luke," Joe says with gruff approval. He likes Luke, though he does not know him well. Luke and Joe are similar—family men by nature, with deep sentiment and unusual reserves of physical strength. They each tend to pit their strength against emotional stress, and can be found at times of crisis struggling to conquer grief or marital conflict or job dissatisfaction by moving boulders, felling trees, and building fences.

Eben seems to me more like Matt or Garrett. He loves the outdoors and outdoor work, but reminds me more of a Thoreau in the woods than a Paul Bunyan. Matt, Garrett, and Eben are thinkers and travelers, thin, restless men too impatient with themselves ever to put on weight, or, in Garrett's case and Matt's, to stay in one place for long. And yet when these men are home with their wives, all alone, I believe there are mo-

ments of surpassing tenderness when they are not restless at
all.

"If you call Luke he may get on a plane and come east,"
says Helen. "But I guess there's no reason why he shouldn't
get involved if he wants to. I do know that Matt left for Chile a
week ago, so we can't talk to him, and Mark is heaven knows
where. . . ."

"Mark is in Prince William Sound," I tell her. "He called
this afternoon—well, it was Sarah who talked to him. She said
Mark was cleaning oil off an otter."

"Are they really able to do that effectively?" Eben swivels
to look at me.

"To an extent, I gather, from what he told Sarah. But in
many cases it's too late, apparently. There's already a breakdown of the hair follicles, and . . . wait a minute, I'll remember
. . . a loss of impermeability. Sarah gave me the whole report—
I guess they talked for quite a while."

"Impermeability," Eben murmurs. "What a terrible thing to
lose." Eben will save this phrase, I am guessing. He will use it
in one of his lectures at the university or in an essay on something unrelated to cleaning otters. I have often done this kind
of thing myself: remembered a phrase from a conversation,
savored it, used it later on. Writers are magpies, collecting little
beads of bright things from everyday experience to feather their
literary nests.

Helen shakes her head.

"If Mark is cleaning otters he won't come. He'll think that's
much more important than Alicia's memory loss."

"Maybe it is," says Eben.

"What do you mean by that?" His wife turns on him, and
he blinks in surprise. Eben is sitting closest to the fire with his
shoulders forward and his arms around his knees. I wonder for
an instant if Eben himself has suffered a loss of impermeability
since his marriage to Helen. But he just smiles at her.

"I don't mean anything critical, not of you two, or your mother, or even the Japanese television people. But as I'm listening here I wonder if you aren't really trying to turn back a process that is, in fact, very natural. Mark, in a sense, is at least making an attempt to redress an *unnatural* situation."

"You don't think it's natural to save our mother from embarrassment and humiliation?" Helen persists. Don't get upset, Helen, I think to myself with unbecoming glee. We're all concerned.

"Is that really what you're doing, though?" Eben asks her. "That's all I'm questioning here, and it's not my business to question, so I'll stop soon. What are you trying to accomplish? And are you sure you should be doing it at all? I don't know your mother, really, but it seems to me there might be a question here of, well, I suppose one might call it entitlement, on her side."

"Entitlement to what? What do you mean, Eben?" Helen is nettled, getting angry. "Talk like a human being, not a professor, for once." She turns to me and Joe now. "The real trouble is, Eben thinks we all worship Alicia too much," she says. "He thinks it's unnatural."

"Okay," I say, "I can see how he might think that. But entitlement to what, Eben?"

Eben had opened his mouth to answer Helen, but looks toward me now, perhaps relieved. "An entitlement to forget, Cress. I feel that she may be entitled to cancel the interview if she wishes, entitled to let it go. That's my sense—that she has the right to choose to let go."

"Wait a minute!" Helen breaks in. "You're the one who said that it would be embarrassing for everybody if she cancelled! Even the Japanese . . ."

"I think I've changed my mind," says Eben now. "I'm trying to put myself in your mother's place. And you misrepresent me, Helen. I never said you worshipped your mother, any of you. I have noticed that people in your family seem to speak of her in a way that in *my* opinion holds her at a distance. And at one time, yes, I may have compared that attitude to the ways in which people approach holy figures."

"Like the Dalai Lama," Helen says. "Don't deny it. You said we all behaved as if Alicia were the Dalai Lama."

Joe starts to laugh, and then we all follow. Alicia in saffron robes, enthroned and beaming, while the family arrives in a hush of slippered feet, each determined to do proper homage.

"It's really not the worshipping that troubles me," says Eben finally. "It's the sense of sacred trust. It robs her of something, I think." Sensing our bewilderment, he goes on. "Let me try something, by way of explanation. Can each of you tell me what you consider to be the most important thing about Alicia's life? Right off the top of your head, if you would. Helen?"

"That she has survived it," Helen says quickly, less irritated and more willing, but touchy. "No, I'm not joking, don't smile. That she came through it intact—well, almost. I'm sure she'd say almost."

"I would agree," says Joe. "Your mother has not succumbed, whatever the trials she has met in her life. She has prevailed." I watch him closely. Yes, his eyes are filling. This is the way Joe is. His eyes fill.

Eben looks in my direction.

"Cress?"

I am uncomfortable with this exercise, not in the mood for a classroom atmosphere, even if it's Eben's classroom. I try to find something to say, nevertheless, that I believe.

"That she has chosen to live her life in a *conscious* way: that whatever has happened to her, she has tried to be fully aware of it. I don't know anybody else who lives as consciously as she does. She doesn't close herself off from life at all." But I am assailed by doubts as I say this. What about right now? Maybe she is closing herself off now, starting today.

"All right, then." Eben has the voice of a very good lecturer who has come to the end of class. He knows that he will produce his point before the bell rings. "I respect all of your responses, but I would contend that none of them, excellent though they are, can possibly matter as much as this: The most important thing about your mother's life, as with any human being, is that it is *hers.*"

There is a silence, which seems right for the moment Eben has created. Then Helen speaks again.

"I'm not sure I agree with you, Eben. I can see what you mean, but I don't know if I agree. Maybe our lives are ours and maybe they're not. Maybe they are our children's, or God's, or maybe we just all belong to each other. I don't know. But I can tell you this much: If Alicia's life is really her own, then our job is to help her keep on living it, for as long as she can, any way she wants to. And as far as I'm concerned that's all we're trying to do."

"You're absolutely right," I say. "That's exactly what we're trying to do."

Now the wives are in agreement, and the husbands hold their peace, and even the fire burns without spitting or sparking as we watch it. By the time Helen and Eben have left at the end of the evening, the logs have burned down to just a few embers, but when Joe and I put the fire screen in place before going to bed, we linger by the hearth because the embers still give out so much warmth and light that it is hard to go away and leave them.

# Chapter

# 4

SPRING arrives unexpectedly the next morning, in the barn, with the birth of twin lambs. The mother is one of our youngest ewes, no more than a year old herself, and a flighty creature. She takes no notice of her offspring once the messy struggle of childbirth is over, leaving them in a wet heap on the floor while she rejoins the flock at the hay feeder.

Luckily, Joe is in the barn checking on the sheep only moments after the delivery, and comes back to the house to get me. I bring towels out to dry off and warm up the newborns, who at first are just inert, slimy lumps in the hay, as ugly as a pair of drowned house cats. But they gulp and sputter blindly as we clean their faces, clear their nostrils, and rub away at their tiny, thin-ribbed chests. Then they begin to shudder into life. Soon the ears stick out, no longer slicked back seal-like along their skulls, and the eyes open, and the little legs flail against my body as I rub. There is more movement, a struggle to stand up, and a protesting miniature bleat. That's it! The infants have taken hold of life. Instantly they are different. At this point I remember what lambs are supposed to be: adorable, calendar-photograph barnyard babies. But it takes persuasion and patience. The hardest part of raising sheep is getting them to agree to be alive in the first place.

I pour a little iodine on their umbilical cords as my first weaver/sheep-owner friend taught me to do back in the 1970s, and I settle the two lambs on a pile of fresh hay inside one of the "lambing pens" Joe has built along one wall of the barn. These are roofless enclosures about the size of a shower stall, with waist-high solid walls on three sides and a wooden gate that can slide across the fourth as a door. Joe brings a bucket of warm water laced with molasses from the house, and I get a scoop of grain to tempt the recalcitrant mother into the pen. Most sheep are grain addicts; they'll follow me anywhere for a taste of it. In she goes.

The skittish ewe remains confined with her lambs for twenty-four hours. We keep her well supplied with hay, grain, and water, and squeeze into the pen ourselves every two hours for feedings. Joe holds the mother still while I bring over first one baby and then the other, positioning each in its turn under her body, guiding each eager, sucking mouth to a nipple that I have first milked by hand to start the process. I am kneeling right under the ewe to do this, and I can smell the lanolin in her wool and feel how warm and full the udder is. The milk squirts out all at once—a thick, creamy stream—onto my hand and the head of the lamb I am holding. The lamb is frantic, bobbing its head in every direction to find the milk. It sucks at my fingers, the cuff of my wool jacket, and finally, the nipple.

Lambing is an unpredictable, sloppy business, but of all the rituals that take place in our small farmyard during the year, this baptism by sheep's milk early in the springtime is the one I love best.

This is also the time of year when I miss my father most. He loved the seasonal details of country life, and when I first lived in Vermont with Garrett, during the last years of Cal's life, he and Alicia would visit us often, and he would compare rural life in our part of the country with what he had known at the beginning of the century in the Midwest. He talked of deep, enveloping snows and bitter, subzero winter days, of plowing and planting in the springtime, of honeysuckle and lilacs blooming all around his mother's house in summer, and of the animals, year-round. Aside from cattle and hogs, which we don't have, he raised chickens (leghorns), geese (Toulouse, like ours), and sheep (Shropshires). He told me that lambing was a busy time for him, too, and that because some of his sheep were not good mothers (always we blame the mothers) he would walk around the farm on early spring mornings collecting their abandoned babies. I treasure a photograph I have of Cal on the farm in 1918, a sixteen-year-old boy in a dark jacket and a peaked cap, holding up a bushel basket full of lambs.

After a day of forced intimacy with his mother and regular meals, our stronger male twin can butt and bleat his way to an udder without assistance to drink whenever he wants to. He is now tolerated by the ewe, but the smaller, weaker female, who still needs our help, is a source of nervous irritation. When we go out to check the family the second morning we find the mother stamping and pawing at the smaller lamb, and we remove it from the pen. Then Joe reluctantly, and I with impractical delight, decide that to survive at all this will have to be a "bottle lamb," fed by our family with a mixture of warm water and milk-replacer powder from the feed store, and it will have to sleep in a box by the stove.

"They usually don't do too well, you know," Joe warns us as Sarah and Megan and I bend protectively over the lamb in the kitchen, and Nicky sits on the floor beside it. The little lamb is curled up, full of milk, on a piece of cotton flannel inside a cardboard box. The children and I are about to leave for Connecticut, and I want to be sure the lamb has been fed before the trip. Megan is holding the empty bottle, recycled from a six-pack of Molson ale returnables in our pantry. A thick black rubber lamb nipple, also from the feed store, has been squeezed tightly over the lip.

"They don't get the immunities from lamb replacer that they would from ewe's milk," Joe says. "Bottle lambs tend to be more susceptible to disease."

I knew this already, having had bottle lambs to care for in past springs. Many of them succumb to pneumonia or intestinal ailments, some are just too weak to thrive. Still, some do.

"She had ewe's milk for the first twenty-four hours," I point out. "She got colostrum, and that's the important thing."

"She's going to be fine," Sarah says with confidence. "She'll survive everything. She's tough—I can tell. She's like this province I'm reading about in my Latin class that never gave in to the Barbarians. Numantia. Hey! Can we call her that? Numantia?"

"Why not?" I smile at Sarah. "Maybe it will bring her luck."

"But can we call her Numie, for short?" Megan pleads. "It's more cuddly. Here, Numie Numie Numie!"

"She's not a kitten, Meg!" Sarah rolls her eyes heavenward. "And besides, she's trying to sleep!"

"Numie, Numie," Megan persists, but softly.

"Mee-mee, mee-mee!" Nicky repeats, leaning heavily against the carton. I nudge him back. I don't want him to cave in the side of the box.

"Call her whatever you like," says Joe. "But I don't want you to get your hopes up . . ."

He sounds the way Garrett always used to sound at lambing time, and the way my friends' husbands sound: kindly, but not optimistic. It is my experience that men adopt a fatalistic attitude in barnyard matters, as, in fact, do most of the animals, whereas women are unashamedly and fanatically maternal, and as a result save more lives.

After Jason's illness and death I would have expected to become more fatalistic myself, at least about lambs, but I found that the reverse was true. The first year I could hardly bear to see a weak, staggering newborn, or one that lay unpromisingly limp after birth. That year I cried my way through lambing, but the next year, oddly, I went numb about the lambs and became enraged with their mothers instead—those ewes, however inexperienced, who rejected lambs that were small or imperfect. "This one goes to the slaughterhouse for sure," I'd snarl. "She has *no* maternal instinct." Finally, by the third year, by the time I had Nicholas, I recovered my old affection for spring lambs and arrived at my present attitude of tolerance for ewes' failures. Still, after Jason I know I will never give up any life without a fight. And I know that I don't have it in me to step back at any point before death itself and acknowledge the inevitable.

The lamb and the children and I are going to see not only Alicia, but my brother Luke as well. He is flying east today, as he said, to "get a feel for the situation." When I called Luke, I found his voice and manner curiously flat, though he said just what I had expected. Yes, he could see why Helen and I were concerned, and yes, it would be a good idea to come east. He had a few arrangements to make, but he could probably get there by the weekend. He mentioned the children and sent his regards to Joe. Then he said good-bye, and hung up.

It was unlike him. Usually, in a Linley family crisis, Luke is the quickest to react, the most energetic and comprehensive, and, like Cal, the one who talks. He formulates plans and

checks schedules and makes telephone calls far and wide if
necessary: to venerable family lawyers, to childhood friends of
Alicia's or to old airline buddies of Cal's, to archivists at the
various museums and universities holding Linley papers, or if
it is a more mundane, household crisis, to plumbers and electri-
cians and people who install furnaces. Luke always knows
whom to call. This time he offered no plans to phone anybody,
and during the whole conversation seemed to be speaking
through a fog, like someone who has been sleeping too much.

Communication with Alicia, on the other hand, has been
very clear. I have called her three times during the past two
days, each time identifying myself at once and then sprinkling
bits of personal information throughout the call just to make
sure she remembers me. I don't want her to know I'm worried,
so I use a breezy, playful tone of voice as I deal out facts and
hope they stick: "Hello, Mother, this is your daughter Cress.
Guess what? Your granddaughter Sarah just got a part in a
play! *Guys and Dolls*. At the high school." . . . "Hello Mother,
this is Cress again. On the farm. We have lambs! Yes, they're
doing fine. Your granddaughter Megan is out in the barn with
them now. She just got home from junior high! It's so hard to
believe she's actually in eighth grade now." . . . "Hello, Mother.
Cress here. Yes, your daughter on the farm. One of our baby
lambs is here with me in the kitchen. She wasn't doing well in
the barn, so she's going to be living right here for a while. We
have to feed her every two hours. Nicky loves it, as you can
imagine. He holds the lamb in his lap, and Megan helps him
feed it. She is really wonderful with Nicky, *and* the lamb. Sarah
too, but she hasn't been home as much. High school seniors are
so busy. Did I tell you about the play? Listen, Mother, is it all
right if we bring the lamb with us this weekend?" . . .

Except for sounding a little rushed, Alicia has responded
normally to all of my calls, and seems to remember everything
we talk about. (I haven't brought up the interview, though. I

just can't do it. There will be time in Connecticut, I tell myself, when Luke is there.) She loves the idea of the lamb and its bottle, and has no objection to our bringing it to visit. She did ask once whether I, myself, was feeling quite well. She said I seemed overexcited. Was it the lambs?

Joe is not enthusiastic about our taking the lamb to Connecticut. As we prepare to leave the house, he questions me one more time.

"Are you sure you want to take this animal all the way to your mother's? It's suburbia down there, Cress. They probably have an ordinance against farm animals. And it could be a real pain in the neck. I can keep it here and feed it, and then if anything happens . . ." He eyes Nicky. "Nobody will get as upset. Sometimes you have to let nature take its course . . ."

Sensing male opposition, my spine stiffens even as I recognize the truth of what he says. I am feeling the old, familiar blend of guilt and defiance. There probably is an ordinance. There always is. But I have stood my ground with two husbands and Calvin Linley, and I will not retreat at any man's opinion, ordinance or not.

Apart from my own stubbornness, I don't really believe that these men mean what they say. They just feel they have to say it. I once had an argument with Cal about feeding an emaciated stray hound in Hawaii, a mother with puppies hidden somewhere near Cal and Alicia's house during his last spring there. (He was already very ill then, and certainly must have known it, but we did not.) He saw me giving food to this dog one afternoon, and lectured me on interfering with the way of nature. There were so many stray dogs near where he and Alicia lived, he pointed out, half-wild products of the lackadaisical but charming local culture, and well able to survive on their own unless some bleeding-heart non-Hawaiian got involved. Did I think I could feed them all? I told him that I didn't approve of the way of nature, that it was just another name for human negligence. Since abusing nature was sacrilege to Cal, we ended the discussion on bad terms. But late at night, after Alicia and I and the children had gone to bed, I woke up because of a light flickering outside my window, and looked down to see Cal sitting alone on the open, tiled porch overlooking the ocean, with a kerosene lamp set down beside him. His face was turned toward the Pacific, invisible but immense in the Hawaiian darkness, and with his right hand he was feeding dinner scraps to the very same dog. I never told him I had seen it, but I won't forget that vision of my father. I will continue to take care of my lambs.

"It's only for a weekend," I tell Joe. "And Alicia's looking forward to it, Joe—she said so. Besides, think what a nuisance it would be for you to have her here, with all the sheep in the barn about to have babies, too. And you have an article to finish by the end of the week, remember? I should take the whole flock!"

My husband starts to smile at me, and keeps on smiling.

"I see," he says. "The circus is coming to town again, Cress?"

Joe has a theory that whenever I am upset in any way I create fantastic diversions around myself involving animals. He compares me to a nervous ringmaster, calling in juggling seals, acrobatic elephants, and dancing bears to distract from the fact that the big top is on fire. I understand what he's saying, and think maybe he says it because I brought my farm animals with me when I divorced Garrett and married him. Joe says he likes the animals; he's just never known anyone who incorporates them into her life in quite the same way. But I think his theory is unfair and ignores the facts. For one thing, I only brought animals into my second marriage because I had to. They were an important part of daily life for both me and the girls, and what would have become of them otherwise? Garrett was working on assignment all over the world by the time we got divorced. Who would have taken responsibility for seven old chickens and four sheep and the horse, if not I? Let alone the gander, whose temper is uncertain. Joe doesn't stop to consider, either, that if one writes rhyming picture books for young children, which is in fact what I do, one *needs* farm animals. Where would Mother Goose have been without her gander? I don't have time to argue this out now, so I try another tack.

"It's not the circus, Joe, just a little piece of the farm. And it's not coming to town, either; it's going to Grandma's house ... over the river and through the woods, remember? She'll love it! What could be more appealing than a little abandoned lamb that needs to be fed with a bottle?"

"Won't it wake Leesha up at night?" Sarah asks. She has come into the room with her backpack and her school bag stuffed to its straw capacity with homework, ready to go. I frown at her for treachery.

"Your grandmother has a deaf ear. She sleeps on the good one, so she won't hear noises at night. She always has. She won't hear a peep."

"A peep, Cress? A *peep?*" Still that smile on Joe's face. "What, you want to take the chickens, too?"

"She won't hear a *sheep.*" Sarah giggles.

"It will remind Alicia of her childhood," Megan offers, wandering out of the bathroom with the lamb's bottle and her dreamiest voice, "long, long ago . . ."

"She grew up in New York and Mexico, didn't she?" says Joe. "Private seminaries for young ladies and embassy balls? There wasn't much 4-H in Alicia's childhood, if I remember correctly." But Megan has reminded me of Cal and his bushel basket, so I look fondly at her, and agree.

"It's the *idea* of childhood! It's the idea of spring! Life! Hope! New beginnings!" I pick up the box and move toward the kitchen door.

"Yes, but do you really think she'll like it?" Sarah looks

down into the carton with the doubtful eyes of the family real-
ist, as we carry the lamb out to the car. It is indeed a scrawny,
tentative thing that shivers in the March air. Megan quickly
climbs in the car and settles the carton in her lap, wrapping the
lamb more closely in its blanket, a remnant of an old nightgown
of mine that was a Christmas present from Alicia about the
time Megan herself was born. The material is red with hearts
and flowers and little men and women printed on it, holding
hands stiffly in all directions.

"She'll love it," I say with conviction.

"Love it," Nicky murmurs behind me, then sneezes.

The drive south is always easy for the first few hours. The
clean gray highway has little traffic on it, and the quiet, snowy
Vermont landscape lulls us along. The lamb is asleep, Nicholas
is dozing too, and the girls are lost in their own thoughts or, in
Sarah's case, in the tape she is playing on her Walkman. I look
at the hills as they go by. The distant ones pass slowly, sleeping
beasts with a haze of bare trees for fur, while the ones close to
the highway flash past with brief, sharp silhouettes of tree
trunks running down their spines like harp strings. It is getting
late in the day, though, so I can't see any mountains at all.

Driving south on Route 91 means moving backward in time
for me. This highway takes me near the first town in Vermont
where Garrett and I lived and taught in our early twenties,
before the girls were born. We moved north after college in the
late sixties, he to teach English and art in a regional high school,
while I taught a dozen well-scrubbed second graders in a community down the valley. My school was small but new, and its
construction marked the first time the children in the elementary grades were all together under one educational roof, rather
than in one-room schoolhouses spread out over a wide area.
The town itself had been settled by Italian families of a generation back who had come to build the railways at the turn of
the century. Lombardy poplars lined the roads that wound up

into the hills, and a band played on the town green in the summer. There was a river and a furniture factory that employed most of the town's citizens. Nobody was wealthy, everybody was related to everybody else in some way, and the whole community was proud of the school. Not only did all the parents show up at school functions, but all the grandparents and uncles and aunts and cousins as well. It was a wonderful place to teach, and maybe the school was what knit the town together so well, the way the railroad had stitched together the two sides of the valley, joining the community and the generations.

"What is it about Leesha, anyway?"

I am startled back to the present moment, and to Sarah in the seat next to me. She has removed her earphones and is looking at me in a piercingly inquisitive way.

"What do you mean?" I want a little time before I answer, and after all, she could be asking about any of a number of things. But of course, being Sarah, she goes straight to the point.

"Why are you always calling her, and talking to Aunt Helen about her? Why were you on the phone with Uncle Luke? What's going on? Does she have cancer or something?"

I take a deep breath. "No, Sarah, she doesn't have cancer. Nothing like that. I don't really know what's going on. Nothing much, I hope. We've been a little worried about her lately, that's all. I should have known you'd guess that."

"Guess! Anybody would! You act like she's dying or losing her mind or something."

"I do?" I am genuinely surprised. "How could I? She's certainly not dying, and I don't think she's losing her mind at all."

"Then what is it?" Sarah is impatient. She wants to get the air cleared of whatever nonsensical adult mystery this might be and continue with her own life.

"I'm not—we're not sure. It seems as if your grandmother is having a little memory loss. Her memory is just sort of . . . fading away, I guess." I look at the horizon as I tell Sarah this. I wonder how she'll take it. Will she feel the threat of being erased, lost along with memory, as I have felt it?

She doesn't say anything for a moment, then clears her throat. "And?"

I look over at her, puzzled. "What do you mean, 'And'?"

"And what else? That isn't it, is it? That isn't all? Memory loss?" She sounds incredulous. How could anyone worry about a little memory loss? What's the big deal? I am trying to think of a way to explain.

"Well, of course it's normal to have some memory loss as you get older, but it seems worrisome to Alicia because it's so new. She's forgotten an interview that's been scheduled for some time. It's supposed to take place next week, in fact, and if it doesn't it will be very awkward, especially for the television people."

"Television people!" Sarah mutters, making me want to laugh because she sounds so much like Cal. "Why can't she just forget it? I mean really, just cancel it?"

"We talked about that, but it seemed too tricky." This sounds lame and wishy-washy to me. I try again. "Helen thought Alicia would hate to know we'd done that, if she ever found out." Sarah admires Helen, so she considers this.

"Maybe . . . What else is going on?"

I can't think. What else? Then I remember the mountains, and I begin to tell Sarah about the drive last autumn, how different it was to have Alicia asking me the names of the mountains. Sarah listens respectfully now. She can tell this is important to me, and she pays attention the way any other woman would, any sympathetic friend. Then when I finish talking she shakes her head.

"But don't you see, Mom? It doesn't matter now. She

doesn't have to know the names of those mountains anymore. Those aren't her mountains, they're *our* mountains. Don't you see?"

"Oh, Sarah, what a thing to say!" Then I reconsider. "Maybe so," I say slowly. "Maybe I do see."

What I can definitely see is Sarah herself, patient and perfectly convinced, putting the earphones back on again. All I can hear is the echo of her voice, which is my own. My own voice, raised in anxious conviction, coming back at me from all the years at home and all of my long-distance telephone conversations with Alicia over the years, reverberating along the wires and down the generations, into the front seat of my own car.

"Hi, Nick! I'm the tickle monster—watch out for the tickle monster! Wheeeee!" The backseat passengers have woken up, and Megan nuzzles her head and a sweep of shining hair into her little brother's face and shoulder until he chokes and hiccups with laughter, pushing her away with hands still damp from an apple he has partly eaten and then discarded in some invisible spot in his car seat. We are moving along now, through Springfield, Massachusetts, with cars coming in and around me every which way as Megan feeds the lamb another bottle—tepid, but welcome—and Sarah points out the Basketball Hall of Fame. (Who in her life plays basketball?)

Finally we get to Hartford, then after a quiet stretch there is New Haven, and at last the turn for the Wilbur Cross Parkway. I dive into the exit like a rabbit into its own familiar burrow, away from the fearful whine and rumble of the other highway, where accumulated trucks and traffic are roaring on without me toward New York.

Here on this road are the old bridges I love with the faces or the flower-and-fruit motifs carved into the center arches. Here the trees already have a fuzz of almost-budding branches in a reddish haze along the sides of the macadam. The Wilbur Cross, and the Merritt Parkway to which it courteously surrenders, do not seem as terrifyingly fast as the interstates. Perhaps it is because there are no trucks on the highway, belonging as it does to the family rather than to commerce. I have traveled the Merritt beside these trees and under these bridges since I was Nicky's age. Alicia used to take us to *her* mother's house, from Connecticut to New Jersey, across the George Washington Bridge. The Little Red Lighthouse stood beneath it, a sight we would crane our necks to aching point to see, and just about then Hamilton would throw up in the back of the station wagon. None of the children in the family got car sick, but the dog did, almost always. Why had we brought him? Was he Alicia's circus?

The final roads are little ones. Subdued, early evening suburban driving, from highway exit along quiet streets in the company of station wagons smaller now than the ones Alicia and my friends' mothers used to drive, but with the same destinations, I'm sure: baseball practice, dancing school, birthday parties, the train station. I remember Alicia waiting with the other mothers at dancing school, sitting in a folding chair near the open door to the studio, wearing a boiled-wool jacket with silver buttons and a pair of soft boots (après-ski, Alicia called them). I remember driving with Alicia to buy clothes for summer camp at the sports shop, and I remember her sewing name tapes on all of them—shorts, shirts, even socks—late into the night. I remember Alicia behind the wheel of her station wagon, she so small and it so enormous, painted "Gun-Metal Gray," a color Cal had chosen because he said it was inconspicuous. She was the only mother driving a battleship to football games. I remember a hint of 1950s fins over the taillights, nothing flashy.

Finally I pull into my mother's driveway, hearing the satisfying crunch of tires on gravel and then silence as the car comes to a stop before the children realize where they are and tumble out excitedly. Up the steps I carry Nicholas, sleepily protected in his quilt and blinking at the light over the doorway. We are met there by my brother, Luke.

"Luke! I didn't think you'd be here yet! How's Emma?" I speak over the bustle of daughters behind me, Megan hurrying the lamb to shelter, Sarah complaining that she is being shoved.

"Gone, departed. I don't know where she is," he answers me in a low voice. His face looks gaunt and newly lined. I have never seen him look so worn.

The girls rush past us both to greet their grandmother Alicia, who is standing a little further back in the light of the kitchen. She is entirely present, embracing, laughing, delighted to see them and exclaiming at the lamb.

I set Nicky down inside the door and close it behind us, then hug my brother Luke as tightly as I can, giving him an embrace that does not ask who in the family is missing or malfunctioning or even misinformed, but simply establishes that here I am, for whatever that might be worth to him, for whatever good his sister can do.

# Chapter

## 5

ALICIA'S house this evening is a commotion of greetings.
After the first embraces at the door, Luke and I follow our
mother as she urges the chattering children along the hall toward her living room.

"Yes, Nicky, I do see the lamb. What a sweet little creature!
I'm so glad you brought him to visit me. What did you say,
Megan? Her? I'm sorry, I didn't know. A little ewe. And you
really nurse her with a bottle? Yourself? My! What a lot you
children have learned growing up in the country. Sarah, I think
the way you're wearing your hair now is *terribly* becoming. And
you keep it so nicely, too. You must have a great many beaux."
She calls back to us over her shoulder, "Violet is here! Isn't that

lovely?" Aunt Violet? I had no idea she was visiting. I look at
Luke, but he just raises his eyebrows and shrugs. I think he
must have lost ten pounds since I last saw him a year ago. His
face is more like Matt's now, not enough flesh on it to smooth
over and hide the bones. I notice the sharp edge to his jaw, and
my eyes are drawn again to the lines in his forehead.

Alicia moves before us lightly wearing a floor-length house-
coat or "wrapper," as she calls any piece of clothing that can
be worn over a nightgown or a slip. This one is cotton, a bright
print, designed perhaps along the lines of a Chinese worker's
jacket, but much more colorfully. It has at least fifty cloth-
covered buttons going all the way down the front of it, and a
climbing lattice of deeper pink, hibiscuslike flowers on slim
dark vines going all the way up. Inside the loose sleeves my
mother's arms wave winglike behind her grandchildren, whom
she fans with attentive gestures and shoos forward at the same
time.

Before we have quite reached the other room Felix is upon
us, a rush of bouncing terrier fur, barking and jumping at the
carton in Megan's arms until Luke, at Alicia's bidding, lets him
out the way we came in.

"Don't worry about him, dear," Alicia reassures Megan,
who is holding the lamb's box high in her arms, her small face
fierce with protective alarm. "He's just terribly excited. I really
don't think he'll hurt the little lamb."

"I'm sorry. We shouldn't have brought it," I begin, but
Megan and Sarah both glare at me, so I say no more.

"Don't be silly, dear!" Alicia says. "We'll let Felix run
around outside and get it all out of his system, and when he
comes in again I can put him in my bedroom."

"Oh, no. That's not fair to Felix. The girls can take the lamb
upstairs!" Out of the corner of my eye I see that Luke is beginning to smile. I think of Joe and move purposefully on into the
living room.

The quiet teatime beauty and order of Alicia's house rees-
tablishes itself here, and I take in its atmosphere with awe, as I
do each time I enter this room. It has such peace, my mother's
own essence: stillness, containment, a wordless sufficiency.
Here there is no need for Alicia to write or even to speak. The
room speaks for her and of her. There are the books, hundreds
of them, packed too tightly into twin bookshelves on either side
of her desk under the window, and spilling over into piles on
the tables below. Represented here are writers whose works
she has loved for years: Saint Exupéry, Virginia Woolf, Teil-
hard de Chardin, Rilke. Here also are the books other people
have sent to her to read, writers who have become honored
guests on her shelf, if not family: Doris Lessing, John McPhee,
Gretel Ehrlich. Then there are the books sent by hopeful editors
for her review, the reference books, and finally the books she
buys for her reading group, which consists of a half-dozen close
friends and contemporaries who meet once a month at Aunt
Violet's apartment in New York. They started years ago with
Isak Dinesen's *Seven Gothic Tales,* and are currently following
Joseph Campbell's bliss.

The walls make a mixed statement: A black and white Polish tapestry with a pattern of cranelike birds hangs on the long
wall by the stairway; a fin de siècle mirror in the gilded shape
of a hot-air balloon hangs over the Chinese chest by the front
door; and an oil painting of a French farmhouse at dusk deco-
rates the opposite wall above the fireplace. The tapestry was a
gift from Helen. Both my mother and sister like having fabrics
to warm their walls the way an Oriental rug warms a floor.
The oil painting, somber in tone but with an unusual light in
its background sky, is one my parents bought in France before
the war, but the balloon mirror, with its associations of buoyancy, self-examination, reflectiveness, and ornament, must have
been inherited from my maternal grandmother.

There are always flowers in Alicia's house: an indigo blue

bowl of crocus on one windowsill and two plain clay pots of paperwhite narcissus on another. Between these like an altar-piece stands a wooden statue of St. Francis facing toward the room but placed directly in front of the bird feeder outside. In the daytime chickadees dive and flutter behind the saint's head. Beside the statue I can see a dish of pebbles on the windowsill, probably forgotten at the time the bulbs were put in their pots. But the dish now seems to belong where it is, ritually, an offering to or from the saint. Like everything that has been put down anywhere in this house, it has eventually acquired position and validity as if by appointment. A tall crystal vase on the mantle by the oil painting has its particular role: in another woman's house it might hold a bouquet of roses, but in Alicia's it proudly carries one branch of forsythia, budded but not quite blooming.

Even the little pewter dish that sits on a round table near where I enter the room lends a special perspective. It could be an ashtray or an hors d'oeuvres plate, but is too virginally empty of food or ashes for any such purpose. It is just there because that is where it is supposed to be. At its center, like a statue in a tiny park fountain gone dry for the winter season, is the fixed pewter form of a single deer, a doe. She is at once sensual and ascetic, her legs tucked in under the curve of her haunch, and her head erect. This little figure has always seemed to me a perfect thing, silent and entirely self-possessed, minding its own business. When I run my finger along its back as I stand in my mother's living room, I am not surprised to find that the metal is warm.

Alicia's house remains this way year after year: essential and inviolate. It was built in the early 1960s after we children had all left home, when our parents decided it was time to sell the big stone house to another family with growing children and build this one nearby on a section of the original, ample parcel of land. According to my father's design, the new house was to be much smaller and much closer to sea level than the old one. It was hidden, tucked in among the marsh grasses with the shore birds of Long Island Sound. During the last few years of his life Cal had more time for birds. Most of his letters from this period ended like this: "The Canadian geese are flying over the cove, with love, Father." I liked the mingling of his love with the flight of birds, and kept the letters.

The house was Cal's final fortress, compact and practical above all earlier homes. Alicia thought he must have designed it as a kind of cockpit for old age, putting everything he could think of within easy reach: cabinets, stove, kitchen counter all as readily accessible to the user as any control panel he had known during a lifetime of flying. The master bedroom, for instance, is on the ground floor, conveniently close to the kitchen, bathroom, telephone, and two of the three doors that open to the outside world.

Having lots of doors was critical for Cal because of fire. Before the house with the red roof in Minnesota, there had been one that burned to the ground when he was no older than Nicky. He spent the rest of his life knowing that the world can go up in smoke without warning. There are fire extinguishers everywhere in this house, and three exits at ground-floor level, while the basement below, including the garage and Cal's own study, offers another. Upstairs in the guest rooms, he not only installed an extinguisher in the hallway and smoke alarms on each ceiling, but also strong hooks at the windows of each of the two guest bedrooms on which rope ladders were hung. (Apart from the safety considerations, my father never planned anything in his life that he couldn't get out of in a hurry, and it was only natural that he would offer his guests the same opportunity.)

After Cal's death the house became Alicia's alone, and it mellowed, as everything does, under her influence. There are accumulations now, for instance, that my father would never have permitted: those piles of books, and the magazines in slippery heaps on tables much too near the fireplace, and the knee-high vases of flowers in spring set on the floor in spots that compromise access to doors. There are pots of wintering geraniums crowding each other along the windowsills of the upstairs bedrooms, and nobody has seen the rope ladders for a long time.

Even the fallout shelter has eroded in purpose. A few years ago Alicia began to store wine and sherry in its entrance because she felt sorry for the delivery boy who had to climb the steep steps to the kitchen door. The basement was so much closer, and the fallout shelter was the only part of it where she had not already stored something else. Now a case of Pedro Domecq and another of Robert Mondavi are stacked in the concrete entranceway of the shelter. Behind the wine the structure gathers cobwebs just like any widowed toolshed in suburbia, signalling the end of much more than the cold war.

This is the house I came home to that fall weekend during my freshman year at college, when John F. Kennedy was assassinated. This is where Cal first became ill in the early seventies, and this is where Jason died five years ago, in the middle of the 1980s, in the middle of the night. The house has absorbed and weathered all these events, and has remained fundamentally undamaged by them. It runs, like the little saltwater cove on which it was constructed, according to its own secret and cleansing tides. Whatever else happens in the family or in the world, the books will stay in place on their shelves here where Alicia lives, and the glass vase will remain intact on the mantlepiece, always with something in it that is just about to bloom.

The only newspaper Alicia ever looks at, *The New York Times,* sits now on top of a pile of magazines *(Audubon, The American Scholar)* at one end of the low wooden bench that serves as a coffee table in front of the sofa. At the other end of the bench there is a tray with tea things on it, and on the sofa itself, settled and smiling in a Chanel suit the very color of her name, sits Aunt Violet with her arms outstretched.

"Kiss me, Cress!" she commands, laughing. I come forward to be enveloped by her laughter, her perfume, and her purples. Aunt Violet is not much bigger than Alicia, but fully capable of enveloping anyone she cares to. And though we all tease her about wearing purple, she does it well. The blouse today is close to gray, and surely silk, the suit a subtle but determined lavender with a braided silky trim that matches the blouse. She wears a pearl pin and earrings that belonged to her mother and Alicia's, and the ring on her finger is one Uncle George gave her, with diamonds circling a large sapphire. It is the first sapphire I ever remember seeing, and it defined for me forever both the color—blue at its very best—and the intoxicating glamor of precious stones. I used to gawk at this ring, and I can see as Aunt Violet releases me that Sarah is gawking at it now. The perfume tickling my nostrils is Chanel also—No. 5 or No. 20. I can't remember which is which, but Aunt Violet will enlighten me. She takes pleasure in the names and numbers associated with what she owns and wears, but as she is also very generous she will happily keep track of such things for others as well: "your grandmother's Limoges," "the Balenciaga Aunt Lily wore to the cotillion," "Waterford, I suspect . . . certainly not Steuben—what an idea!" Or best of all, "A little Dior underwear, my sweet, is exactly what you need at a time like this!" It could be any time, a birthday or graduation as easily as a wedding or divorce.

I know that after this exuberant, scented hug I will find a feathery lipstick stain on my cheek if I look into the balloon mirror. I don't think Aunt Violet ever blots her lipstick on tissues the way other women do; she prefers to leave it on the flesh of those she loves. In childhood, Helen and I used to carry her kisses on our unwashed faces all day long, feeling superior to the boys because they were honor bound, being boys in the

1950s, to grin and shuffle and wipe the mark off right away on the backs of their hands. Helen and I already knew that Aunt Violet's kisses were trophies to be carried proudly and with joy: bright marks of family affection, generously applied.

"And what is this *delightful* parade all about, my love?" Aunt Violet asks, her eyes bright with amusement at the crowd gathered in the room now, Luke and all the children and Alicia lined up with their backs to the fireplace, the lamb removed from its carton and bleating in Megan's arms. "Who are you rescuing today, Cressida? Or need I ask?" my aunt continues, fixing me with a steady gaze. I am startled.

"Nobody, I hope!" I smile at her. "We came to see Luke."

"All of you?" Luke grins at me openly now. "How nice for me." He comes over to sit down next to Aunt Violet and stretches out his legs under the bench. He is wearing cowboy boots. Even in New England he maintains his Western allegiance. Cal came from the Midwest to settle here near New York, a choice that would have stunned his own rural populist father; and Luke has traveled back toward our grandfather's roots again and further. Children do this. I myself moved to northern New England twenty years ago in a self-righteous mood, ridding myself of the cities and suburbs of the Eastern Seaboard for the sake of my unborn children. (There would be no pollution, greed, competitive materialistic life-style of the upper-middle class in Fairfield and Westchester counties for *my* kids!) Now the same children are yearning for the places I left. ("I really think I want to go to NYU, Mom! New York is great!" "Hey! Alicia! I love your town! They've got a zillion kids in the high school, I bet! Things are really *happening* here!") When Sarah drives her children to visit their grandmother twenty years from now, I assume she will be going north, believing that Connecticut is the land of mature adulthood, Vermont a childish regression. Given time and opportunity, every child turns the parent upside down.

"Well, as for me, I want my tea," Aunt Violet says. "Would you like some? You, Luke? The rest of them can settle down, first. Here—I see cookies, too." She indicates the tea tray complete with teapot, cups, saucers, and a plate of lemon slices as well as the cookies.

"Cookie . . ." Nicholas leaves the lamb and his sisters at once. "Cookie!" He says again, deep in his throat like the monster on *Sesame Street.* Aunt Violet hands him a cookie and he sits with it at her feet.

"Tea?" Alicia speaks to Aunt Violet from across the room, where she is watching Megan pour the milk-replacer powder into the lamb's bottle as Sarah holds the animal. "Please do pour, Vi. Everyone must be exhausted." Nobody looks exhausted, but we are glad to hear her say this. Every afternoon of her life, at five o'clock, Alicia counters exhaustion with tea and cookies.

"I *am* pouring. Come sit with us, Alicia," Aunt Violet says. "Let the children fuss with that creature and you come over here!"

Alicia comes over, casting a nervous eye toward the door and Felix's bark from the other side. I offer to put the lamb upstairs again, but she waves the suggestion away.

"He can wait," she says, and sits down in a straight-backed chair near Luke.

"Did you come through Chicago?" Aunt Violet asks Luke, "And do you take sugar?"

"No," he begins, and then, "Yes, I do. I came through Minneapolis, then Pittsburgh. It would have been fine but we were backed up for over an hour on the runway in the Twin Cities. I don't know what the problem was. Anyway, I'm here." He looks over at Alicia. "Do you know there's a big photograph of you and Cal in the Minneapolis/St. Paul airport? You look about fifteen years old!"

"And as if I weighed about three hundred pounds!" Alicia

says, taking a cup of tea from Aunt Violet. "I know that photograph. It was those old flying suits—I drowned in them. I
don't know why your father always looks so trim and I so
enormous. It doesn't seem fair."

"It's just because you were shorter," I say. "But you look
very pretty in those old photographs, and much more relaxed
than Cal. He's always deadly serious, and you're beaming! You
look as if you're having the time of your life."

"I was. Such an adventure! That really was the best part of
our marriage. The flying was wonderful." She looks into her
teacup, leaving a pause in the conversation for two of her children to ponder. If that was the best part, then what about us?
What were we?

"There are two pictures of Leesha in my American History
book," Sarah says, kneeling in front of the tea table and reaching for a cookie. Megan has filled the bottle with warm water
from the kitchen and is conscientiously feeding the lamb. Each
time Megan looks our way, Alicia nods admiration at her across
the top of her teacup, and Megan smiles.

"It looks like you have a helmet on, or something, in one
of them, and you're in the back of an airplane with Grandfather.
And in the other you're bowing to a Japanese lady."

I hold my breath at the Japanese lady, but Alicia is not
affected in any way.

"That's right. That was when your grandfather and I flew
to the Orient. The Japanese were so beautifully polite, and I
found it hard to know when to *stop* bowing." Before Sarah can
remind her grandmother that it is now internationally correct
to say "Asia," not "the Orient," Alicia acts out the dilemma of
not knowing when to stop bowing, dipping over the tea table
many times in her wrapper as we laugh.

"It was such an extraordinarily courteous culture," she finishes, smiling at us. "We had been so . . . mobbed, everywhere.
It was rather frightening. And then, in Japan, it was different.

So restrained and polite, such a relief. Such courtesy! I'll never forget it."

"Does it seem to you as if the culture has changed in that way? I mean, were they just as courteous in the interview last week?" I can't stop myself from rushing in here, and Alicia moves to respond, but Aunt Violet has spoken first, and louder.

"Well, I don't know about that, Alicia, but I read in today's *Times* that they are courteously continuing to undermine our economy. This article"—she taps at the *Times* in front of her— "claims that our auto-parts people can't sell their products to Japanese car companies producing cars right here in the U.S. There's a kind of cartel, or whatever you call it, and they only buy from their own people. American businesses don't know what to do."

"Yes, Aunt Vi, but that's because American businesses don't know how to make a quality product themselves," Luke breaks in. "All they've been after for years in this country is short-term profits, and it shows. Nobody wants to admit that, so we have a wave of protectionism and Japanese bashing instead."

"That's what Joe thinks," I say. "He keeps complaining that we don't actually make things in this country anymore, we just . . . manipulate finance."

"That's exactly the problem!" Luke warms to his subject as Nicky munches a cookie and leans against his uncle's knee, fat cheek against blue denim. "We're not competitive with other producers because we've forgotten how to produce. The farmers are the only ones who produce anything anymore, as a matter of fact, and it's not helping them much. What we've done over the years is to create a nation of consumers—deliberately. Now that's all Americans know how to do."

"And when the economy is in trouble, we're being told we're not consuming enough," Aunt Violet chimes in now. "I listen every night to newscasters who worry about getting Americans to start spending again, and it just makes my blood boil. Spend what, may I ask?" Her fingers open with the question, and the sapphire flashes. "Nobody has any money . . . except the Japanese."

"Oh dear, how dreadful," Alicia sighs. "I read that article about the automobile companies too, Vi, but probably not as carefully as you did. You have such a fine analytical mind. Father always said so."

Aunt Violet likes this. She settles herself into the sofa cushions.

"I do hate to see us at odds with the Japanese, though," Alicia says. And once again, "They are such a courteous people." She looks down and is silent. Aunt Violet looks sharply at her.

"Did they touch on any of these issues in your interview, or was it entirely about the past?" I am addressing Alicia directly, leaning forward, but she does not answer right away. "In the Japanese interview," I continue, "the one you just had?"

"I expect it was about the past, wasn't it Alicia? The old flying days with Cal," Violet prompts her. "It always is, isn't it?"

Alicia still has not spoken, is still looking down.

"I wonder what the second interview will be like," I say, looking over at Luke for help. I am floundering. "Next week, is that when it is?"

Luke, his expression unchanged, winks at me, and puts a hand on Nicky's head.

Alicia finally looks up and answers. "What did you say? Oh, no. I don't think so, dear." She speaks in a vague, sweet way, her smile taking us all in as we sit near her and at her feet: her sister, her son and daughter, her grandchildren gathered around. She considers us carefully, with gentle eyes. In her pink wrapper she is by far the brightest thing in the room. "But they are a very courteous people."

The other adults say nothing for a moment or two, and the children begin to look uneasy. After a while I speak.

"A friend of mine spent a year in Japan in some kind of exchange program for teachers. She said that there is a whole different attitude toward . . . I think she said spatial relationships. She said that they designed checkers games for children where the checkerboard squares are too small for the checkers, just a little bit, so the kids will learn to manage difficult spaces."

"Because of the crowding?" Luke clears his throat. "Is that the idea? I've heard that the cities are unbelievably crowded over there."

"Cities are terribly crowded everywhere," Aunt Violet puts in. "New York is more and more impossible. I tell George we should move to the country."

"Move to the country! How could you leave New York?" Sarah is amazed. I pick up the tea tray and take it out to the kitchen, and when I return Sarah is asking her grandmother about the early flying days with Cal, and the pictures in the American History book. Who was the lady she bowed to? Did the people speak English or was there an interpreter? Alicia is now animated again and answers the questions with details and laughter. She was given a silk kimono by her hostess; neither she nor Cal could manage the chopsticks and so they ate very little at meals; when they were served saki, Cal waited until nobody was looking, and then poured it into his shoe. Yes, his shoe! Cal never drank alcohol, but did not want to offend his host.

The lamb has gone upstairs after its meal, and Megan sits on the floor beside us and listens too, with Nicky in her lap. Felix is allowed to come in, and retires without comment to a cushion under Alicia's desk.

"It's so long ago! It seems like another life," Alicia protests finally, smiling at the girls. "I was another person then!"

"No you weren't," Aunt Violet contradicts her sharply.

"Don't say that! You were exactly the same person. Remember, I knew you then, and I know you now. We all think we change because we change inside, but we're really just the same. You're not really different at all, Alicia."

"Why, no . . . I suppose not, Vi." Alicia looks taken aback. "But sometimes I think that we lead many lives in one lifetime. One life after the other, or perhaps one life on top of the other, many layered. The changes we experience are so enormous. They create a great gulf between one period of life and another. We have to die and be reborn many times, I feel." She turns to Luke. "What do you think, Luke?"

He is jiggling his boot, with Nicky attached.

"I think I'll have to think about it some more. But I'll build a fire in the meantime. How about it, Nicky? Shall we get some wood?"

"Get some wood," Nicky echoes, scrambling up with the help of his two sisters, who volunteer to get wood too. Luke and the children go outside together.

"He's wonderful with children, isn't he?" Aunt Violet comments as the door closes behind them. "He always was."

"And animals," adds Alicia. "All those snakes and turtles!"

"But wait—that was Mark!" I remind her quickly, alarmed. "It was Mark who had the snakes and turtles, Mother, not Luke."

"And the raccoon!" Alicia finishes, barely paying attention. "I was thinking about that little raccoon. Do you remember the raccoon, Cress? Luke kept it in the basement in the old house in an enormous cage full of tree branches and platforms that he made himself. It had such a lovely face, but it was terribly fierce —it bit everybody—and Luke had to feed it with asbestos gloves. Finally he took it to a wilderness area and let it go."

"That's right," I say, "that was Luke's raccoon. And Mark had . . ."

"Mark had snakes, lots of them." Aunt Violet shudders. "He

loved them so much. He always invited me to hold one and was rather hurt that I declined."

"Mrs. Evans met one on the stairs," I reminisce, with a little smile. Mrs. Evans worked briefly as a secretary for Cal and Alicia both, typing manuscripts. She had not been prepared for snakes.

"You can't keep raccoons—or any wild animal—confined anymore," I say. "It's against the law, at least in Vermont."

"I wish it had been against the law then!" says Alicia. "But that's the way it is with boys. My brother loved that raccoon, and nobody could make him change his mind."

"My brother, you mean," I correct her gently. Just a slip of the tongue, this time. Uncle Stewart, Violet and Alicia's younger brother, died of a stroke ten years ago.

Aunt Violet chuckles. "Certainly not *our* brother, Alicia. Stewart was oblivious to the natural world. I don't think he ever looked up from a book long enough to notice it, and I remember when his ashes were buried by that beautiful little stream on his place, we all joked that he never would have walked that far away from the library. I must say he had a lovely sense of humor," she reflects.

Alicia is thoughtful. "Yes," she says, "And he did love that raccoon."

Aunt Violet sends a brief, startled look my way. I speak slowly to my mother.

"My brother," I say. "Your son, Luke. It was Luke who loved the raccoon."

Alicia turns to me, eyebrows raised just a little. "Of course, Cress, dear. Mark had the snakes and turtles."

The front door opens with a gust of cold air, and Nicky appears with an armload of kindling, some of it dropping as he crosses the threshold.

"Wood!" he crows, delighted, and stops in his tracks.

"Hurry up, Nick—you're blocking the door!" Sarah protests loudly behind him. Ignoring her, he drops the rest of the kindling in the doorway.

"Wood!" he announces again. "One, two, three, eight, nine. Wood!" He points to each stick in the pile at his feet.

"Please, Nicky! I'm freezing!" Megan calls from the darkness behind him. Luke's deep laugh can be heard. He and the girls come in to help Nicky gather up the kindling, and soon they have built a fire.

Luke brushes the bark off his hands as we all watch the flames leap up around the pile of logs and kindling. Everyone is quiet, watching the dancing fire.

"How can it be so hazardous and so comforting at the same time?" asks Aunt Violet, staring directly into the fire.

"Like love," murmurs Alicia. Luke shifts in his chair.

We eat dinner in this room too, bringing out our plates from the kitchen. The meal is a comprehensive kind of casserole made by Alicia's neighbor Martha, with noodles and chicken and peas and carrots mixed together and bubbling under crisped breadcrumbs. We have ice cream and cookies for dessert, and afterwards we sit sleepily watching the fire until Alicia gets up from the sofa and yawns.

"I don't know about the rest of you, but it's getting close to my bedtime, and I'm really rather tired. I think I'll go turn on my heat pad and get ready for bed. Goodnight, everybody. It's lovely to have you all here."

As soon as she has left the room Aunt Violet says in a very low voice, "I thought I was imagining it, but I'm not, am I?"

"I don't think so," I say. "But it doesn't happen all the time . . ."

"It may just have to do with a hearing problem," Luke tells us both. "Or fatigue. It's the end of the day. There are a lot of people in the house."

"What are you all talking about?" Sarah's eyes narrow. She is the oldest of the children here, and at seventeen has a sensi-

tivity to atmosphere that the others lack. Low voices mean
nothing good, in her experience. She is sitting in the middle of
the floor with her hands around her knees, studying the grown-
ups, while Megan and Nicky, both still too young to be interested in adult conversation, lean half-asleep beside one another,
against my feet.

"Alicia seems tired," I say, with a reassuring smile.

"Of course she does. She just *said* she was tired. I am too,"
Sarah responds in a cross way. "Come on, Megan, let's go to
bed. Nicky, you too. We'll get him ready, Mom," she offers,
with deft generosity silencing any comment I might have made
about her tone of voice.

Aunt Violet goes out to the kitchen to look for her overnight bag, which she thinks she left there when she arrived
earlier today.

I stay with Luke to help him put the screen in front of the
fire and move the extra kindling, logs, and other debris away
from the hearth. We are alone in the room now, and I am about
to ask him what it is that has happened in his own life, when
Alicia appears again, walking into the living room in her raincoat with Felix's leash in her hand.

"Oh!" she says, startled to see us. "I didn't realize anyone
was here." It is an old raincoat, I see, one that must have been
hanging in the back of her bedroom closet. It is not the one she
usually wears and keeps in the coat closet in the hall. It isn't
raining, anyway.

"Are you going out?" Luke asks, surprised.

She seems both embarrassed and confused. "Well, it's so
foolish of me, really. I never forget to pick it up, normally,
because they can only fit one copy in the mailbox and I don't
like to have newspapers flung on the driveway the way they
do. With everyone coming today, I simply forgot."

"You're going out to the mailbox?" Now I understand the

leash. Felix is behind Alicia, wagging hopefully. Whatever the hour, no dog wants to miss a walk, and if Alicia walks any-where at all, Felix does too.

"Today's *Times?* Don't we have it?" Luke asks. "I'm sure we do. We were just discussing it, before dinner," he reminds her. "That was today's *Times* we were talking about with Aunt Violet, wasn't it?" She doesn't answer, so he looks at me for one questioning instant, unsure of his own memory. Then Luke seems to pull himself together and shake off doubt like a dog shedding water. He says to Alicia positively, "You must have picked up the paper. I'm sure you did."

"Here it is." I go over to get the newspaper from the coffee table by the sofa where we were all sitting just minutes ago. "Look, here's the piece on Japanese automakers, under the fold."

"Oh! Why, of course! How foolish of me!" Alicia says, but uncertainly, like a person newly awake. She makes no move to take off the unfamiliar raincoat or the boots, and Felix is still looking hopefully at her. The leash is looped several times around her right hand.

She obviously does not know what to do next, and I find it unbearable to see my mother in such an ambiguous condition: so unsteady in time, so well prepared for rain.

I rush into speech, babbling comforts as if strewing flowers. "It's so easy to forget things when you're tired. Isn't it funny that the things we do every day are the hardest to remember? I have the worst trouble with my pills. I've taken them at bedtime every day for ten years, but I never feel sure whether I've remembered to take today's pill, or if I'm about to take yester-day's over again."

"You live with children," Alicia reminds me, with a look of reminiscent forgiveness. "It is the most distracted time in one's life, Cressida. How well I remember!"

"Ah, yes!" says Aunt Violet, who has been standing in the kitchen doorway. "Distraction! I don't understand why more people don't talk about *that* aspect of child rearing. For ten years my life was just one long series of interruptions. When the children were small I never *completed* a thing." She eyes the raincoat as Alicia removes it, but she does not comment.

"You completed the children," Alicia tells her sister as she hangs up the coat and stows the boots away in the hall closet, "and you did it beautifully, I might add. Four intelligent and creative children with a wonderful upbringing."

"Hah!" Aunt Violet replies. "They would hardly agree with you. But I appreciate the thought, dear. I truly do."

Shortly afterwards, following a second cheerful exchange of bedtime good wishes with her children and her sister, Alicia retires to her room and her bed. Felix follows slowly, disappointed at missing the extra walk, but he is an old dog and has learned to take disappointment philosophically.

"Well," says Aunt Violet finally, "I couldn't help hearing all that, about *The New York Times,* I mean. I was just in the kitchen. It would have been hard to miss it."

Luke nods in understanding. Aunt Violet sighs and begins again. "You see what I mean, then." But she has not told us what she means, and does not seem able to go on. She just looks at Luke.

"I'm not sure that I do," he says, tightly. "I think that she's extremely tired, which is very natural."

I find it difficult to speak, and my eyes are filled with tears that will neither fall nor abate. I am not sad, I tell myself. I don't know enough to be sad. I'm confused.

"Well, this wouldn't trouble me a bit, frankly," Aunt Violet says, "except that she also came to see me in the city this week and got lost."

Luke and I both look at her, appalled.

"What are you talking about?" I envision my mother drifting off into the heart of Manhattan like a released balloon, directionless, out of all of our hands.

"Not lost in a *dangerous* part of the city," Violet quickly amends. "Lost in a place that should have been familiar to her. The doorman told me he found her walking back and forth on our block, right on Seventy-seventh Street, not sure where she was or why she was there. That's what she told him herself! He knew her, of course, and he had noticed the taxi pull up earlier, but he was with some other people and didn't see who the passenger was. He thinks she gave the driver the right address but then couldn't remember where she was when she got there. It just seemed crazy."

I don't like hearing the doorman's views, and defend Alicia here. "All right, Aunt Violet, but look at it this way. Maybe it seemed crazy to him, but it seems to *me* that walking up and down the block is a very sensible way to behave when you're trying to remember where you are. It's not as if she wandered across Fifth Avenue in traffic, or—"

"For how long?" Luke breaks in. "How long was she walking back and forth like that?"

"Well, not long I suppose . . . a few minutes. The doorman said 'Oh, hello, Mrs. Linley, your sister has just returned,' or something of that sort, and then brought her up to the apartment. She was perfectly all right by the time I saw her. I didn't know anything about her getting lost until the doorman told me later that afternoon. Maybe he exaggerated, as you say. I don't mean to make trouble, for heaven's sake." Aunt Violet is bristling defensively under cross-examination. I notice that her overnight bag has her own initials monogrammed on it as well as Yves Saint Laurent's.

"She didn't mention to you that she had been lost?" Luke quizzes her.

"Not once. And I suppose she probably didn't think she *was* lost. She's been to the apartment hundreds of times. It was just that time between the taxi and the doorman . . . she seemed to have lost *that,* altogether. It must have been like a . . . a blackout of some kind."

"Or like a seizure," I say, thinking about it in a context familiar to me. The pills that I take every night are for a seizure disorder resulting from a head injury I received falling off a horse almost twenty years ago. To my knowledge I have had only two seizures in all that time, but the memory of them is vivid. There was a period of simple absence, just absence, and then I returned to consciousness and into a frightening aware-ness of the seizure's effect on other people—witnesses, family members, medical personnel. There was a lot of rushing, and hushing, and hovering over me, but at the same time a tendency among these people to speak to each other rather than directly to me, so that I felt as if I were dreaming it all, or invisible, more absent in the aftermath than during the event. It is ex-traordinarily disorienting.

"Have you ever actually talked to Alicia about all this?" I ask Aunt Violet. "About everything that's been worrying you? I mean, wouldn't you talk to her about anything else that both-ered you? Why not this?"

Aunt Violet continues to looked uncomfortable.

"I don't mean to burden you. I know you're worried." I continue. "We are too. But what I'm trying to say is, why does it seem so terrible for us just to come out and say 'I've been worrying about some memory lapses I've noticed in you lately'? I know it isn't the kind of thing you want to confront somebody with, but I keep wondering if it isn't cruel and be-wildering not to just *tell* her."

"I think it would be too frightening for her," Luke says immediately. "She'd be watching herself all the time. She'd be in a constant state of anxiety. I don't think it's a good idea."

"I think it might be a huge relief," I argue. "Look at us! We're all talking about her behind her back and tiptoeing around her when we're with her, waiting for a slip. How can she not be aware of it?"

"I don't tiptoe around her, and I don't talk behind her back!" Luke protests. "I just don't want her frightened unnecessarily. She'll be upset. What good does it do? I think this is a time when we should be very careful."

"I think we should be honest. That's what I'd want in her place."

"Shall I tell you what I think?" Aunt Violet interrupts us at this point.

"Well?" Luke asks, a bit sharply, because Aunt Violet is looking thoughtfully at the painting over Alicia's fireplace: the French farmhouse with its hills receding into the background and the evening light, a village with its church spire in the middle distance, and a gray-brown wing of clouds overhead. Alicia loves it, though she once confessed that the artist was obscure and the subject overfamiliar, as landscapes go, so she wasn't sure why. Perhaps it was the absence of human figures, the strange wild lightness of the sky, or the fine, faded gold of the old frame. Or perhaps, she said, it was just that any work of art that has been in a family for half a century acquires a dignity beyond its original merit, like a beloved, undistinguished uncle.

"This is what I think," Aunt Violet says when she brings her gaze back to her niece and nephew. "I think she already knows."

"That's not possible," says Luke. "It doesn't make any sense. Why are we all here, then? What is this all about?" But I listen, because it strikes me that what Aunt Violet says might well be true.

"She doesn't know everything," I say slowly, watching for a reaction from my aunt. "But she knows there's something going on. Is that what you mean?"

Aunt Violet nods. "I think so. You see, your mother has

always been the most *private* person, ever since childhood. Private and often . . . preoccupied. And she has always had periods of, well, withdrawal. You know how it is when you talk to her sometimes and it takes quite a while for her to respond? It always has. She's thoughtful. She doesn't gush, and she doesn't speak without considering."

I smile because I love this quality in my mother. It implies such thoughtful attention to whatever the person she is with is trying to say.

But Aunt Violet has a different interpretation. "I think that she's always been distracted at times—she's had so much to think about and all you children too! Why, she said it herself just now. But there's also been the occasional retreat—from her own sensitivity, you know. She's so unusually, *painfully* sensitive." Aunt Violet stretches her arms wide to embrace Alicia's sensitivity. She is proud of it, her sister's sensitivity, protective of it, as I am of Helen's magic. "That's why she is such a wonderful writer, of course, and reaches so many people. But it's exhausting for her—it always has been—and she learned early on to withdraw, thank God. And not to let people notice. But now she's older—we're all older—and she can't bring herself back as quickly as she once did. It takes more time and more effort now, and people are beginning to notice."

"And she notices it herself, you think."

"Yes, she does. She talks from time to time about feeling 'vaguer' as she gets older, but after she has had one of these memory lapses, she doesn't talk about vagueness at all. She talks about everything else. She doesn't act bewildered then, she acts . . ." Aunt Violet searches for the word, and I find it for her.

"Brave."

"Exactly. She acts brave, and I don't care what anyone says; you don't act brave unless you know there is something to be brave about. She knows." Aunt Violet has a toothbrush poking out of the side pocket of her overnight bag, and it is purple too. Hard to believe.

"She has always been brave," Luke points out. "And there has always been plenty to be brave about."

"This is different," says Aunt Violet. "She can't just be brave about this. She *must* let people help her. She could endanger herself."

"What kind of help?" I sink at this, thinking of hired companions, garrulous knitters in white uniforms sitting in all the quiet corners of my mother's house, knitting and talking and rocking in rocking chairs, watching and talking and rocking and knitting while Alicia dwindles and grows silenter by the day.

I cannot imagine Alicia living with a constant companion. An intermittent companion, perhaps. Her marriage to Cal survived through intermittency, as much by virtue of the intense mutual privacy it provided as through the romantic early companionship that had so entranced the public. Without the privacy they offered one another, without the consuming need for a certain kind of freedom each could recognize in the other and therefore could permit, however difficult it was to tailor this need to their own work and to the family they created together and to social expectation of all kinds, without this freedom I don't believe either one of them could have been married at all, to anyone. (But I have wondered so often about this freedom, too. I don't feel sure that I like it, in retrospect. Tell me, wherever you were, wherever you are, soaring into the air alone or swimming sleek as a mermaid among the waves and eddies of creative consciousness, weren't you ever lonely?)

"Well, I'm not sure what kind of help she needs." Violet says. "But I know that there are people who can analyze these things and set up programs. Perhaps a doctor she trusts . . ."

"Wait a minute!" Luke says. "What doctor? She had a complete physical a month ago. She's in great shape, remarkable for her age, they said. She doesn't need a doctor. I'm sorry,

Aunt Violet, but this is just too much. She has occasional memory lapses—that's it. You acquire a certain number of years, you lose a certain number of brain cells—that's the deal, from what I'm told. And it happens to everybody. What's left to work with, at least in Alicia's case, is pretty damn good, but once in a while the old memory just kicks out—and considering all her years and all her memories, why not? Why do we suddenly have to call in the surgeon general?"

"You just don't understand, Luke." Aunt Violet shakes her head at him. "At our age, everything is risky. You can't afford a memory lapse at the wrong time. What if she were crossing a street, or driving a car?"

"Or doing an interview," I say quietly. Luke hears me, but is impatient.

"Right, right, I know, the interview . . . but I wonder if maybe the trouble with *that* is that she just doesn't want to do it. Why should she have to? Is there any graceful way to get her out of it?"

I shrug. "I don't know, I guess so. But I think she told them during the first one that she'd be delighted to see their correspondent from Kyoto—next week, in fact. Helen thinks it would be humiliating if we went ahead and cancelled something she'd agreed to—not just for them, but for her too. What if we cancel, and then she remembers?"

"Dreadfully humiliating." Aunt Violet shudders. She begins to look tired. She is only six years younger than Alicia, and each is the only member of the family that the other has left.

"Well, anyway," says Luke, "I don't think there's any danger of her walking out into the street, or driving off the road. It's the things she *says* that upset people, not the things she does."

I think of Alicia standing in the center of this darkening room in her rain gear.

"I think we should all go to bed," I say, "and see what

happens tomorrow. Aunt Violet, why don't you use the bathroom first—I'll help Luke here if there's anything left to do."

Aunt Violet agrees gratefully to this suggestion, and starts up the stairs. She will sleep in the little bedroom across the hall from the one where the children and the lamb already are settled, the girls in sleeping bags on the floor and Nicky probably sprawled across the pillows of the double bed, where I will join him as soon as I possibly can.

Luke had finished with the fireplace before Alicia left the room the first time; there really is nothing to help him with, but I linger now anyway. This might be his only chance to speak if he wants to. I wait, trying to suppress the hope that he will be too tired to unburden himself tonight so that I can just go up to bed.

"It's Emma," he says finally. "She left last week, and I don't know if she's coming back." Emma. My own dear friend for twenty years and more, who loved and tickled and read stories to my children when they were tiny, who let me visit her for weeks on end when I was a worshipping teenager. Emma, with her dark hair and her silver bracelets and her laughter. Having Emma in our family was like making a new window in an old house, bringing light into places where you had never thought to expect it.

"Where did she go?"

"I don't know," he says, then corrects himself with a laugh. "Well, that's not true. I know she's been driving across the country and stopping to see friends, because that's where the books come from. One from Lois in St. Paul and another from Jill—she lives in Omaha."

"What books? What do you mean?"

"Oh, all those books—" he gestures largely, *"Men in Need and the Women Who Need Them, Dysfunctional Partnerships,* that kind of stuff. I keep hoping maybe I can figure out what she's been saying to people about me, just from the titles."

"I remember that," I tell him, "people sending books, and articles, and long letters. The minute you want to get divorced, everybody you know is an expert."

Luke winces, and before I have finished my sentence I know why. I shouldn't have said "divorced." I remember now. It's much too soon. The wife has just left, the books are just beginning to arrive, a Hansel and Gretel trail provided by concerned friends, crumbs when one needs real nourishment and yet has no appetite, especially not for words like "divorce."

"Do you have any ideas why?" This is the question that will keep me from my bed, because it's the one people want to answer most at this time, even though they don't know the answer. It's only fair to ask, no matter how sleepy I am. I remember what it was like, and how many people listened to me. You have to pay your dues to the process . . .

Luke takes a deep breath and begins.

"Plenty of ideas. They way I see it, all this goes way back. We were married right out of college—Emma never had a chance to establish herself independently . . ." That's right, you talk about how it was for Emma, you tell me all about what went wrong for Emma and what was going on inside Emma's head and how difficult Emma's childhood was. You pretend this is wholly and completely about Emma, nothing to do with Luke. "We always did the things that advanced my career, not hers, and now it's twenty years later and she feels it. She's been out of the art world for two decades; the kids are grown and gone; I'm preoccupied with my own work. She's been feeling abandoned, like it's all a waste, and . . ."

"Angry?" I suggest. I am asking about Emma, but Luke misunderstands.

"Never." He is emphatic. "I'm not at all angry with her. In a way I think I can really understand this, even if I can't understand all of it. I'm not angry in the least. I know that it's been tough in some ways to be married to someone like me. And not only that—" He stops, looks at me appraisingly—Can I take this?—"but it's tough to be married into our family."

"Yes, that's what they tell me."

They. Yes, both husbands have said it is hard to cope with the Linleys, with the Linley heritage, the Linley family obsession with itself. But family influences weigh just as heavily on each of these husbands, too—I know they do—only there isn't the fame to label the weight. And family background, on either side, is just one among so many things that can slowly freeze and weigh down a marriage over the years, like ice on its wings.

Alicia once said that all first marriages may be doomed from the beginning because they are both an escape from and a reflection of the marriage in which each partner was raised. What an impossible duality! In my mother's marriage, I can see the escape part of the equation, but not the reflection part. Where in Cal with his Nordic height and his eagle's eye was the tiny, absentminded, owlish, and endearing scholar: my mother's father? Where in Alicia were the suspicious whisperings and jealous rages of Cal's mother, so possessive of her son during all of his growing years that she even went to college with him, installing herself in a house near campus. Finally he dropped out of school and took to the air, his only escape on wings, with his most famous plane a monoplane, single engined and single seated, with no room for a mother or any other copilot. His only true copilot, later, was Alicia, who like him could drink in the solitude like water and breathe it out like air, two humans gilled alike, a first marriage that lasted forty years, doomed or not.

Was Garrett another Cal for me, an echo of the early, boyish Cal from the old photographs? Young man of freedom, genius, and long, entitled absences? Prince of the arts and the air? And who was I for him? Some version of his mother, years ago? No, this doesn't ring true to me. We were too much brother and sister, Hansel and Gretel ourselves, leaving home hand in hand to travel into the forest. We were not parents for one another but siblings, comrades-in-arms, allies, second selves.

"You must miss her," I say to Luke. "It must seem so quiet without Emma. It must be awful."

"I don't know," he tells me. "It's still too new and it just seems weird. I wish I could talk to her—I just don't know what's in her mind."

"You didn't talk about it? What do you mean? I thought you said you understood."

"Well, sure, we talked about it when she was still home. There was almost too much talking at first—it kind of wears you out, and you can't stop. You talk all the time."

"I remember. It's wonderful, in a way. You feel so close to each other, you feel you can say anything."

"Yes, that's true. We stayed up half that first night, and we got out everything between us, even things we hadn't talked about during all the years of our marriage. It was really good, I thought. I felt like no matter what happened after that, we really understood each other. It was great. But the next day it got weird—she was so mad at me. It's like she has all these old grudges, things I didn't even remember, stuff she's been holding in for years. I never let her make any decisions, she said. Where to live, what our life was going to be like—it was all set by me, because of my work, or because I was going to school, before that. She says she never got to *choose* anything. It was all me." He shakes his head. "I just kept listening; she went on and on."

"Does that make sense to you, though?" I ask him. "I mean, do you agree that you chose everything and that you made all the decisions?"

"Well . . . I had to . . . I just listened." He laughs now. "The awful thing is, she was so mad about it, and I just couldn't even remember."

Remember . . . remember back . . . What were the various complaints, the arguments back and forth, the reasons we each built up separately in our minds and then clung to like rafts on rough seas? When the impossible rifts began to appear, what were the names we gave them? How did we try to apply logic to the separateness as it grew, by itself, always eluding us, grew and took on a life of its own with its own illogical, irreversible momentum? Estrangement and divorce happen to us, like accidents and disease. We are not in charge. We like to believe that the reverse is true, that we cause these things and that we can control them even as they occur, but it is not true. We work hard to name the problems, we struggle to name the probable causes of the disaster, we name and label our history, saying the names to ourselves and to our friends over and over, like charms memorized against the advent of chaos, which is nameless. But then later on, and not so very much later on at that, we stop all naming, and then we stop referring to the names, and finally they fade from us and we forget the names altogether. Because they were never true but only comforting, and only for a little while during the period when the roofs of our lives had been torn off from over our heads, and we were suddenly all alone with the wind and our fears and the faraway brightness of the stars.

"God! I don't know, Cress!" Luke's forehead is furrowed, his hands spread open toward me. He looks as if poised to catch a basketball or a small child being tossed in the air. Knees bent, arms crooked to receive. "I never thought of it as making choices. I thought of it as living, you know? Daily living, growing up, being a responsible husband and father. I didn't feel that I was . . . hogging all the power, or the good stuff, or anything like that at all. It wasn't all such good stuff anyway," he adds.

We stand at the bottom of the staircase, but I have not put my hand on the rail.

"I don't know why this happens," I say, after a silence. "It

just does. I don't think anybody else knows why it happens
either—not your friends, not Emma's friends, or the people
who write the books. Nobody. But what amazed me when I
was going through it was finding out that it gets better after a
while. I didn't think it would, but it did." I feel foolish saying
this, even though I am so sure it is true. What can it mean to
him, "It gets better after a while"? Not good enough, little
sister.

He stiffens. "If you mean . . . I'm not pursuing her for a
reconciliation," he says in a formal way. "Emma and I may
never get together again. I don't know what the future holds."

I almost laugh, but do not. "That's not what I mean at all,"
I say, and pull down Luke's resistant shoulder so that I can kiss
his cheek. "But it does get better. It's true, that's all. It gets
better. It stops feeling so crazy. It just gets better. I know."

"I'm not looking for another marriage," he says, not quite
as stiff. "It's not like you and Joe. It's completely different.
There isn't anybody else in the picture."

How sad, I am thinking. Nobody at all? Not one comforting
body in the picture?

"That's not what I mean either. I don't mean the marriage
gets better, or a new relationship makes everything better. It's
you I'm talking about, Luke. *You* get better. I promise. You get
better, that's all, no matter what happens to Emma or the marriage or anything else. It's like . . . recovery from a long illness,
or a bad dream, or anything in your life that has gotten stuck
and doesn't change and you don't know how to change it. What
I'm trying to say is that *you* will get better, Luke. You feel
awful now because it *is* awful. And you think you'll always feel
awful, but you won't. You'll get better and you'll be fine."

I'm not saying what I want to say well enough, and I expect
him to be annoyed, at least irritated with me. But the look on
his face is complex: surprise, unwillingness, fear, and a glimmer
of maniacal hope. Then he bends down and kisses my cheek.

His face is rough, the way I remember Cal's, and the bones are hard against my face. If he comes to visit us, I am thinking, Joe and I will give Luke pancakes and maple syrup, and beer in the evening, and he can eat while he talks to us about Emma, and get fatter. Luke is too thin. It would be nice to have him come to the farm.

Luke goes off to sleep downstairs in our father's former office with its fold-out bed, and I step over my two daughters and the lamb, blessing the quietness, undressing in the dark. I move Nicholas aside just a little to make room for myself next to him, a warm and sweet-breathing bundle of pajamas and a blanket. Then I lie on my back for a long time and look out the window, listening to the sounds of the cove with its Canada geese and its marsh grasses, watching the Connecticut crescent moon climb up into my mother's favorite elm tree and entangle its twin horns among the branches. I watch and listen and, hardly knowing it, inhale and exhale exactly at the same time that Nicky does, matching my breathing with my child's, in and out, in and out, breath for breath, perfectly synchronized, until at last I fall asleep.

# Chapter

## 6

In the morning I wake to clear skies and sunlight. I know that the air outside my window is not really warm, but the sun streaming into the room is so bright that I can almost believe its promise of warmth. This feels like just the kind of early spring Vermont morning when the girls persuade me to let them wear denim jackets instead of winter parkas to school for the first time in the season.

My bare feet move pleasurably through the pale rhomboids of sunshine projected on the floor near each window I pass and go downstairs to let Felix out. The dog is bouncing eagerly ahead of me, already brimming with excitement. He came upstairs early to greet me and the children, as he always does when we visit. Then, with us, he rediscovered the lamb. Together they caused a pandemonium of bleating and barking that only stopped when I shut the lamb into the upstairs bathroom with Megan, sleepy but good natured in her red flannel nightshirt. As I left them she was mixing the early morning bottle while the lamb stood unsteadily on the bath mat, sniffing the backs of her knees.

Nicky and Sarah have scarcely stirred, though Nicky rolled over and Sarah mumbled briefly while Felix frisked around them. Now they both lie curled in sleep again, and Aunt Violet, across the hall, has not made an appearance at all, whether from obliviousness or tact I am not sure. When I get downstairs I hear no sound from Alicia's bedroom either, or from Cal's study down on the basement level.

I close the door behind Felix and a chilly breeze fans into the house. I step back quickly and wrap myself more closely in the oversized blue and white Japanese kimono I am wearing over my nightgown. The kimono does not belong to me, but I have borrowed it on my visits here ever since the day I found it, years ago, during some pregnancy when nothing of my own fit me. It was hanging in the back of the closet in the room where I usually sleep, comfortably enormous, with great sleeves that would have enhanced the dignity of the proper wearer as I imagined him or her, some exquisite Japanese person, but seemed to droop in an implausible way from my own arms like the cloth on those continuous towel dispensers in public restrooms. The fabric itself is gossamer light, though, which made the robe a pleasure to wear despite its size and mine at the time. I have worn it again and again, and I have never actually seen anyone else in this garment. Because of that and its hugeness, I wonder if it could have belonged to Cal. When I questioned Alicia she was vague, and in fact this seems unlikely. Cal avoided bathrobes the way he avoided dinner napkins. ("No, thank you. I have my pocket handkerchief, and

that's all I need." All that anyone needs, was the implication.)
He disapproved of using more paper or wearing more cloth on
one's person than was strictly necessary, just as he disapproved
of hunting except to feed one's family. This robe may have
been a relic from the trips to Japan with Alicia, however, a gift
he could neither use nor decently refuse, left at the back of the
closet out of mixed respect and uncertainty.

Alone in a giant's "wrapper" I listen to the morning noises
around me: geese arguing on the cove, Felix barking at a pheas-
ant, early traffic going by on the road with a characteristically
suburban hum and swish, so different from the sound of cars
on the dirt roads in Vermont, where the hearer can feel each
bump and vibrate to every protesting rattle.

Far away, at the back of all the sounds, there is the faint
noise of a telephone ringing, like an alarm clock muffled under
a pillow. It takes a moment for me to realize that this must be
Alicia's phone in the kitchen, separated only by a thin wall
from the bedroom where she is sleeping. My instinct to save
and spare my mother leaps instantly to life. I rush to answer
the phone before it awakens her. Kimono sleeves aflap, I run as
silently as I can through the hallway between the living room
and the kitchen. When I get there I can see that a pillow is
wedged over the phone, and is also stuffed into the little square
windowlike opening between kitchen and master bedroom.
This window in the wall above the counter is often a surprise
to visitors. Cal put it there after the house was built so that one
could push the telephone back and forth between the two
rooms and use it in either one. He did not design this feature
into the house originally, because Cal himself did not telephone
from his bedroom. Bedrooms were for sleeping, not for chatter,
he felt. But Alicia disagreed. She thought it would be nice to
be able to talk to her family, for instance, while resting in
her bedroom or even in her bed. She managed to persuade Cal
that a bedroom telephone would ensure privacy as well as

comfort, but as he was only half convinced he never installed a phone jack in the bedroom. He simply cut a hole in the wall.

Breathless and barefoot, I answer the phone. It is my brother Mark, the last person I would have expected.

"Thank God somebody finally answered!" he says. "I was getting worried. Alicia is usually up with the birds."

"Hi, Mark. We're the only birds here," I pant, "me and the kids. She's probably sleeping late because we wore her out coming in last night. Aunt Violet's here too, and Luke, and even a nursing lamb—the children insisted we bring it along. What a crowd!"

I am talking too much and too fast, feeling pleased and surprised and defensive all at the same time. This is the brother closest to me in age, the one who always catches me off guard.

"Hi, little girl," he says. (He says this every time we talk or meet, whatever the interval. He will say it when I'm sixty-five.) "Tell me what's going on with Alicia, okay? Don't hide anything: I hate that." He sounds alarmingly wide awake and pumped full of fresh air, as if he has been up for hours already patrolling the arctic tundra. Mark always gets up too early. I've never been completely sure that he sleeps at all.

I stall. "Where are you? Alaska?" It is easy to imagine Mark in Alaska, squinting out of a fur-lined parka with the wind whipping his hair, leaning on the inner wall of a phone booth thick framed in ice, like a refrigerator overdue for defrosting.

"Washington, D.C. I came here to testify at the congressional hearings. Didn't Alicia tell you?"

No, she didn't. Why didn't she? It should have been the first thing out of her mouth. (Cress, dear, your brother Mark is in Washington. Yes, a congressional hearing! Isn't he extraordinary? One never knows where he'll turn up next.) Because she said none of those things I'm not sure what to say myself.

"She didn't really have a chance," I lie. "We just got in last night. Late." I don't want Mark's feelings to be hurt, but he is far ahead of me, as usual.

"Oh, boy," he sighs. "It's still the same, then. When I telephoned last week she kept forgetting who I was. She called me Stewart three times. Once I would have understood. After I hung up I felt like a ghost, you know?"

"Oh, Mark . . ." My voice cracks and stops. "Absolutely. I know just what you mean." I am looking at the pillow and the hole in the wall. Is our mother awake? Is she listening?

"You do? Is she forgetting stuff a lot?" Mark asks. "Doesn't it seem pretty strange to you? And really new? Or is it just me? Maybe I've been gone too long."

"No, it isn't," I say. "You haven't. You're right. That's the way it is, or anyway I think that's the way it is. I don't have any idea what it means, though."

"No. I guess you wouldn't." What does he mean by that exactly? "It must be hard to figure out what's going on," Mark continues. "Is that why you're all there?"

"Absolutely. You're absolutely right," I say again, to the pillow. "About me and Luke, anyway. I don't know about Aunt Violet."

"Aunt Violet? That's right, you said she was there, And a *lamb?*" He sounds just the way Helen does with me, delighted but satirical. Mark, for all his work with endangered species, is dogmatically unsentimental about animals. He spends his life with animals, yes, but God forbid he should be taken for a bleeding heart! His cause is the preservation of biological diversity, and his positions are ecologically correct. He maintains a certain degree of scholarly detachment even from his own dogs and cats (though I've noticed the few times I've visited Mark that his animals follow him everywhere and stay as close to him as they can, so maybe his behavior is different when he thinks nobody is watching, the way Cal's was).

"A baby lamb, yes. Why not?" I ask stiffly.

Mark does not answer. He is laughing.

"Never mind. Good old Cressida. Tell me more, will you ? Give me a picture of what's going on. Is she sick, do you think? Alzheimer's setting in?"

"God, no! How can you even—" I start to protest, then lower my voice. "Mark, look. I'm standing right in the kitchen. Everybody else is asleep . . . I think. And my feet are freezing." This is true. The red-tiled floor in Alicia's kitchen, which gives the visual effect of sun-baked earth and of Mexico at noon, actually holds no heat at all, as Joe once pointed out to me when I suggested a tiled floor for the farmhouse. Ever since that day my feet have been cold in my mother's kitchen, and this for some reason makes me irritated with my husband, not my mother.

"You never wear socks. That's your problem, Cress," Mark tells me. "Go put on a pair of socks and come back to the phone, why don't you? No, actually, maybe not. I gather you can't talk now anyway, right?"

"Right. I'm in the kitchen," I murmur. "If you want to just ask me questions, I'll answer. That way it will be quieter. I don't want to wake anybody up."

"I don't have to ask any questions. I'm coming to see for myself. This afternoon, with Matt."

Mark is impossible. "What are you talking about? This afternoon? Matthew is in Chile, Mark!"

"Was. Right now he's in Miami, en route to D.C. Something got cancelled down there, I think, and he's coming back. He left a message for me at the hotel. Apparently he called home and Gwen said Helen has been trying to reach him about Alicia. He wants us both to hop on Amtrak as soon as he gets here. Can you meet us in Stamford at five?"

"Yes, but wait, Mark! I don't even—Yes, of course I can. What about beds, though? Where are you two going to sleep? We're all piled up on top of each other here as it is."

"I can imagine! Who sleeps with the sheep?" Mark laughs again. "No, we'll stay at Jake and Penelope's. We're just coming to visit Alicia for an hour or so. We're gentlemen callers."

I brighten at this news. Jake and Penelope, Matthew's oldest daughter and her husband, live in Rye, New York. Penelope is an editorial assistant at a Manhattan publishing house, Jake works for public television, and they have a sad-eyed Irish setter named Cervantes whom they bring over on weekends occasionally to go out walking with Alicia and Felix. Jake and Penelope are expecting their first baby in the fall.

"So all of you will be here for tea?" Teatime at Alicia's spreads a kind of cloak of sense and order over everything, even the family.

"All two of us. It's just Matt and me."

"That's fine, I'm sure," I say to him now. As is so often true, I relax into this conversation with Mark just as it is about to end. "I can't wait to see you! And Mark, if you're very good to Megan, maybe she'll let you bottle feed the lamb."

"I can hardly wait, little girl," says Mark. I can feel that he is smiling, not satirically, and I cradle the phone as he says good-bye.

To hang up I have to untangle the phone cord from the kimono sleeve, shaking my arm free. The blues of this kimono are several shades, with a pattern of cranes flying, or maybe they are dancing. That's the way it looks when I move and can see the pattern in reverse, from inside out, through the filling sails of the sleeves.

I walk within this space of light and airiness, feeling the material billow and flow as I move, and I think of the old photographs of Alicia in *National Geographic.* I bow as my mother did in the pictures, but that does not create enough movement to satisfy me. Leaving the kitchen, I take an extravagant step, than another. I turn and turn again in the little hallway, until I am just a little dizzy. Ahhh, better! The kimono becomes voluminous, the big sleeves fill, I turn again and step through the door into the living room, all blossoming air and blue-white wings.

"Chassé, pirouette, développé!" cries Megan, who stands before me in jeans and a T-shirt, the lamb in her arms. "Now you should take a bow, Mom, like this." She hands the lamb to me and gestures grandly, holding out the skirts of an invisible gown and sinking slowly toward the floor, her head bowed, beautiful.

I laugh aloud with the pleasure this gives me.

"Megan! Show me what to do in this kimono. Should I bow like a Japanese lady?" I attempt the little sharp bowing motions Alicia showed us last night, but Megan frowns at once and shakes her head.

"No, you should bow like a bird—that's the way you were dancing." She turns and dips, bows and sweeps. I find everything about her breathtaking—wrists, elbows, pale forehead, bent knee—and hope she won't stop. But she does, abruptly, no longer a bird but a thirteen-year-old girl in blue jeans, her bangs falling across her eyes. "Can I have something to eat? Numie had breakfast already, and everybody else is asleep."

"Yes, of course! We'll have to sneak into the kitchen, though. Alicia's still asleep. And I'm not so sure about Numie." I look at the lamb, whose mouth and nose still show traces of her recent meal. "Will she be noisy?"

"Of course not. Why should she? She's been fed, she's been cuddled. What's there for her to be noisy about?"

"What, indeed?" I have to agree, and the lamb is as quiet as we could wish, except when Megan puts her down on the floor while I open the refrigerator door to get milk for our cereal. At once the four tiny cloven hooves slide on the slippery tiles, and the lamb sinks into a small clattering collapse.

"Poor Numie." Megan rushes to pick up the lamb, checks her legs for injury, and holds her securely in her arms while I put breakfast things on a tray to take them out into the living room.

"You can put her down here on the carpet," I tell Megan when we are settled. "She shouldn't have any trouble standing." Megan, though, looks doubtful.

"On the carpet? Really? What about pee?" she asks. "She's not exactly house-trained."

"I'll tell you a secret." I smile at her. "Neither is Felix."

Megan grins back. "I know. Felix goes outdoors and everything, but when he comes back in he just lifts his leg wherever he wants to anyway. Sarah and I didn't want to say anything about it because we thought Alicia didn't notice."

"I think maybe she knows," I say, and then I am thinking about what Aunt Violet said last night about Alicia herself. "She just doesn't mention it."

Megan nods. "Maybe she doesn't want to hurt Felix's feelings," she says.

"Maybe," I reply. "You know what? That was your Uncle Mark on the phone just now. He's coming this afternoon for tea. With your Uncle Matt. Isn't that amazing? More uncles!"

"Wow!" Megan speaks through a mouthful of cereal, and then, swallowing, says, "Three uncles at once! I've never seen them all together before. And they're so handsome, Mom!" She leans closer to me, flirtatious, a girl in love with uncles. "I just wish I'd brought my camera." She sighs and stares at nothing. This is a side of Megan I have not seen before.

"Maybe somebody else will have one," I suggest, pleased. I imagine Megan lining up the uncles for a group portrait on the stairs, like a glee club.

"I thought Uncle Mark was at the North Pole, anyway. What's he doing here?"

"He's coming to see your grandmother like all the rest of us. He was in Alaska, not the North Pole, with an international study group tracking the long-term effects of the oil spill up there. The Exxon *Valdez*—remember?"

Megan looks vague. "I guess. How long since we've seen him, though? I was pretty little the last time, I think."

I have to stop and think. Three years? Four years? Could it have been so long? I don't like to count; it makes me sad. When you are in the middle of life, the long absences from family members seem like squanderings of time. It is unthinkable now, but when Helen lived in Europe and I was teaching in a Vermont elementary school, we often would go for a year or two without seeing each other at all. I remember receiving Helen's thick, airmail envelopes from Paris full of news about her very young children, even sketches of the boats on the Seine and the people in the parks where they walked (the Luxembourg Gardens, the Tuileries, the hidden tiny parks on the Ile de la Cité). Years later, asked about those times, one of Helen's children said to me, "It was so *gloomy* in Paris—all old ladies and pigeons and rain." I was speechless. To me Helen's life there always seemed so lighthearted and light filled, a Raoul Dufy painting of boats and balloons, and my little bilingual niece dancing through it all with ribbons flying from her wide-brimmed straw hat.

"Three years, I think," I say to Megan. "I can't wait to see them all together myself. We should call Helen right away. Maybe she could drive down this afternoon—then we'd *all* be here."

"We all *are* here," Sarah announces from the top of the stairs, still wearing her nightgown. "Who else is coming?"

"Uncle Mark and Uncle Matt!" Megan calls to her. "And maybe Helen!" My children do not call my sister "Aunt Helen" —just "Helen," just as they call Alicia by her first name. They have always done it, perhaps because I do, and because I have never thought to ask them to do otherwise. This is a family in which we not only speak the same language, but often speak in one voice.

"I don't know about Helen for sure," I caution them. "I don't know what she was planning to do this weekend, and it may be that she'll come later, after we leave. Besides, if we all show up at the same time, what will Alicia think?"

"She'll probably think she's dead," Sarah says, from half-way down the stairs.

"Sarah!"

"Sorry. But doesn't it sound like a funeral? The family gathered . . ."

"Why couldn't it be a reunion?" I protest. "Lots of families have reunions."

"Ours doesn't, does it? I've never been to one." Sarah, having fully descended, sits down next to me on the sofa, takes a piece of toast from the tray, and looks at me dolefully.

"You *plan* a reunion. For funerals, you just gather. The family ga—"

"Sarah, stop it! It was awful the *first* time," I say to her, exasperated. "You sound like a radio announcer from the fifties. It gives me the creeps."

"But I'm right! When you die it happens really suddenly, so everybody just arrives out of the blue, like the uncles today. But if it's a reunion, everybody plans for months ahead, and they write and ask you to find pictures for an album, with photographs of everybody from when they were little, stuff like that. Like we did for Nana. You see what I mean?"

Nana is Garrett's mother, whose friendship I have been missing since the divorce. There is no bad feeling between us; we have maintained contact over the years, exchanged birthday greetings and news of family activity with hardly an interruption, but there is on both sides a reticence now, a restraint that is only right and proper, born of unspoken loyalties. That certain things we do not anticipate losing are also sacrificed through a divorce is inevitable, though the smaller losses are overshadowed at first by the large ones, and by the time we discover their nature, they are already irreversible, a small sad surprise that we accept along with everything else there is to be accepted, like the twinge that lingers after the injury is gone.

"Yes, I see. But you know, your uncles aren't coming from out of the blue. Mark has been in Washington at a congressional hearing, and Matt is en route from Miami."

The girls give me disbelieving stares.

"You don't call that out of the blue?" says Megan.

It is obvious that they do. So, it appears later, does Alicia.

"But where *are* they?" she asks me, as did Aunt Violet and Luke at intervals during breakfast when the girls had gone upstairs with Nicky. Luke, without a fire to tend, is nervous. His left leg is crossed over the right one, and on the free-swinging foot his cowboy boot jiggles so fast that his whole leg vibrates.

"They're on their way here," I explain.

"It will be such a joy for you to see all your sons together!" says Aunt Violet. Alicia has risen late this morning but still looks tired, as if she did not sleep well. I am feeling tired myself, having tried to explain the pending arrivals to my mother twice already. The trouble for Alicia seems to lie in placing Matt and Mark geographically, the same difficulty she has had with Helen.

"You say Matthew is in South America? I thought he was living in the Northwest. Has he moved? I feel so terribly vague today . . ." Alicia says.

"What do you mean, Mother? Don't you feel well? Can I get you anything?" I become tense, alert. I am wondering if Alicia is having a stroke. A very small, undetectable stroke right this very minute as we sit talking together.

"I feel fine, dear . . . just rather stupid." Alicia is smiling at me. "Tell me again, Cress. Everyone seems to be arriving at once, and it makes me feel rather confused."

Maybe she can retrain her mind, practice tricks and techniques to improve her memory. B. F. Skinner wrote a book about training oneself to deal with the aging process in this way. I leafed through it and though it very funny, charming but silly, when I picked it up at the house of an old friend's father at Christmas one year. It described in minute detail many appallingly obvious practical systems for not forgetting your umbrella when it rains, taking your pills at the right time, dressing appropriately for the weather, and so on. I thought it was only for B. F. Skinner himself, and other absentminded professor types. Now I am thinking I should look for a copy of the book and get it somehow, tactfully, to Alicia.

"Mark and Matthew are coming in from Washington this afternoon, just to have tea," I explain to her one more time. "They've both been traveling, and they both happened to be in Washington at the same time, so they met there and they're coming up here. For tea. They'll stay overnight at Jake and Penelope's house, not here."

"Overnight?" Alicia seems more distressed, not less. "Surely more than one night—it's such a long way!"

"From Washington? Not these days, really. It's just an hour on the shuttle—people do it every day. And I'm sure it's much nicer to have tea with you and spend a night with Jake and Penelope than stay over in some hotel in Washington, anyway." How long will this go on? I look at Aunt Violet for help, but she is looking away.

"In a hotel? But Matt *lives* there!" Alicia finally cries out in protest, and she puts her almost-empty cup of Twining's English Breakfast tea on top of yesterday's copy of *The New York Times*.

I stare at the teacup and then at my mother, completely bewildered. What should I try next? I can't think.

"Matthew *lives* in Washington!" Alicia repeats. "Why should he stay in a hotel at all? Has something happened you're not telling me? Gwen? Has she—"

"Seattle!" Luke interrupts sharply. "Washington. Seattle, Washington, Cress. You forget. Matt and Gwen live in Seattle. Washington."

"*I* forg—Oh, my God." I stop myself, begin to feel my face heating, know that soon it will bright red—flushed all over.

"Washington, *D.C.* They're in D.C. I'm so sorry, Mother. I didn't understand. Matthew and Mark both had business in Washington, D.C. this week. I wasn't talking about Seattle. Didn't I ever say D.C?" Aunt Violet shakes her head while Luke puts both cowboy boots on the floor, pats my shoulder, and stands up.

Alicia smiles comfortingly at me, and reaches over to pat my hand. "Never mind, Cress. It's a natural enough mistake, isn't it?" I feel the dry warmth of her hand on top of my own.

"I think we should all take a walk!" says Luke, up and striding toward the door. "Any chance we can unglue those kids from the tube?"

"Wait, Luke! I have to get the dog's leash." Alicia laughs and rises from her own seat, though more slowly. It is easy to see that she loves the eager strength of her son, as I love Nicky's. Mothers feel this way about sons, I think. Daughters also give us joy in their movement—Megan dancing, the bend of Sarah's neck when she bows it in shyness, so lovely, so gentle a curve of that soft neck from this clever girl who likes to bristle. But it is a different pleasure with sons. For some reason we love their physical arrogance, the swing of their arms and the swagger of their legs, the very motions that finally take them away from us.

"The leash *and* the dog, I hope," Aunt Violet says to Alicia, heaving herself up out of her chair. "I'll come with you."

"The children should come, too. Luke is right. They've watched TV long enough."

I go upstairs and find the girls willing enough to come along, while Nicholas is already restless and has begun taking books out of the lower bookshelves along the bedroom wall. Nicky is not very interested in television, which is sometimes a disappointment to me. He is an energetic, active toddler for whom I would have welcomed even the partial, blessed supervision that "Sesame Street" and "Mr. Rogers" provided in the late afternoon when the girls were his age. Nicholas is tolerant of, but never mesmerized by, the screen, so I have to check on him often at home to be sure he has not abandoned it in favor of weeding Joe's tender seedlings, temptingly laid out on trays in their tiny individual green plastic pots by the big kitchen window at the farmhouse, or trying to feed gravel to the hamsters, or putting the flyswatter in the oven.

I emphatically believe that a child's upbringing should include television, probably because mine did not. Cal would not have one in the house, but we all watched it anyway, greedily and indiscriminately, at the homes of neighboring friends. I adored television as one does anything forbidden by one's parent's, and can still sing every word of every theme song of every Western I watched on the neighbor's TV in the late fifties. I loved them all—*Maverick* and *Sugarfoot, Bonanza, The Lawman,* and *Have Gun, Will Travel*—equally, though there was one friendship-straining fight with my closest friend one night when she slept over about whether the words *Wire Paladin— San Francisco,* printed on the calling card of *Have Gun, Will Travel*'s hero gunslinger, indicated directions for sending Mr. Paladin a telegram, or simply spelled his name.

"Nobody's name is Wire," I argued. "It's ridiculous! That's a *verb.*"

"I don't care what it is, it's his name. I think it's a *cool* name. I'm going to name *my* son Wire," my friend Irena argued back.

"It's an Old West name, I bet. Wire Paladin is a real cowboy name like . . . like John Wayne, or something—ask anybody."

I asked only Mark, who knew everything, but all he volunteered to the discussion was that John Wayne's real name was not John but Marion, and this shocked us both so much that we stopped arguing entirely.

The children have left the lamb quietly settled in its box, and when they have put on their jackets and come downstairs, Nicholas looks over the assembled relatives in outdoor clothes and makes his way to his grandmother.

"Go for a walk, Ganna?" he asks Alicia, using his own name for her, which she accepts without question, as she does his proprietary attitude.

"Yes," she says to him. "But first I think a kiss would be quite nice." I am relieved to see that Alicia is wearing a bright red jacket this morning and a flowered scarf on her head. Her colors are those of a Russian matreshka doll with no drab raincoat or boots in sight.

"KISS!" cries Nicholas, and runs to her throwing his arms around her stomach. This is the greeting that makes me cringe, but they are both accustomed to it. When Alicia recovers from the first rush and bends over to Nicky, he gives her a wet and very noisy kiss on the cheek. Sarah makes a face.

"He's just *slobbering*, Mom. Can't we teach him not to?"

"Maybe," I laugh. "But he thinks it doesn't count unless you can hear it."

"Yucch," says Megan, moving toward the door.

"Are you almost ready, Cressida?" My mother is speaking in a tactful, reminding way. Reminding me of what? I look around at everyone here, Alicia in her bright colors, Aunt Violet in a plum-colored ankle-length coat, Luke in a denim jacket lined with sheepskin, and my children in their parkas. Then I look down at myself and realize that my jacket is still upstairs.

"What a *dingbat* I am! I can't believe how absentminded I'm getting! You all go ahead out. I'll be right there, I promise. What a dummy!"

I am talking too fast again, stammering with embarrassment. Too much embarrassment, a flood. Luke looks at me and I am overcome. I will start to blush again, I know it. I can't manage anything today. I make an awkward plunge toward the stairs, aware of every bumbling cell in my body.

"I'll be right back," I call out once more. "You go ahead— I'll catch up."

As I take the stairs two at a time, I can hear my mother's quiet voice floating up with me. "Don't rush, Cress. You'll fall. We'll wait. It's nothing to fret about, for heaven's sake. I forget things all the time . . ."

# Chapter
# 7

W E are walking toward the tidal inlet where Alicia's neighbors keep their boats in summer: windsurfers and Sunfish and Boston Whalers dragged up above high-water mark over the mussels and the sharp-edged shore grass, unostentatious cabin cruisers tethered like well-behaved thoroughbreds in mid-channel. Alicia likes to look for shore birds here: a family of ducks diving and splashing in the rush of turning tide under the cement bridge where the road crosses the inlet; a solitary egret or great blue heron stalking the mud flats farther out; once in a while a pair or two of Canada geese who have spent the night in a marshy field by the water.

We tramp along, Alicia bright as a tanager herself, Luke in

his cowboy boots, the children rosy and well warmed by their own goose-down parkas, and Aunt Violet in her long city coat. She alone seems weary, and though I think I can sense the nature of her weariness, I know I am the wrong person, the wrong age, to offer comfort. The city coat, too, has a dull look in this morning's brightness, and its color is the tired purple of an old bruise. Still she keeps up with the rest of us, uncomplaining, and we make a formidable family procession on the road.

This is the same black-tar road that was our bicycle road, our bus-stop road, the road to my friend Irena's house. I walked this way every morning in my camel's hair coat in junior high school, too, after Irena had moved to Bethesda, Maryland at the end of sixth grade. I would meet Teri Schultz at a point just halfway between my house and the bus stop under the big chestnut tree, half a mile farther on. Teri was in ninth grade when I was in seventh, and I was amazed that she would even walk with me, a lowly preteen. Under Teri's camel's hair coat she wore a much tighter sweater than I would have dared to own or could have done justice to: a fuzzy cardigan worn backwards and buttoned down her spine, as the ninth-grade girls wore them that year—terrifyingly provocative. On Teri's mouth there was more Tangee lipstick than any seventh grader would dream of being allowed to wear.

I did try it once, picking up a tube of Tangee at the drugstore after school and applying it the way I thought Teri did when I got home. But Cal came out of his office and roared with laughter, then—much worse—made me go back into the office with him again and lectured for an hour on the atavistic yet disastrously expensive materialism of Western civilization. After the first ten minutes he really hit his stride, and by the time twenty more had passed he was no longer laughing, but instead asking me in his Wrath-of-God voice why I didn't just go out, pick berries, and squeeze the juice on my face in stripes the way tribal women did. (His travels had taken him to East

Africa and the Philippines recently, and we were to hear a lot of talk about tribal peoples and simpler cultures.) At least it wouldn't be such a waste of money, he said. I listened to all of this in a shivering panic, because I thought I was going to have to answer the question about picking berries—one never knew which questions were rhetorical, with Cal, and which were the ones that would leave him waiting, glowering, for a response. I couldn't think of a thing to say in this case (What berries? Rhododendron berries? Pachysandra berries? Poison ivy berries? We're talking November in Fairfield County, Cal!) except that Tangee was a lot less expensive than Revlon or Max Factor. Fortunately Cal made the leap, as he sometimes did, from Western civilization to materialism Right Here At Home, to women and shopping, and then, of all things, to Mother's Day. (Crass commercial exploitation of family values by the forces of the marketplace.) By the time he had run through all of that, by some happy miracle, he was in a better mood again, jovially quoting Alicia's father (or was it Calvin Coolidge?) who once had said "Where there are women, there will be commerce!" Years away from any feminist consciousness, I was simply relieved and grateful for this turn in the conversation, and for the chance to be sent away, finally, with a pat on the back.

Two years later, when I had my ears pierced, he began exactly the same lecture, in the same mood, starting with the laughing promise that he would forgive me if I pierced my nose too, as tribal women did. By then I was ready for him, though, and staved off the Wrath of God by saying that I couldn't possibly pierce my nose because I had to blow it so often, living in this cold, inhospitable, and unhealthy New England climate. He liked that, as he was already leaning toward the simple, wholesome life of the Pacific Islands, so my ears—after only fifteen minutes or so—were safe.

Teri and I used to meet at the crossroads that my family is now passing in its promenade. When I was walking to school

in seventh grade, someone had just built a red cedar ranch
house here, the first split-level ranch house that I saw in our
area, though ten years later the town was covered with them,
as well as the oversized rambling Capes and massive Colonials
with white clapboards and black shutters that sprang up as the
town became a bedroom community for New York City.

When Cal and Alicia first came here, this part of Connecticut was still partially rural, with only the wealthy, weekend
millionaires in their fieldstone-and-plaster or timbered mock-
Tudor retreats living down by the cove and the inlet. The
suburb grew up all around me as I was growing up myself, and
I welcomed it. Instead of great gloomy mansions nobody ever
lived in at the end of spooky driveways lined with dry-leaved
shrubs that always seemed to need dusting, there were real
houses, houses for families, just like the ones in my Ginn &
Company First-Grade Reader, houses for Dick and Jane and
Baby Sally, with television aerials on the roofs and baseball
bats left on green, regularly mowed lawns. How I loved the
lawns! The one we are about to pass now used to have a family
of painted deer on it, later replaced by a smiling man with a
black face and a jockey's red coat and hat, holding at the end of
his outstretched arm a metal ring to which one could tie a
visiting horse. I never did see a horse there, but refused to give
up hope. A horse grazing on a lawn in my own neighborhood!
I did not know at the time that this brand-new suburb, like
many of its era, held equally discouraging views on horses and
black faces in certain neighborhoods, and mine was one of
those neighborhoods. I was content to love these lawns and
their ornaments. Every time I came this way I wished again
that Cal and Alicia could be more like other people, people who
had television sets and outdoor statuary. All Cal would allow
on his lawn were trees and bushes and grass that grew too
long. Why didn't we have a jockey with an invisible horse? Or
painted deer? Why couldn't we have little porcelain gnomes, at

least, like those I'd seen occasionally in town, with painted porcelain stocking caps? Or those ducks on sticks, whose wings perpetually churned in their wooden circle, even if they couldn't fly? It wasn't fair.

In Cal's wilderness of a nonlawn—his sleeping-beauty thicket of untended Connecticut jungle that he grew for the sake of privacy between the house and the tar road, between his family and The Press—there were real deer once. They were there when Cal and Alicia first moved to the stone house. The animals would browse in the tangle of brambles and sumac that had once been a weekend millionaire's tennis court, and Cal had placed a salt lick in a clearing he made there. He would take us to see them at night, one by one so as not to frighten the wild creatures, and we would watch the deer come like shadows—does and fawns and tense, shy bucks behind them, all bending their necks to the taste. I know that the deer are back again in unwelcome numbers, and that they are now pests that carry Lyme disease and eat the flowering shrubs in all the suburban neighborhoods around New York, but what I remember was different. Even now I can see the shadows and a white patch on the ground with a quiet head dipped to it, and I can feel the worn leather coat that smelled like mothballs and motorboats, with somebody's arms around me.

"I can't believe the way this place has changed!" Luke says to Alicia. "New houses everywhere!"

"It has changed a good deal since you lived here, yes." Alicia looks exhilarated with the exercise, walking in eager step with her son and daughter. Aunt Violet has dropped back to meander more slowly with the girls and Nicky, who are collecting pinecones while Felix rummages in dry leaves at the side of the road.

"But it hasn't changed much lately, has it?" I ask. "Weren't these houses here the last time you came, Luke? It's not exactly *new* construction."

"It's all totally different! I can hardly recognize these roads —you never used to be able to see across to the inlet from here. And everybody's property is so civilized!"

I look where he is pointing, over a stone wall and across an expanse of terraced landscaping that seems, I have to admit, very civilized indeed. I notice too that one well-trimmed cascade of bushes is composed of a group of tenacious, fast-spreading little pines that we call ground hemlock in Vermont. How the farmers curse and wrestle with this at home! Ground hemlock unchecked covers the pastures like a plague of rooted nests and makes the land unfit for grazing. Here in Connecticut I suppose somebody gets paid, handsomely, for planting and tending it.

Still, this view has been the same for some time, I am almost sure. Perhaps not quite since the time I was a child, but certainly since my own children were born. Fifteen years, at least. What does Luke remember? What was it like here before he went away to college? Again I work to recover memory, and it comes. There was a big field with marsh grass thick in places because the land was so low that it was often flooded. There were also hurricanes in the fifties, making this property look like a giant's pond, with a stone wall circling it. The hurricanes killed the apple trees that once grew here, though as I recall these were withered and unproductive anyway. The land was too salt laden for any fruit tree to thrive.

I recognize the place where Luke is pointing as the field of my flying dreams. After seeing Mary Martin in *Peter Pan* with Irena, in New York, I dreamed night after night of running through the marsh grass that grew here, trying to fly. I ran faster and faster in these dreams, with my arms flapping and my hopes high, running through the marsh's mud and reaching for the open sky. I would run toward the sea wall at the far end of the wild field and become airborne just before hitting the wall, or tripping over it into the water. If I kept at it long enough and if I didn't wake up first, I flew. And that was bliss, nothing less. I soared over the mud flats and the great blue herons of Long Island Sound, high and free, without wings, without arms, without weight or thought. And that feeling of having lifted myself from lowest earth to highest air lingered through my waking hours.

The land is much higher now, obviously no longer a field but an extended and elegant lawn, "grounds" for one of the old mansions we knew when they were empty, this one renovated in the seventies for a well-to-do investment banker and his family. Someone twenty years ago must have brought in quantities of fill to eradicate the marsh grass and create the bushy terraces, and a whole generation of dreaming children has grown up since.

"There was no road beyond the inlet," Luke is saying to Alicia. "It was all woods, and there was a water tower."

"The water tower!" I cry out, my attention riveted. "With the mad monk! You terrified me so much with that story, Luke. Do you remember?"

Luke laughs. "The mad monk! I'd forgotten all about him."

"There was rust, or something, a long red stain of it running down the side of the water tower," I explain to Sarah and Megan, who have caught up with us. "But your uncle Luke said a mad monk had jumped from the tower and dashed himself on the rocks. That was his blood on the side of the tower, Luke said. I was too scared to go near the place, even in the daytime!"

"Poor Cressida!" Alicia says, shaking her head. "Brothers are really terrible!" She makes a sympathetic, cooing noise, but I'm not fooled by it. I know that she is on the side of mad monks and strong sons today. Quite a way behind us Aunt Violet and Nicky have their heads bowed together over something he is holding in his hand and is describing to her authoritatively but unintelligibly from this distance.

"But it doesn't make sense!" Sarah objects. "If the mad monk jumped from the tower and dashed himself on the rocks, then there would have been blood on the rocks—not the tower."

I stop in my tracks. "That's true! Why didn't I think of that? Luke, if only I'd had my daughter's brains I would have foiled you!" We are playful. We are noisy. Our faces are red and our breath is coming fast. We have been walking quickly.

Luke turns on Sarah. "Foiled? Foiled, you say? I hate being foiled!" He shifts his eyebrows and twists a nonexistent mustache. He crouches low then rises up and moves toward Sarah and Megan with his hands curled into threatening claws. "Aha!" he says, "Shazam! Booga-booga! Foiled? I'll show you foiled!"

Alicia chuckles, and Sarah, too old for this, grins in spite of herself. Nicky looks up from lecturing his great aunt and rushes at his uncle like a cannonball, butting him with his head so that Luke staggers and begins to fall. It all happens too quickly for anyone to catch him, and Felix barks twice as Luke starts to go down. He steadies himself at the last minute with a scrabble of cowboy boots on the tar, however, and is able to remain upright.

"Nicky! careful!" Sarah catches her brother around the waist, looking quickly at Luke and then over at me for one solicitous, breath-holding moment. We of our generation are vulnerable too, in our children's eyes.

"He was just trying to protect you from an evil magician, Lady. Give the kid a break," says Luke, ruffling Nicky's hair.

"If only you magicians would learn to use your power for good instead of evil . . ." I sigh.

"Why should we?" says Luke. "What fun would that be?"

"Hey, Sarah," Megan calls out, "remember these?" She has taken off her glove and holds the tasselled head of a stalk of pampas grass. It is as soft as a nosegay of feathers, wheatlike in color and configuration.

"Of course," says Sarah. "Featherbeds!"

"Featherbeds?" I question. "What do you mean?"

"We used to make beds out of these for our dolls. We'd put them in little boxes and cover them with Kleenex. Sometimes we'd have piles of them in one box. They made wonderful, puffy beds. We used to always pick them when we came here."

Irena and I used to pick stalks of pampas grass, as close to the ground as possible, and we used them as great big paintbrushes, trailing them in puddles and then along the road behind us, their bedraggled heads leaving thin, swiftly vanishing wet lines on the tar. We also brandished them in war, riding imaginary palfreys through the fields while we waved the stalks like banners or charged one another with them like lances. Sometimes they were used in sword play, but that was unsatisfactory because the stalks splintered and broke into sharp little shafts. I am wondering now if I should have exposed my girls to a little less Laura Ingalls Wilder and a little more Sir Walter Scott. But I suspect they would find their own uses for the pampas grass anyway.

"Peek-a-boo!" Nicky says from under his uncle's coat, nuzzling at the sheepskin.

"Peek-a-boo *you!*" says Aunt Violet who has now caught up, her mittened hands over her eyes.

Alicia smiles at the two of them. "I wonder how old a game that is," she says. "Peek-a-boo. It must go back much further even than our own childhood, don't you think so, Violet? I can certainly remember it, among others."

Aunt Violet is considering. We have stopped walking, and stand together at the beginning of the inlet, with no egrets or other birds yet in evidence. "Do you remember 'Miss Jenny-A-Jones,' Alicia?" she asks.

"Of course!" Alicia at once begins to sing, in her well-bred, well-trained light voice (she studied singing at one time, though she is too self-conscious to sing, except with the family), on tune and with just a little vibrato.

" 'I've come to see Miss Jenny-A-Jones, and how is she today?' "

" 'She's got a sore throat!' " says Aunt Violet, gruffly and with an accent—part English butler and part growling beast. Both she and Alicia laugh while the rest of the group stares.

"It was really the most wonderful game!" Alicia wipes her eyes. "How often I think of it, when someone wants to see me and I can't think of a way to say no. Miss Jenny-A-Jones and all her ailments: the measles, a broken leg, *leprosy!* Oh, Violet," she stops in midrecollection, "wasn't it awful? We were so afraid of leprosy. The thought that one could just rot away, starting with the tips of one's fingers. I suppose now it wouldn't even cross these children's minds."

"They have to worry about AIDS, though," I remind her darkly, then turn to Sarah for help. "Would you say that the kids you know are afraid of AIDS, Sarah? Do they think about it at all, or is it just a media thing for them, something outside their experience?"

Sarah frowns at me. I think I know why—Miss Jenny-A-Jones was lovely. Did I have to bring up AIDS? I look out across the inlet. I can see moving shapes far out in the water among the tidal pools and marshy hummocks at the edge of the inlet, near the open sound. Luke is also pointing them out to Alicia. Herons? Geese?

"It isn't that kids don't think about it," Sarah says. "It's more that they think about it for somebody else. Nobody I know is afraid of getting AIDS, I mean even people who are really sexually active." Sexually active! Well, I asked for this. But if she says "sexually active" so easily, does that mean she will be sexually active soon? Better not to think. "But a lot of people think that they may know somebody *else* who's going to get AIDS," she goes on. "It's kind of weird."

"And that seems frightening enough just in itself, I bet," says Luke, with Nicky still clinging to him, leaning his back now against Luke's long legs and looking out to sea as everyone else is doing. Sarah nods at Luke, and gives him a shy smile.

"What if you run out of excuses?" Megan, standing near her grandmother, asks. Alicia says nothing. She looks as if her eyes are bothering her—too much wind? A breeze has come up.

"What if Miss Jenny-A-Jones runs out of excuses?" Megan asks again. "Then does she have to see the person, Leesha? Or what?"

Alicia still does not respond.

Megan looks around to the rest of us for guidance, but before she can repeat the question for the second time Sarah breaks in with impatience.

"She can just forget! She can forget she ever heard of you and tell you to go away!" Sarah speaks grumpily and loud, furrowing her brow at Megan, who is not offended but only surprised—she knows Sarah too well to waste time on hurt feelings.

"No! That's too easy!" Megan says. "The game wouldn't work. It's like saying you just don't feel like being at home. The whole point is that she has to have a good excuse."

"Why isn't that a good excuse? People forget things just as often as they get the measles or break their legs—more often! Why does it have to be such a big deal?" I recognize this tone at once, the sound of Sarah's ax grinding.

"But it wouldn't be *fair!*" Megan's voice climbs to fighting pitch. "Anybody could say that—there wouldn't be any reason for the game at all."

Alicia stands blinking with wind or water in her eyes, not

responding to the argument, not looking at the movement far out in the water.

"What do you think, Aunt Violet?" I ask. My aunt does not respond either, for she and Luke are training all their attention upon the activity across the cove. I alone watch Alicia, in my private confusion. Is something significant happening in my mother's mind right this minute, something dangerous? Or is the trouble in *my* mind?

The girls are caught up in their argument now and no longer notice their grandmother's silence. What a curse it is, this noticing: what a mine field of potential hurt. I wish I could give it up. Instead I pursue Alicia; I can't help it. "What are the rules for this game, anyway? Do you take turns singing verses, or are there consequences if you're the one with no excuses? How do you play?"

She does not answer me, but even as I stand suffering in the empty air around my words, she turns her head toward the water, alert to a noise there. I hear it too, and then at once there is a great rushing of wings and a great splashing of water, with a wild, loud series of honking cries that would do credit to the biggest barnyard in Vermont, as the shapes on the water marshall and reveal themselves at last. The Canada geese have risen up out of the mud flats, have circled the inlet, and now are landing right here beside us in the channel, right in front of our eyes.

The whole family stands still, hardly breathing. Even Nicky is quiet as he clings to Luke. Megan has the good sense to catch Felix up in her arms before he can rush over the bank on top of the intruders, and his barks of protest can be heard only faintly beneath the clamor of geese as they honk and preen and settle, so close that one of us could reach down and pluck a trophy from any feathered back. They gossip with one another for a moment or two, fluttering and hissing as they stretch their necks like so many snakes in a pit. Then they turn our way, peer nearsightedly at us, and evidently decide against the location after all. With just as much commotion as they created on arrival, they depart. A few geese, the ones who barely landed at all, have taken flight in alarm, but the others are more relaxed. We have crowded, not frightened them, and they make their way down to the water again with leisurely waddlings and honkings. Finally, all assembled—about fifty of them, I think —the whole flotilla drifts to the middle of the channel again and off into the black-rippled distances of the inlet.

"It's a blessing," I hear my mother whisper. Felix has stopped barking or even struggling in Megan's arms. Instead he is now quietly licking her chin.

"It's a blessing," Alicia says again, "when wild birds land so close to humans. It's a gift."

"I've never seen so many geese all at once," I whisper back to her.

"Forty-three," says Sarah, in her normal tone of voice. "That's what I counted. What about you, Megan?" Sisters. Comparing numbers, counting cars as the freight train rolls by, counting geese.

"Hmmm? Oh, I don't know," says Megan, still dreamy with the visitation, her chin wet from Felix's attentions, her imagination far out in the inlet with the geese.

"Some people don't like them, you know." Aunt Violet remarks. "Or ducks either. They feel there are too many now and they've become too tame with everyone feeding them. It's gotten out of hand, I've heard people say—just too messy, with the feathers and whatnot everywhere. Overpopulation must be the main complaint, I suppose."

"I'll bet the main complaint is the whatnot," says Luke, next to her. We are walking back toward Alicia's house, Nicky riding on Luke's shoulders. "There was a problem in the Twin

Cities, I heard on the plane. St. Paul, I think it was that they have so many little parks with lakes and ponds in the middle of the city, and that they are all full of goose sh—droppings."

Megan giggles. She has released Felix, who runs ahead of us now, homeward bound.

"There is something so wonderful about feathered creatures," says Alicia. "Anything with feathers."

"Only birds have feathers." says Sarah. "I remember when I learned that. I was really little, and they had it on Sesame Street—What makes a bird a bird? They kept asking questions, like 'Is it the nests they build?' or 'Is it that they lay eggs?' and they'd tell you the other animals that did those things. Feathers were the one thing birds had, but nobody else."

"What about angels?" Aunt Violet asks. "They have feathers."

"Well, I guess so." Sarah looks embarrassed. She had not necessarily intended her reminiscence to turn into a conversation.

"Vi, I once told you that I wanted to be reincarnated as a bird. Do you remember?" Alicia asks. "A rose-breasted grosbeak. It was when we were both reading about reincarnation, but you were much better informed. Do you remember what you said to me?"

"I hate to think," says Aunt Violet. "I used to read volumes and volumes on reincarnation. I can't remember any of it now, although I still approve of the idea."

She approves. Only Aunt Violet could approve of reincarnation.

"You said that only saints in this life were entitled to feathers in the next," her sister reminds her. "I gave up the idea at once, of course." Alicia's eyes are bright with amusement, her hands deep in the pockets of the red jacket. Just like Helen's and mine in brisk weather, her nose has a red tip from the cold.

I wonder if she still has in her right pocket a smooth horse chestnut, with one flat side that is shiny as if oiled, because she has been rubbing it over and over with her thumb for years. We used to get flat-sided horse chestnuts for her from the bus-stop chestnut tree, when we could find them, just as we would search the beaches of Maine in summer for "lucky stones"— the ones with a white ring that ran all the way around them, unbroken, bright as halos. See? See, Mother? We found this stone, this feather, this special chestnut, just for you.

"How terrible!" says Aunt Violet. "What a priggish thing for me to say! And besides, I'm sure you qualify for sainthood, Alicia."

Alicia laughs, "No, I don't think so."

"Why a rose-breasted grosbeak?" I ask.

"Because they have a lovely song—and a lovely mate who takes equal care of the children," my mother answers promptly.

"And what a wonderful bird he must be!" says Aunt Violet. "Alicia, I want to ask you something. Did your husband ever change a diaper? Ever in his life? George certainly didn't."

"Not that I know of," says Alicia thoughtfully. "He might have, I suppose, if necessary."

"Oh, come now, Alicia. You *know* he didn't," I feel compelled to say here. "I even remember one of his pronouncements on this, because I was so mad at him when he said it. 'Any man who changes diapers isn't a man at all.' Outrageous!"

"Yes, but then he *may* have said if just to irritate you, dear. One never knew," says Alicia, and Luke laughs.

"But it's so unfair!" I persist. "You two were just as busy as they were. You both worked just as hard—Alicia was writing, and Aunt Violet, you had to spend a lot of time at the college during all those years when you were a trustee, for heaven's sake.

"They made sure that we *had* lots of help," Aunt Violet

reminds me. "We were both fortunate enough to be able to afford hired help, and there was more of it available then. It's much harder for your generation."

"I don't know," I say. "I'm not sure that's true. The friends I have who hire people to help with the kids—not just day care, but au pair girls or even nannies, all trained and British and so on—I suppose it's a help, but it's expensive and it's, well, *strange,* you know? It's like having an extra member of the family, but they aren't really family—it doesn't always work."

"Well, that's certainly true," said Violet. "Some of the people we hired were *very* strange and didn't work at all. I always wonder if it's because they're so far from home. It was really more of a mothering job than managing, at times. I remember one poor pregnant Norwegian—oh, dear!"

"You sound just like Leesha!" Sarah says, smiling at her. "She says 'oh, dear!' exactly like that."

"I suppose I must!" Aunt Violet said, pleased. "After all, we're birds of a feather, aren't we. Alicia?"

Alicia does not answer for a moment that becomes long enough to make me nervous once more. "When you were first married, did Cal help with the children?" I want to go on to say, like the rose-breasted grosbeak's husband, Alicia—that's the connection here, remember? What you said about the rose-breasted grosbeak? We're having a conversation that you started yourself. Please don't leave me here.

". . . When I was married," she says finally. "It seems so long ago that I was married. Sometimes it's hard to believe I ever *was* married."

I felt it again, the chill, creeping sense of annihilation. Alicia is erasing us all—Cal, and then the rest of us, in her retreat into the mist.

"Do you ever feel that way, Vi? Oh, look! There's Martha!" Alicia's face clears and brightens. She waves to a tall person approaching briskly in a bright blue parka.

Felix barks and jumps around her as she comes closer. Nicky wiggles to get down from Luke's shoulders. I am aware that Alicia has just asked her sister to compare experiences of widowhood, but Aunt Violet is not a widow. Uncle George is very much alive and waiting for her on East 77th Street.

"Hi, Martha!" I call out. Martha Elsen is, in fact, a widow, with a son about Sarah's age. Having moved next door to Alicia five years ago, she has developed a friendship with our mother that is both sensitive and practical. Martha may telephone Helen or me on the spur of the moment to say, "Your mom's a little down today. Why don't you give her a call?" Or she might notice that the furnace doesn't seem to be running well. Or she will invite Alicia to go swimming at her health club, or to a movie, or out to dinner with friends who won't be inclined to worship or overwhelm. Martha is the kind of friend who lends strength rather than taking it, though she claims that the benefits of the relationship are all on her side: Alicia gives her perspective and makes her laugh.

Martha waves at us, an encompassing wave, big enough to greet an ocean liner or a kindergarten on a field trip.

"Hi all! What a great morning!" She grins at everybody, then addresses Alicia. "Are you all Linley'd out, or are you ready for one more?"

"You're always welcome, however many of us there are," Luke says to Martha. "Good to see you again, Martha."

"You, too," she says, and pivots cheerfully in her white tennis shoes to fall in step beside him. The shoes are big, probably men's, probably inexpensive.

"I like your shoes," I tell her truthfully. "Very nice."

"They're Noah's," she confesses. "He'll kill me. Except they're so clean now he may not recognize them when he gets home. He's on a weekend with his environmental club at school. Hiking boots and frostbite. I took a chance and put these in the machine while he's gone."

"Noah's not here?" Sarah asks, disappointed. Noah and Sarah are good friends, sharing certain character traits (shyness, sarcasm) and interests (acting, photography) without seeing each other often enough to let the relationship get complicated. ("Don't be ridiculous, Mom! Half my friends are boys. It's not *like* that.")

"Nope, but he gets back today, he has midterms coming up —come over and visit. You guys must be swamped in that little house. Look at this crowd! And there's another one coming tonight!" She puts a hand to her forehead and staggers back, clutching Alicia's arm.

"Another *two* coming, actually," I correct her. "Mark and Matthew are both planning to come this afternoon, but not for the night. They're staying at Jake and Penelope's."

Martha waves away this information. "I know. Helen called last night: She's coming too! Don't fret; she called to see if she could stay with me, which is great—I'd love it. She should be here anytime. You will have *all* your children here by the end of the day, Alicia. Want to hop a flight to the Bahamas?"

Alicia stops walking at this and looks at Martha with a decided frown. With her nose and cheeks and jacket all red she is suddenly fierce and small, an angry elf in a red coat. I, for my part, feel betrayed. Why is Helen doing this? We agreed that we would take turns here, to make our visits seem at least a little bit normal, and that was back when Luke was going to be the only other sibling present. Now we're all going to be here at once. This is crazy.

Luke is shaking his head at Martha, amused. "What a circus!" he says. I flinch.

"It's too much!" says Alicia finally. Here it comes, I can feel it. Here's where we all get nailed. Who do we think we are, the five of us, descending upon her, tampering with her quiet life, greedily sucking the milk of her memory? She's going to send us all to our rooms without supper. Actually, Alicia was not a disciplinarian, nor did she need to be. One word of disappointment or unhappiness would put us in our places immediately. I believe that she once spanked Mark, for putting a family of turtles in her bed at night, giving her an indescribable fright when she climbed in on top of them. Cal was away at the time and Alicia felt compelled to take some action, but she was remorseful afterwards when Mark told her, tearfully, that he hadn't meant to frighten her—he just thought the turtles would like it there and that she might want some company too.

"You have so little time alone, Martha," she says now. "It isn't fair to you. Helen can stay with us. We'll make room. You mustn't give up your one free weekend to take care of my family."

"Don't be silly, Alicia! Helen and I are old friends. Besides, she has Melissa with her, and that's more than your house can handle."

"Melissa's coming?" Sarah perks right up, as does Megan. The three girls are close companions during any of the time that Melissa is home from boarding school, although Megan has lately grown very close to Helen's son Michael, only one year younger than she is.

"Maybe. She's having a crisis of some sort at her school, I believe. They have just notified Helen, but she says she won't know much about it until she gets there." Melissa's school in Connecticut is an easy hour's drive from Alicia's house, so Helen's presence here is explained.

"Well, I'm leaving before lunch," Aunt Violet announces. "That should help."

"Oh, no!" Alicia cries. "What will I do without you?"

I am beginning to feel some irritation. Who does Alicia think her children are, anyway: a pack of invading Visigoths? We're her flesh and blood!

"George needs me," Aunt Violet says. "And I need George, too." She adds this as if it surprises her. Uncle George is now in a wheelchair, and there are nurse's aides who come in by the day to help Violet attend to him. She once confessed to me that she would have preferred to continue doing it alone, even though her own doctor has forbidden her to. She said she liked having her house and her husband all to herself, whatever the difficulties.

"I don't like to be away for more than twenty-four hours," she says. "You'll be just fine, Alicia. You have your children."

"Yes, and so many of them," says Alicia in a small voice, and after that, for a while, we all just keep on walking.

# Chapter

# 8

I A M drinking coffee with my mother and my sister in Martha's house, after lunch. For lunch Martha gave us French bread and Dutch cheese, green salad with Italian dressing, and her own home-made vegetable soup that originated, as Martha did, in Waterville, Maine.

Martha lives in the very stone house where I grew up. She does not own the house, but lives there rent free, house-sitting for a paternal cousin and his wife, the same pair who bought the house from Cal and Alicia the year I went away to college. Now this couple's children, too, have grown and gone, and the parents live year-round in Jacksonville, Florida. When Martha returned from Europe five years ago as a widow with a boy and little means, the cousins offered it to her for as long as everyone found the arrangement convenient. Martha got a part-time job in the language department of a private school in Greenwich, enrolled Noah tuition free, and moved in.

It always feels a little odd to be in this house, superimposed as it is upon my own past. And yet the house and property are so different from the way I remember them that I feel released from the past, not betrayed. My business here is over. I like sitting in my old home surrounded by someone else's furniture, secure in the certainty that the stone house has not stood still in time while I moved. On the contrary: It has given itself as wholly to other families as I have given myself to other homes, and we have both been made lighter by the process.

I remember darkness in this room, a comfortable Linley cave of it: thick red curtains, heavy European paintings—more oil paintings of evenings with enormous frames—and chests that were almost black, with carving half an inch deep and dull bronze locks and fittings. The off-white walls at the far end of the room wore a complicated reddish tapestry, as big as a double bedspread, and there was a grand piano back in a corner on one side, and the Victrola with all the records in a cabinet on the other. The chairs and the sofas were upholstered in fabric that had a texture you could feel with your hand, like corduroy, but with little hairs you could see if you looked very closely. There were no patterns on the fabric, just colors—red, blue, red again for the curtains. Then there were lamps and books and statues: the wooden Saint Francis, a bronze head, a Chinese horse, a whole wall of encyclopedias. You wouldn't have wanted to drop any object from this room on your foot in my time. And although Cal and Alicia did not like the "fuss" of overfurnished houses, and there was not a great deal of furniture in any room of ours, still it seemed to me that every single thing in the stone house was heavier than I was. I could feel the accumulation of weight and time hover over me during all the years I lived here. On the other hand, when I came home from college I loved to see each piece of furniture standing in its familiar spot, substantial as an ancestor, reminding me where I came from.

Now the walls are painted in pastel shades, the kitchen cabinets are winter white, not ivory, and the overstuffed sofas and armchairs have flowery cushions. All these things, and the feeling they convey—a not-too-serious summer—belong to the couple from Jacksonville. I prefer Alicia's furniture to this lighthearted collection, and yet I like knowing that this has been here for as long as hers was, and has nothing to do with us or our time here. I do like the lightness. Even the stain on the wide boards of this wooden floor is three shades less somber than when I walked carefully into the room as a child, looking for Cal or Alicia, trying not to step on the cracks.

The stone house has a real lawn now, too, and although there is no statuary, there is a birdbath on a pedestal and a stone pathway through a rock garden. These may be small touches, but they lend a certain air. They make me think of rose arbors and topiary and other horticultural elegancies. When I walk over from Alicia's present house, as we did this morning, I am pleased for the old house's sake. I feel that it has served well and long, and deserves this kind of attention.

Drinking Martha's coffee, I watch first Alicia and then my sister Helen, who is describing Melissa's current crisis at boarding school. Helen looks at Alicia only, although she is speaking to everyone in the room. Whenever Alicia is present for a family conversation this happens. It doesn't matter who the speaker is, or who the ostensible listeners might be: Alicia is the focal point.

Helen sits on a wide, white bench with blue cushions that extends the full length of the big picture window overlooking the cove. Her legs are curled up under her, and a full window's expanse of Long Island Sound merges in a gray way with the

sky behind her head. Because of the view and because her legs
are not visible, she reminds me of the Little Mermaid statue
that is always on postcards from Copenhagen. It is impossible
to tell what the mermaid sees, or even to know what she might
be looking for, though one can guess. Helen, when not actually
looking at our mother, looks down at the polished floor in a
worrying, intense sort of way. I remember this habit of hers—
eyes on the floor, staring anxiety down.

The school has asked Helen to remove Melissa for this
weekend and possibly longer, as Melissa's behavior is "having
an adverse effect upon the other students," according to the
letter from the headmaster. In fact, Melissa has organized a
schoolwide boycott of classes in protest against her boyfriend's
expulsion. He was, actually, not expelled but suspended, pending a charge of illegal drinking and substance abuse (marijuana)
in a day student's home. Both boys claim innocence and the
school is investigating.

"I don't know how to treat this," says Helen. "I want to
encourage her to stand behind her friends and her principles,
but I don't think this is the way to do it. She's causing so much
trouble for herself! And who's to know what the truth is,
anyway? What if these guys are just lying? What if she's
wrong?"

Helen looks at Alicia again, a look of appeal. Alicia smiles
at her, and Helen, heartened, goes on.

"This is the story, basically . . ."

Here in the quiet room with its window overlooking the
water now dribbling in among the muddy little coves and bays
of the inlet at low tide, Martha and I listen to Helen's story, but
Alicia does not. I don't think Helen knows this, because our
mother's face is attentively turned in her direction. But from
where I sit it is easy to see that Alicia is really looking over all
of our heads, watching two high-circling gulls—almost too
high to fit within the frame of Martha's big window—soaring

and gliding over the cove, far above the marsh grass and the jack pines, between the shore and the horizon.

"I don't know," Helen says finally. "It's a real dilemma. I'm not sure what happens next."

Martha nods with sympathy. Alicia brings her gaze back from the horizon and into the living room, where it rests on the one object that could have been hers—a large, heavy-looking wooden statue of a bearded head. (A saint? A prophet?) The work is old and certainly European. It sits at eye level—the statue's eyes are level with the human ones—on an even more massive wooden chest that stands between Alicia's armchair and Helen's seat in the window. The statue and the chest remind me of the way the room used to be. They are both Martha's, from her life abroad.

"This is really such a lovely piece," Alicia says, reaching out one hand to the sculpture, not quite touching it. Martha smiles affirmation, then turns again to Helen.

"It's quite a dilemma you've got there," Martha says.

"A dilly of a dilemma," I echo in a mock-sober voice, but not without compassion. Helen grins at me and then passes a quick puzzled glance in the direction of the statue.

I don't know what more to say. Helen's daughter Melissa is the defender in her generation, the one child of all the cousins who fights on in the very teeth of the evidence . . . fights for the dog who obviously *did* bite the U.P.S. man, for the cat who certainly *has* just had diarrhea on her mother's pillow. The boys are probably guilty, in my opinion, but there isn't any need to say so.

Helen relates her conversation with Melissa's guidance counselor, and quotes him. " 'I think there is a real opportunity for validation and growth here, Mrs. Stone,' " she says. "Dear God, I hope and pray he's mistaken. There's nothing I need less than another 'growth experience' in my life. Validation, my foot!" She heaves a big sigh. "Oh, Melissa, what next?"

Melissa at that moment is with Megan and Sarah in Alicia's house next door. The three girls are playing cards and baby-sitting the lamb and Nicky, both of whom were asleep when we left the house. Luke has borrowed my car to "drive around and do some thinking," which sounds to me like a combination of looking for more changes in the neighborhood and brooding about Emma. Aunt Violet went home to Uncle George before lunch as promised, having first distributed lipstick among all her assembled kin.

As Helen talks and Martha and I listen, I watch Alicia pretend to listen, and find myself wondering whether she had always just pretended. Had she feigned the appearance of hearing us all along, for the whole oblivious length of our chattering and eager lives? When she was younger she pretended more skillfully, was that it? Were we simply too preoccupied with our own stories, as Helen is now, to notice her disregard? And yet she must have listened, because her responses were always right: "Oh, my! How on earth do you accomplish all that you do, Cressida? I can't imagine!" "I think you're doing it very well, dear!" "Of course, I understand. It must be terribly hard. You handle these things so much better than I did when I was young!" Each of the responses was a whiff of sweet fragrance, a breath from her own garden, an Alicia scent—syringa or lily of the valley—just a whisper, enhancing the particular benediction.

But weren't they all interchangeable? Did they really mean anything? Didn't they just come out of Alicia's own copy of the universal Mother's Phrase Book, useful in family conversation the way small talk is useful at a bridge-club luncheon? And Alicia's specialty has always been big talk—Love, Marriage, God, Life, Death.

I am startled to hear her voice, not expecting it.

"Did it come from a church?" Alicia speaks into the general

sympathetic lull following Helen's last words. She has surprised all of us, but Martha is the first to respond.

"I'm sorry, Alicia, what did you ask?" Martha swivels slightly where she sits, so that she now faces Alicia as well as Helen.

"It's so beautiful. Did it come from a church?"

It takes a moment to realize that Alicia is asking about the sculpted head. Smoothly, Martha slides into a story about the acquisition of this piece during a vacation trip to Italy with her husband Franck, many years ago. There was an antique dealer in Ascona, Franck's old friend, who had found this head and had praised it so highly that there was nothing for Franck to do but travel immediately to see it.

"It was found in a sacristy, forgotten and neglected behind cobwebs, in a cathedral in France—a hidden treasure. But traveling with Franck, as you might imagine, meant that we got lost in a hundred northern Italian villages before we ever got near Ascona—what a vacation!"

Alicia sits upright and smiling, seeming to enjoy the tale. Martha was once an exchange student in Austria, where she met and married a man twenty-five years older than herself. He was a Viennese historian and a diplomat: Franck von Elsen. She lived with him for eighteen years in Vienna, where their son Noah was born. Franck was like Alicia's father, a hopelessly absentminded man, widely loved, and universally treated by those who knew him with affectionate protectiveness. He once left his dinner jacket at an embassy party and went home wearing the ambassador's wife's evening cloak; another time he got on the wrong bus and traveled all the way to the border of Czechoslovakia, where the guard—a woman—pinned his new ticket to his jacket with a note to Martha at home—"Gnädige Frau, I return to you your husband. You must watch him more carefully."

One day in Germany, wandering back to his hotel from a conference in a tiny town in Bavaria, Franck was struck and killed instantly by a train. It was entirely his own fault, the investigating officials concluded respectfully, in the report they sent to Martha: "Gnädige Frau . . ."

She came home with her son and a few belongings about a month after her husband's death, and ultimately settled in Connecticut in the old stone house.

Helen asks her, "What is a sacristy, exactly? Pardon my ignorance, Martha." Helen is beginning to relax a little, warmed by the light, benign blanket of Martha's attention.

"It's a little room at the back of the church, usually, where they keep all the robes and vestments and so forth. Like a sort of ecclesiastical dressing room." She leans forward to Alicia, who looks thoughtful, questioning.

"Well, it's so lovely, that's all," our mother says to Martha then. "And I keep wondering . . . does it come from a church?"

There is a pause, a waiting in suspense, but it is soon obvious that yes, it is the same question again. Alicia is still looking at the carved head, reaching out her arm to it again, and raising her face to Martha with a polite smile, but with the question still there.

"Well," Martha begins again, more slowly, louder, "It came from that antique dealer in Ascona, Franck's friend, who picked it up in a cathedral in southern France. Of course I think we had as much trouble on our crazy journey, just getting to Ascona, as Franck's friend ever could have had bringing that sculpture out of France!"

Martha tells the story more tentatively this time. I can feel her hesitation. While she speaks, I watch Martha's hands. They are storyteller's hands, long and beautifully tapered, moving like two pale, paired fish swimming in an ocean all their own. When Martha finishes the story of the carved head for the second time, she sits back in her chair. Alicia beams at her and leans forward in hers.

"Yes, I see," she says. "It's absolutely lovely. And did it come from a church?"

"Yes," says Martha.

Helen begins to speak now, her voice loud and bright and the words coming fast. "What a place that school of Melissa's is! I can't believe how hysterical they all are! I mean the administration, the guidance counselors—everybody! They're all about twenty-five years old, and they have this sort of pop-psych-Zen Buddhist attitude that makes me crazy. If one more person tells me that the Chinese characters for "crisis" really mean "danger" and "opportunity," I swear I'm going to flush the *I Ching* down the toilet!"

Martha and I both laugh. Somehow nobody can look at Alicia. Animated, agitated, the three younger women talk to each other.

"Remember when people used the *I Ching* as a kind of oracle?" I say. "They threw coins at it or let it fall open at random, mostly."

"God yes!" says Helen, but Martha shakes her head.

"I was away for the sixties," she says. "I feel as if I've missed out on my generation."

"Forget it," I reassure her. "So did most people—the media invented all that 'sixties generation' stuff anyway. Except for the politics—that was true—but even so it was a minority. Most people were just growing up the way they always do. But I wish I knew how many of the old *I Ching* crowd is reading 'Dear Abby' and the daily horoscopes now."

"More than would admit it, I bet," Helen says.

"Oh! that reminds me . . ."—me again, a new thought, how do I sound to Helen? Loud? Fast?—"Does anybody read the fine print on the food packages anymore? Do you? I mean really read it, top to bottom? I have the feeling that people don't do that now, and it used to be you'd read every written word before taking something to the cash register. I mean *militantly,* people would spend hours in the aisles at the supermarket— you met everybody you knew, standing around reading labels —it was like the library. Now nobody does it. I never hear about cyclamates and phosphates and nitrates and nitrites any- more, either. Where did they go? How come nobody reads the fine print any more?"

"That's easy," says Helen, "We can't. We're all middle-aged and need glasses."

This time Alicia laughs too.

Martha asks Helen, "What does Melissa say about what's going on? Never mind the headmaster and the guidance coun- selor and all the rest of them."

"She says nobody understands." Helen looks at me—the other mother of teenage daughters—and smiles. "What else?"

"Kids. Nothing but trouble." I smile back at Helen. We are mothers who have children now, not children who have moth- ers. "Now what happens?"

"Now Helen finds a way to fix it." Martha smiles too. "Isn't that right?"

"I don't know," Helen says. "Maybe . . . I guess Helen tries, anyway. What amazes me at times like this is the way every- thing seems to happen all at once, you know?" She is still not looking at Alicia. "I can't work on things one by one, and I hate that. I like to take one thing at a time."

"Life never works that way, though, does it?" Martha says with sympathy.

"No, of course life doesn't work that way." Helen gives a short laugh. "But I do!"

This is true. Helen likes things to happen one at a time, and she likes people one by one. She is like Alicia in this. They both prefer small dinner parties to large social affairs, almost any kind of concert to an athletic event, and one intimate contact with one relative, whether little loved or long lost, then the organized chaos of a family reunion. For Helen and for Alicia, just being in the presence of too many people at once is a punishment to their particular sensitivity, the way cacophony is punishment for people with acute hearing.

"I don't think The Brothers will be here very long," I offer. "They were pretty clear about that on the telephone—Mark was."

"I'm not sure," says Helen. "He may stay a while. He's got something on his mind. I could tell when I talked to him. There's something going on with Mark."

"There's always something going on with Mark," I say crossly. How can Helen tell that there is something going on with Mark? When did she talk to him? How could she have picked up something I missed?

"No, it's different. He had this tone in his voice . . . I know! I remember now: It's the way he always sounded when he'd found something really unusual—a painted turtle or a big king snake. He has something to show us, but he's not telling yet."

She is pleased, indulgent. Helen is Mark's older sister, after all.

"Show and Tell," I say grumpily. Martha laughs right at me. But what does she know? She was an only child.

"How long is it since all of you have been together?" Martha looks inquiringly at both of us, briefly at Alicia. Everybody is silent.

"Well, it must have been two years," I begin finally. "Alicia's eightieth birthday party."

But Martha dismisses the birthday. "No, not that—that was Violet's big restaurant bash in the city, and there must have been a hundred other people there. What I mean is family time, together—all of you sitting down next door in the living room, with Felix and the dinner trays . . ."

Alicia nods, smiling, "He does love that," she says.

"Five years? Penelope's wedding?" Helen looks at me for affirmation. I shake my head.

"Only Matthew and Luke. Remember? Mark had an international whaling thing."

Not a birthday, not a wedding, I am thinking. Maybe a funeral . . . Unwillingly I recall Sarah's suggestions of this morning. A funeral: little Jason's funeral? No, it was in Vermont, and neither Luke nor Mark could get there. Jason's funeral could not be counted as a full family gathering. Farther back, then . . . Ten years? Fifteen? That would be Cal's funeral, but that too could not be counted.

Cal did not have a funeral, or at least not in the usual sense. There were Hawaiian hymns sung at a service in the little Hawaiian churchyard immediately following his burial, but Helen and I only heard them on tape afterwards. We were together in a rented house in Maine that August, calling Hawaii every evening until the day before Cal died, which also turned out to be the date of Helen's return to France at the end of her summer vacation. We were not together, though we had expected to be, when he died.

Helen and I filled our role as The Daughters very well that summer: women together with small children (and I was heavily pregnant with Megan), far away from our father's dying, living a feminine day-to-day life with ripe raspberries and pine trees and stony beaches and the sweet, sad song of the white-throated sparrow—"Old Sam Peabody, Peabody, Peabody"—lifting itself into the salty, driftwood-dry midday sunshine. We walked and watched our children and waited for the telephone calls. Helen and I were listeners but not witnesses at this death. Cal's three sons were his couriers and his bearers, on hand to carry his stretcher on and off airplanes and to watch with our mother as he lay dying on a tropical island, within the sound of the sea. They had also come to comfort her when he was irascible—alternately irritated by her hovering over him or restless and demanding of her attention.

Cal's trip to the place where he wanted to die was characteristic of him, and of the family. To achieve what he saw as a simple goal (death in a quiet place that he loved) required quantities of effort, inconvenience, red tape, and planning on the part of everyone around him. How was Alicia to get the New York hospital to release him, a man as sick as Cal, in intensive care? Was any carrier even willing to bring him to the island in his condition? And once he got there, where would he stay? How would his care be administered day to day? What about around-the-clock nursing? What about medication and oxygen? Where and how would he be buried? The questions were endless.

The death was accomplished, ultimately, under Cal's own direction. And he directed, as he had always done, under the assumption that this was a simple matter. Planning one's death was as routine as filing a flight plan and going through the checklist before taking off in an airplane. (Medical release negotiated? Check. Passage booked for wife, sons, and stretcher? Check. Local clinic notified, also churchyard trustees and grave digger? Check. Check. Check. All right, then . . . Contact!) Other people, with their worries and unnecessary complexities, were the only complicating factors. My father felt that he was planning a simple death, and I truly think he believed to the moment of that death that he had led a simple life. The complications came from others, from outside.

For Helen and me, there was really nothing to do but wait. And even in Hawaii, the family members just followed orders. In the evening they would telephone us: "He wants to be buried in a Hudson Bay blanket. Where am I going to get a Hudson Bay blanket in Hawaii? Anybody have one to send out?" (Emma found and sent the blanket from Montana, in time for Cal to know that it was there.) "He thinks the hymns Alicia has chosen are too 'corny'—yes, that's exactly what he said. He's had her singing different ones to him all afternoon—it's a rehearsal, for God's sake!" "He's decided to have a Hawaiian service if the congregation here is willing. Apparently they have a wonderful choir, and he loves the idea. The hymns will be in Hawaiian, so nobody will know whether they're corny or not." "He just sent all the grave diggers out for hamburgers. He says heavy work without food is no good in this heat." The grave was a great square hole—big enough for a horse—deep and wide like all Hawaiian graves, with rocks to go on top and all around it. The old man who headed the work crew told Cal it was the best grave he'd ever dug, and vowed he'd climb right in with Cal when the time came; he was sure he would never dig another as good, not even if he could dig one for himself. (The last bill received from Hawaii after Cal's death was from the fast-food stand on the beach in the town nearest the churchyard. Burgers—$16.60.)

Finally the grave was dug, the service planned, the air calm in the aftermath of preparation, and that was when Cal died, just as he had planned, early one morning in Hawaii. Alicia called me, and I called Helen, who had just arrived at her home in Paris.

I remember that the distancing crackle of the telephone call across the Atlantic to France was familiar to me, and more welcome than the hollow echo of Alicia's voice coming from Hawaii only minutes earlier that had been strange, unreal. The Pacific is an alien ocean for me anyway, and I trembled in the delayed space after each word our mother spoke.

So many years ago now, and I know exactly what she said. "Cressida, your father died peacefully early this morning. It was very quiet. I held his hand."

There it was. Half the world gone. My ears rang with the emptiness.

Alicia had been too calm that morning, too brave. How

could she be so brave? And if it was very quiet, as she said, then it was too quiet. When I called Helen in Paris, it was a different story. "Oh, Cress!" she said, in a heavy sigh. Helen's sigh was the right noise.

"I can stand it if you can," I remember saying to my sister across that Atlantic space on the morning of our father's death, and I don't know what I meant by it, either. Surely there was no choice for either of us but to stand it.

"I don't want to think," Helen said back to me, and I could tell she was shutting down and closing in on herself. I had that old sense of all the bedroom doors in our home quietly closing, as everyone in the house retreated into his or her own room.

"I don't think we've been together since Cal died," I tell Martha. Helen thinks about it at some length, and nods.

"I think you're right," she says. "How strange."

But it makes sense, because he was the one who kept us together. Alicia loved, defended, and understood us; she sympathized, was sensitive, and endured, above everything. But Cal's was the hand that held us all—whether we wanted to be held or not. By holding us to him, he held us to one another long after we had left home. His letters were family news bulletins; his voice on the telephone reported, advised, interfered, and bound us to the family: "I just got in from Beirut and I stopped in Seattle. My, your brother is doing a fine job with that little girl of his!" "Held over in Paris—Helen has a good manuscript; she's about to submit it. Fine work..." "I was thinking about your garden, Cress, on my way back from Munich. Have you considered the *varieties* of corn you might want to plant? Back on the farm, when I was a boy, nothing tasted better to me than Golden Bantam." "Your mother and I are here in Denver. Luke and Emma were in an automobile accident twenty-four hours ago. It was a pretty bad one, Cressy. Head-on with a drunk. Luke had quite a knock on the head, and Emma got banged up too. They're out of danger now, but we thought we'd fly out . . ." And his relationship with Mark continued to be stormy, periods of argument, periods of alienation and distance, but always there were letters, back and forth, as long as speeches on both sides. He never stopped talking until he died.

After that one dry telephone call from Hawaii, it was all gone. Cal's voice was gone—Cal's obnoxious, overbearing, inescapable presence (even when he was absent, he was present) was gone. It took me months to believe it. He must be *somewhere*—Munich? The Philippines? Gone were the lectures, gone the bursts of temper, gone the unwanted advice on everything from tampons (he didn't like them—suspected they were bad for women's vaginas, though he admitted he had no proof, and there was no talk of toxic shock in those days) to humidifiers (he believed in using them, but not in buying them). A humidifier could be made with two pans of water and a towel, he said. I never could figure out exactly how. It was like his story about the stick and the piece of string, which Helen loved so much: "Children have too many toys these days! Commercial claptrap . . . Why, when I was a boy I played all day with a stick and a piece of string!" (Played what? Helen has a long list of obscene and outrageous speculations.) Gone were the walks under the maple trees, the nights on the porch looking at the stars ("The Navigator's Circle—look, children: Capella, Castor, Pollux, Procyon, Sirius. Mark, are you paying attention or gathering cobwebs over there?"). Gone were the swimming lessons—arms around his neck, you'd float out into Long Island Sound on his back so you could "get a feel for salt water" long before you could even dog-paddle. Absolute terror and absolute security coexisted for me in those waters when he was there. "I won't let you go," he'd say. I learned to know the depth and buoyancy of the sound, could feel it support me as I floated, my arms around my father's neck, at first so tightly he'd gag, laugh, and loosen them. But then I held more and more loosely, until finally I was ready to let go—he never did —and when I released myself and flailed and fluttered and finally swam after all, he was still there, parting the water out ahead of me with his hands. I moved through water because he did, and he did because he understood it, just another liquid, as easily negotiated as air.

What an airless, hollow place the world became when he died! I think for a while we were all confused, off center, without the interfering, opinionated, exasperating powerhouse and windbag that was Cal. Now everything of his seemed to be gone except for our family's old love and ambivalence, and of these two things we children each took our allotted portion and fled. Left at the center was Alicia, who went back to Connecticut after Cal's burial in Hawaii and lived in the house that he had built for her here. Over the years her children have come one by one to visit her, bringing grandchildren too, the newer ones never having known their grandfather except as a page in the American History textbooks, a silver airplane and a leather helmet and long earflaps and a grin (Or later on, the darker, thicker, middle-aged prewar speaker, as troublesome a figure for his grandchildren as for his children). At different times some of these newer grandchildren will have such a look of him that I am wary, suspecting a reincarnation, (Megan has the grin right now, Helen's son Michael at eleven could have posed for the photos of Cal at that age) but the look always passes, and the children look like themselves again. I've come to think that these fleeting resemblances are Cal's way of keeping us on our toes—a grin here, a dimple there—reminding us whose family this really is, after all.

"The last time we were all together was at Matthew's wedding, I believe," says Alicia now, in Martha's house. "Cressida had a curtain ring in her pocket—I don't know where you got it, dear. She said it was *her* wedding ring, and she dropped it several times during the service. And Helen wore a lovely Lanz dress. From Austria," she defers smilingly to Martha.

"But surely . . ." Helen begins, "surely since then?"

"I think you'll find I'm right, dear."

"It couldn't be. I was nine years old," I say. "There must have been another time. Matt's wedding was more than thirty years ago, in Illinois. We haven't been together for thirty years?"

Alicia nods at us. "Yes, I think that's right."

We are astonished. I am sure she's wrong.

"What about Christmas? There were a couple of Christmases in Colorado, remember? I'm sure we were all present at the same time at least for one of them. That was *much* later." I know I am right; I am sure of it. But I stop anyway, remembering that I was fifteen years old during the last Christmas in Colorado. A quarter of a century has passed since then. Whatever the truth about Colorado may be, this is the first time since our childhood that Alicia's five children have come together at the same time under her roof, as we will come together this afternoon.

"This should be quite an occasion, then," Martha cheerfully remarks. "Would you like me to make something? How about a Viennese coffee cake, Alicia?"

"Well," Alicia says to her, frowning and looking thoughtfully out over the inlet, "I was only wondering, you know, whether I still have enough tea." Looking out behind her, I can see that all the gulls have gone now, and the tide is rapidly coming in.

# Chapter

## 9

' ' Could it be just . . . age?" Helen asks.

"Oh, no, I don't think so," I am quick to answer. "I mean, age is a factor, of course, but there are all kinds of *real* reasons for memory loss, things that can be corrected." I list rapidly the possibilities Joe mentioned at home. "There can be imperceptible little strokes. TIAs, they call them. People Alicia's age can have those and take medication to stop them. Or sometimes it's due to a urinary disorder, and there's also something about pressure on the carotid artery. I've heard that too."

We are waiting together at the train station for Mark and Matthew. Fixed to a vertical beam near us is a steel-framed poster advertising *Phantom of the Opera* on one side and *The*

*Wall Street Journal* on the other. Helen is pushing a small pile of debris past the poster toward the edge of the cement floor of the station platform: match folders, cigarettes, grit, a collection she has been scraping together with the rubber toe of her L.L. Bean boot (leather uppers—I have the same boots in Vermont, but they are sitting outside my kitchen door, covered with sheep manure). As she starts to speak again the pile goes over the edge and down onto the railroad track somewhere.

"But that's exactly what I mean. That's all really just age, isn't it? Part of the process?" Helen sounds impatient and her voice is sharper than I'm used to hearing it.

"Maybe you're right," I answer. "I don't know. I guess I didn't think of it that way." I try to puzzle this out in my mind.

Could Helen be right? Is this what age is? Indiscriminate losses and lapses in attention, in memory, in orientation to life? "The Dwindles," as a nurse practitioner friend of mine describes the generalized ailments of her elderly rural patients: "Rosie's ninety-two, and she's not really sick—she just has The Dwindles." Dwindling eyesight, dwindling hearing, dwindling bladder control, dwindling memory, losing one's place in space and time.

"Well, I don't know either, obviously. But I have to say frankly, Cress, that it looks that way to me. I don't think this is an emergency."

"How can you be sure of that?" I ask. "What if there's something really wrong?" Helen stuffs her hands into the pockets of her parka.

"It doesn't make sense! She just had a medical checkup and they didn't find anything wrong: We know that. And now that I've seen her myself, well, yes, I understand why we were concerned. Things do get a little foggy for her sometimes. But my feeling is that all she needs, at this point anyway, is a little extra help here and there, maybe some kind of assistant, or a secretary again, to keep track of things for her."

"Keep track of things like what? East Seventy-seventh Street?" I ask, appalled. "Come on, Helen. You heard about what Aunt Violet told us. Getting lost in the middle of Manhattan isn't exactly like misplacing your glasses case. And what about the Japanese interview? Do we just sign off on that, too? I thought you were the one talking about embarrassment and humiliation. What are we supposed to do about that?"

Suddenly my sister turns on me. "We're supposed to lead our own lives, for once! God, Cressy, can't you ever let go? Our mother is old; she's getting forgetful; it happens to millions of people all the time. It's going to happen to you and me. Let her do the interview or not do the interview—whatever she wants! It's not going to be the end of the world either way. Why can't we give her some space and let her make up her own mind? Look, I'm sorry, but I really think you're making too much of this. I have a lot of other things to think about right now. I'm not in the mood to preserve the Linley image, okay?"

I rock back on my heels in surprise and catch the corner of the steel poster frame between my shoulder blades. It makes me think differently.

"Okay," I say to Helen, "I'm sorry. I forgot it's been such a crazy weekend for you already. I wasn't thinking about Melissa."

"Don't worry about her. We'll figure it out," Helen says shortly, but whether she is referring to our mother or her daughter I don't know. Now, instead of talking, we shuffle our feet and look off down the westbound track in silence the way the few other people on the platform have been doing all along.

We have left Alicia at the house, napping, and all the rest of the family in Luke's nominal charge. One of his charges is an excited and defiant Melissa wearing a black shirt and jeans and a red bandana around her forehead. She looked to me like Tonto in a *Lone Ranger* rerun as she sat on Sarah's bed straight-

backed and cross-legged, defending her friends to Sarah and
Megan while she watched a Garfield video with Nicky and held
the lamb in her lap.

The five o'clock train is past due now. Finally, about ten
minutes after the hour, the train comes in, just the way I remember it, with all the familiar self-important clankings and
snortings, the heavily burdened, metallic groans I used to
know. Iron Horse of New York, New Haven, and Hartford,
stamping its feet, tossing its steamy mane and hissing hot
breath all along our platform. Suddenly I am confused. I know
I took this train a long time ago, but surely it never ran on
steam? ("Steam from the heating system," Joe tells me later on
the phone. He grew up in a New York–commuting suburb too.
"Air brakes by Mr. Westinghouse. I don't know what the
groaning could be. When I was going into New York every
day it was the coach cars that groaned; they were ancient even
back then, but they've replaced them all now. Maybe it was the
passengers you heard.")

"There they are!" I follow Helen's pointing arm, way up
toward the front of the train. Two of The Brothers, Matthew
and Mark, are walking our way. They have seen us, too, and
are waving. A confusion of warmth and a stinging incipience of
tears in my eyes makes me realize how glad I am to see them.

The first thing I notice is that Matt, the oldest of us all and
by rights the biggest, looks like a small man next to his oversized youngest brother. Next, that Mark seems very free swing-
ing next to Matthew, a golden retriever lolloping along with a
whippet. Matt is slight where Mark is tall; Matt is tight where
Mark is loose limbed and rangy. Matt has thinning dark hair,
wavy and turning gray, while Mark has kept the same light,
straight, unruly thatch he always had, and no hint of a curl
anywhere. Still, if I did not know these men, I think I could
pick them out as brothers. It is not that they look alike, but it is

the way they walk together that shows the kinship, a long-standing trust between body and body as they move along.

Matthew wears a zip-front brown leather bomber jacket, carries a small briefcase, and keeps himself to himself as he always did: arms and shoulders in close to the sides, jaw set thin and grinning, a fan of grin-wrinkles between eye and hairline. There is a slight roll to his walk along the platform today that reminds me of Cal.

Mark is the same old Mark: big and blurry around the edges. He wears faded jeans and a bulky brown sweater (Peruvian?) with fuzzy hairs sticking out of it and woolly animals woven in, maybe llamas.

"Well," says Matthew, stretching the greeting out on a low whistle, and letting loose the grin, "two sisters." He hugs each of us quickly, hard, and we take turns putting hasty kisses on the thin cheek. Mark folds me in the smothering woolliness of the sweater then pulls his head up and away, laughing, when I try to stand on tiptoe to kiss him. I know this movement of his —it's a boy's game. My stepsons play it too: no kisses with "girl germs" on them, no kisses at all, sometimes. Mark used to do this when he was ten years old, and I suppose it was a joke even in those days, but I am abashed to find that it still hurts my feelings. A rejected embrace is never really funny.

As children, if we awoke in the night and were scared of the dark or of our dreams, we ran down the hallway to Cal and Alicia's room, and climbed into bed with them, as we were allowed to do. What was not permitted, however, was any motion at all by children who had achieved the parental bed— not a wiggle, not a thrash, or Cal would reach out from the very depths of sleep, as it seemed, with a binding half-Nelson of a hug across the whole upper torso, pinning the offending offspring into stillness until morning, or until the child voluntarily left the bed. (This may have been our father's intention all along: "Cal? I don't think I'm going to have any more nightmares. Can I go back to my room now?") Alicia, on the other hand, was always warm and sweet smelling in her night-gown, and all fear vanished in the serenity of her sleeping presence. But if you tried to kiss her cheek she would turn her sleeping head away, automatically, as a signal that she had covered her face with night cream and that you should place the kiss on her neck. She explained to us, when awake, that she did not want us to be contaminated by her "grease," as Cal called it. Helen and I, however, comparing notes later, discovered a shared resentment of this. We had wanted to kiss her face, directly, regardless of what was on it. We felt that she should have let us take our chances with the night cream.

The four of us drive to our mother's house talking. Our talk moves homeward the way we ourselves have done, inward toward the center that is our mother, from all the perimeter points of our individual lives. Matthew tells us that he and Gwen have plans to sell the house and build a log cabin, now that all of the children are almost grown. Mark is quick with interest in the details of log-cabin construction. He says that he has lived in a tent, a geodesic dome, a yurt, and several other borrowed or rented structures during his years of research around the world, but he's ready to settle down and build a home of his own now.

For Mark to talk of settling down, after twenty years of itinerant living, is news. I wonder what it means. I glance at Helen to find that she is looking at me in the same speculative way. But then she launches into a description of the advantages and drawbacks in having two homes: what a nuisance it is to live with one's spouse only part-time, as she and Eben too often find themselves doing, but what a relief for each child to have his or her own familiar household to retreat to, a respite from the blended family!

Matt then says that Jake and Penelope, who have just

moved into their new home, have been making changes there because of the expected baby: "Doing every bit of the work themselves! No builders, no unions, no nothing. The kids are saving a pile of money and they're doing a damn nice carpentry job, too." He presents for our consideration Penelope's question about whether her dog understands that she is pregnant. Helen is sure that it does; Mark is skeptical. Somebody mentions the lamb, and the talk turns my way.

"Our lady of the lambs," Mark says. "Saint Cressida." When I look in the rearview mirror at him I see that he is smiling hugely, kindly at me, his eyebrows bobbing up and down like a benevolent clown's. What has come over him?

"Earth Mother," Matthew puts in, "that's our Cressy."

"Earth Grandmother," I contradict him. "This is Megan's baby. You should see her—bottles, blankets, the whole business."

"I'm looking forward to it," says Mark. "It's been a long time since I've seen the kids. Nicky must be quite a handful now!"

Nicky is the one he's never met. How would he know what a three-year-old is like? Helen and I eye each other again as I turn into Alicia's driveway.

It is Luke who meets us at the door with Nicholas attached. Nicky is crawling around Luke's ankles, examining the hand-tooled designs on the cowboy boots. Luke tries to detach him as he greets us, but before he can manage to do this, Nicky is scooped up out of the way by the one uncle he does not know at all. Mark has Nicky in his arms, among the llamas. He smiles the foolish clown's smile at his nephew, and Nicky stares back at him. Luke and Matthew are shaking hands, as The Brothers always do.

I once read in a book that to the end of her life, my father's mother greeted her adult son with a handshake, as he did her, and that this was an example of the way in which his upbringing made it impossible for Cal to "relate to" other people. He had been taught to maintain a physical distance even from those closest to him. The book was right there in the town library, in the history section. The sentence was printed in black-and-white before my eyes, and it gave me the sense I've had often during my lifetime: that history and reality are two completely different things. I knew for a fact that I had never shaken hands with Cal, but I had certainly hugged him a thousand times, and had watched him tussle and laugh and play on the floor with his children the way Joe does now with his own boys. I had also sat upon his knee as a child with obnoxious regularity, and in cheerful disrespect for any physical integrity he might have wished to maintain had braided a long section of his gray hair into a rakish, sideways, Mandarin's queue. This lock of hair was actually a vanity of Cal's. When he began to get bald on top of his head he grew the hair on this one side long enough to part implausibly far down by his ear, and then he would comb it up over the bald spot and over to the other side. It was longer than the hair on the head of any doll I owned, if thinner, and it was a real pleasure to braid.

"Honestly, Mark," says Helen at my elbow, "you'll terrify the poor kid!" Mark is making grotesque faces at Nicky while jiggling him up and down in his arms. "It's about time you had some children of your own—you might learn something!"

But Nicky has broken into a smile and is grabbing his fat little cheeks with both hands. He sticks out his tongue at Mark and chortles with glee. Mark chortles right back at him. Something is up, there's no doubt.

"Oh my! There you all are!" Alicia has appeared behind Luke. She is so small compared to any one of the five of us and seems overjoyed to see us, this pack of giants in her kitchen. We are all here, where we belong. Nothing is wrong, nothing is lost, nothing has changed except for the better: Nicky in Mark's arms, Melissa and my two girls hanging back in the living room, shy at the new adults but eager to be part of the family greeting. Nothing is lost, everything has been recovered.

Teatime, however, in the company of the whole Linley family, is hard to take. I can't get used to so many of us at the same time. Disoriented by the intensity, I have the feeling that the lights here are too bright and the temperature too warm, the coffee cake that Martha has sent over in celebration too sweet, and the tea itself too hot. In a state of mental dizziness, I can do nothing for the first half hour except watch and listen to everyone else.

Alicia too, still flushed with pleasure, is quiet, her eyes bright as they move from one eager speaker to another, back and forth across her living room. I can tell that this is an effort for her. Following, trying to follow, listening, trying to listen. Hearing what? Hoping what? That she will understand, not let the words or their meaning drift? Trying to hold on to the words with her mind as if clinging with fingers to a ledge that is crumbling? Trying, hoping not to let go?

"How do they catch the animals, Uncle Mark?" Megan wants to know about the treatment of affected wildlife after an oil spill.

"Gently, if possible," he says. "We want to be as noninvasive as we can. Sometimes we don't have much choice, but we try." He explains various systems of trapping and treatment, leaning forward as he does so and using his hands to describe the sizes and shapes of the equipment.

Matt and Mark sit together on the sofa, Nicky between them in glory, an uncle at each side. Luke relaxes in a wing chair on one side of the hearth opposite, and the restless cowboy boot swings as he talks. Alicia herself sits with a cup and saucer and a beautifully straight back in the twin of Luke's chair, on the other side. Between them on the floor all three girls are now cross-legged, their backs to the unlit fireplace. Helen stands leaning against the mantle on Luke's side of the three, and I am near her on an ancient, dark little stool that looks as if it came from Martha's sacristy during the Middle Ages.

Megan is feeding the lamb, which sputters now and then, but has become used to her touch and is much less noisy than before. Felix is outside, at Megan's request, for the duration of the lamb's mealtime, at least. ("Ours too, if we're lucky," I muttered to Helen as I encouraged the dog through the door.)

"How rough are these animals to handle?" asks Luke. "A friend of mine has done a lot of research on grizzlies, out in Glacier Park. Some of the stories he tells will scare you to death, but he says you just have to know what you're doing. He's a piece of work, this character. I know for a fact he prefers the bears to the tourists, anyway."

"I don't have to deal with tourists or bears," says Mark, "so far, anyway. It's not too bad. And I'm working with a bunch of other people." He has a hand on Nicky's head, smoothing the curls as I often do myself, not thinking. I watch this, watch also the smile with which he answers Luke, who used to tease him daily, even cruelly, at times, when he was growing up. This smile has no memory of that teasing, nor is it the half-bitter, half-foolish smile with which he faced Cal's fury. This is a new smile.

"I work with a wonderful group of people," he says again. He is looking at Alicia, as we all do. "I'd love to have you meet some of them. There are several of us in the area right now."

"Oh, yes," she says at once, "it sounds so interesting!" She positively shimmers with interest, and yet her expression has not changed for several minutes. I start to feel uneasy.

"Tuesday?" Mark persists. "We'll be around for another day or two, but there's a meeting in New York on Monday so I wouldn't be able to bring anybody over here till Tuesday."

"And Wednesday is Alicia's Japanese interview." I slip this in before I can help myself. Conversation stops, teacups clink.

I see that Nicky has a huge piece of coffee cake—it covers most of his face. Did Mark give him that? Good grief!

"Give it a rest, Cress, will you?" Helen whispers hard in my direction, startling the girls on the floor below us. Their backs stiffen; their bottoms shift. Megan bends low over her lamb. It must be strange to think of their mothers and aunts and uncles as squabbling brothers and sisters like themselves.

"Oh, that's all right, dear," Alicia speaks warmly to me, reassuringly. "It's all over." She turns to Matthew and Mark on the sofa. "That poor man was so nervous—Felix frightened him. I can't think why."

Matthew clears his throat and then speaks in a soft, dry voice to Alicia, his eyes very blue in their focus upon her, and her alone. All the rest of us in the room lean forward. "Gwen had a call today. They were trying to reach me. They couldn't get through to this house, and they couldn't get through to Vermont, either." The blue eyes flicker in our direction, Helen's and mine. "The Japanese group wants to come to see you again on Wednesday, Alicia, but not for a second interview. They are most grateful to you for the one you did last week. It's their network producer who wants to come to see you on Wednesday, to meet you again. He met you once before, sixty years ago, when you and Cal flew to Japan. He was just a young boy then. And he was hoping . . ." Matt clears his throat again. "They said that he was hoping to have the great honor of meeting you again."

"God! How romantic!" says Helen. "Who did you say this man is?"

Matthew. I never would have dreamed it. Matthew, who lives quietly and travels constantly, who felt all the earliest and strongest of the Linley shocks and aftershocks, who is supposed to be in Chile anyway. Matthew has come as a personal family courier with this message, because it wasn't getting through.

Not to Alicia, not to me or to Helen. It was not an interview at all, but a personal meeting that was being requested, again and again, and the request had been misunderstood.

"It's been so many years," Alicia falters, very pink, "I don't remember . . ."

"He was quite a young child when you came," Matthew continues, as we all still lean in his direction like trees in the wind. "And now he is about to retire. He is a highly placed, a highly distinguished Japanese businessman now, and he would very much like to meet you again. If only for a moment. Maybe for tea." He gestures with one arm at all the teacups in the room: Helen's, mine, Luke's, Alicia's own. Our tea ceremony has its own intricacies: Perhaps the Japanese businessman will understand us better than we know.

"Another conquest, Alicia," sighs Luke. "I don't know what Cal would say—it's an endless parade."

"A gentleman caller," says Mark, "All the way from Kyoto. I don't see how you can turn him down, Alicia."

Alicia has her hand at her throat, finger and thumb massaging the width of it lightly, just above her collarbone, moving as if over an invisible wound or an invisible necklace, important to her in either case.

"I can't," she says, "of course. I can't turn him down. It would be much too discourteous—now, you stop that, Luke!" He is laughing at her, and she is of course pleased in spite of her words. "You know I'm much too old for anything like that at *all.* But rudeness doesn't do any good at any time in one's life. Oh dear, I'm so sorry they weren't able to reach me directly. I really can't imagine . . ."

There is a quick knock at the door, then it opens and Martha stands on the step, holding the doorknob and letting only her head enter the room.

"Hi, everybody. I'm sorry to break in like this. Alicia, it's Felix—the Hubbards just called me from across the inlet. He's

down at their place. He's fine, but they've got a bitch in heat—
oops!" She covers her mouth for an instant and then laughs.
"Ignore that, Nicholas, girls."

"But what was he doing so far away? What shall we do?"
Alicia is perturbed, and rises.

"I'll just run down with my car and get him. No big deal.
Girls, if you want to see Noah, he just got home an hour ago
and he'd love it, anytime. I'll be right back there myself as soon
as I pick up your grandmother's little wanderer." She smiles at
us all and starts to close the door on herself again, but Alicia is
standing now.

"Wait," she says. "I'm coming with you. He must feel lost
and confused, and I think I should be there."

Martha stops, considers, and says cautiously, "I'd love your
company, Alicia, but I really don't think that what your dog is
feeling right now is 'lost and confused.'"

The three girls giggle, Luke smiles.

"I'm coming with you," Alicia repeats with decision. "Just
wait while I get my coat." She disappears only for a moment,
and comes back with the red jacket on and her scarf. The
Brothers by now are all standing up and looking polite.

"Martha, we don't like to put you to any trouble," Luke
says. "One of us can get the dog."

"Absolutely," I agree. "Noah just got home; you're busy.
We've got my car right outside . . ."

"No trouble." Martha waves us away. "No problem, really.
It'll take two seconds. Alicia, are you sure you want to come
along? Your kids just got home too, after all!" she laughs. "And
I'm all set to go . . ."

"I'm all set to go too," says Alicia. "We'll be right back,"
she turns to tell us all as she reaches the doorway. Martha
stands behind her with a what-can-I-do-about-this look on her
face. "Please help yourselves to more of everything." The door
closes behind them both.

"Mom?" Melissa is looking up at her mother with eagerness. "Can we go over to Noah's now? Is tea over?"

"I don't know," Helen says helplessly. "I guess maybe it is. What do you think?" She turns to me.

"It is for now, I guess," I say to the girls. "Why don't you kiss any uncles you can grab and go ahead."

Sarah gives me a reproving, resentful look as she rises gracefully from the floor—I'm a *senior,* Mother, don't tell me whom to kiss—but the other two girls need no further encouragement. All three uncles are kissed exuberantly by Melissa and by Megan, who has handed me the lamb. I take him upstairs to his box and come down to see that Sarah too is now quietly, after the other girls have finished, embracing her uncles. When she gets to Luke he holds out his own arms and says, "You'll never have to go grabbing, honey. They'll all be after you." Then the girls are gone.

"Too much cake?" I ask Nicky. He is tilting a little to one side, against Matthew's shoulder, looking seasick. He shakes his head in denial, however.

"Too much Linley?" asks Helen of the room at large, a spiced challenge, delivered with laughter.

"Not for me," says Mark, his hand again on Nicky's head, his expression benign. Maybe he's taking some drug, I think suddenly, unnerved. No, I don't think Mark even takes aspirin.

"Too much Japanese interview," Matthew says, looking grim again. "I hate doing this to her."

There is a general chorus of protest.

"What do you mean? You were wonderful!"

"Don't be crazy, Matt—you saved the day!"

"It was beautifully done," says Helen.

He shakes his head. "I hate to disturb her. At this age you'd think she finally could be left alone."

"You did exactly what you had to do," Helen argues. "And if you ask me, I think she loved it! Now it's over—don't worry, for heaven's sake. Everything is taken care of." And now we can all go home, thank God, I can almost hear her thinking.

"Well, there are still some people I'd really like to bring over," Mark begins, but Matthew had started speaking first.

"It's never over, Helen. That's the terrible thing. I just wish she could have some part of her life free of it all."

"Of the past, you mean?" Helen smiles. "Like divine absolution: Wipe the slate clean of all those bad memories."

Now Luke speaks out from his corner, cowboy boot jiggling fast, voice slow, "Maybe that's what she's doing now." This takes me aback.

"Wait! What about the *good* memories?" I make my plea. "What about all the happy parts? What about their early flying days and those wonderful last years they had, the conservation work they did together? What about the family? They had almost fifty years of family life." From Matthew to Nicky, fifty years of children and grandchildren. Don't we count in the tally of joys and sorrows?

"More, if you count her first baby," Helen reminds me. "That's a memory I'd like to see her released from."

"And the war," Luke says softly, "Cal's speeches."

"That's right," Helen follows up in a matter-of-fact way. "What about all that business of Cal's back then, the bigotry and the racism? That must have been hard to take."

"That was a misrepresentation," says Matthew, as tight as I've ever seen him. "He never should have said what he did— he had no idea what those words meant to people—but he was not a bigot. Look at his personal life. Look at his friends and associates."

"Oh, sure. 'Some of my best friends and associates . . . ,' " I begin, flip and angry, supporting Helen. But Luke is first, quick to back Matthew's position.

"I know what you're saying, Matt. I know exactly what you mean. I can't defend anything he wrote or said at that time, but what I can say, and do say if I ever get myself in a situation where I have to talk to The Press"—he says it as Helen and I do, The Press—"I say that during my lifetime, my father was not a bigot. That's all."

"Well, he sure knew the language," I say, bitterly, "and he certainly used it in the thirties and forties. No, I didn't hear it during my lifetime either. But you can't deny that stuff he said in the thirties and forties: 'Jewish Problem,' 'Western Civilization and racial strength.' Look it up if you want to refresh your memory, Luke. A little reference to 'racial purity' here, a little suspicion of 'intellectuals' there. I don't know what he thought he was talking about then, but I sure know what it sounds like now."

"But Cressy," Mark lectures me gently. "That's just the point. Cal's history is not who he *was,* don't you see? It's what the *country* was. He just got the attention, for some reason. And he drew the fire. I've always felt that Cal was just acting out the great American unconscious—as he did earlier in the airplane, and maybe later with the conservation work, although that hasn't been publicized as much. He was a symbol, a representative, every time."

"Tell it to Anne Frank!" I mutter. "Tell it to Elie Wiesel!"

"Goddamit, Cress," Luke breaks in, "you're judging things that happened fifty years ago! You weren't even born when he made those speeches! He wasn't out to get anybody; he was just lending support to a very popular antiwar movement. He was no diplomat, but he wasn't a bigot."

"Read those speeches," I say. "Read those articles."

Matthew moves in again, reestablishing a quieter tone. "One thing that always gets me is that he was so young—well, almost a generation younger than any of us are now—through most of those years. When he was flying he was not much older than Sarah and Melissa. When he made those speeches he was your age, Cress."

"No excuse," I maintain. "I would know better."

"Well, he *learned* better!" Luke is close to shouting at me now. "Go ahead, Cress, you went through the 1960s, you know everything, go ahead and blast him—it's easy for you!"

"It is *not* easy for her!" Helen furiously confronts Luke now. "Cressy has been through as much as anybody else in this family. It's not easy for any of us."

Luke turns toward Helen in surprise, then leans back in his chair and laughs. "Jesus! What a tiger! I'd forgotten what the women in this family are like," he says to us all. Then he looks over at me. "I'm sorry, Cress. She's absolutely right. It's been hard all the way down the line, for all of us."

And here we are again, all of us, pitting our own memories against the public scrapbook. Who *is* that in the frozen frame, that young couple grinning next to an airplane? Yes there is a family resemblance, but I never knew them. Who is the grim middle-aged stranger on the podium, speaking words that baffle and sting me fifty years later? I have never seen or heard this man; he bears some traces of someone I knew, but is a stranger to me. And yet he is in the scrapbook too. It doesn't matter how hard I try to give it the benefit of the doubt, or how surprised and hurt I am at some of the things in it; there is no solution for me except that it is simply somebody else's scrapbook. I have no memory of it. Mine has different people in it, people who move in time the way the rest of us do: people who are adventurers in their youth, conservative in their middle age, more philosophical and visionary as they get older; people who grow fatter and grayer as time goes on, who wear glasses, comb their hair over bald spots, and get poison ivy from clearing brush or clipping back the rosebushes; people who vote for Adlai Stevenson and argue with me about Andy Warhol or Stokely Carmichael, or discuss Emily Dickinson and Anaïs Nin, who follow the space program and the course of the cold war, and finally, late in life, remember that they love eagles as much as airplanes, and learn to take a little more honey in their tea.

"There was always that dark shadow," muses Mark, with Nicky under the cradle of his hand, "over both of them. And she fought so hard against the darkness. She knew it was there. He tried not to pay attention—he just went on to the next thing."

I am thinking how real Cal was, thinking about his sense of reality and how much I needed him when Jason was six months old, brain damaged by an infant disease that left him unable to move independently, or to talk, feed himself, or even suck his thumb. Through all the terrible days of Jason's illness, the diagnosis of damage, and the weary months of diet and treatment and therapy afterwards, and even during the time of his death here, in Cal's own room in Cal's own house, the person I longed for always, missed the most, was my father. Cal who could never track his own emotions very far, I believe, without running into a danger that was too distant in him for me to understand, could nonetheless look directly at anything real, without flinching. He would have followed my child, his grandson, all the way inside his illness, I was sure. Cal would have gone with him, would have been with Jason right down inside the destroyed brain cells, in a place I could not even bear to imagine. And then Cal would have come back again to tell me all about it, in detail and with love: These are the cells, he would have told me, this is the biology we can understand, and these are the molecular unknowns. This is life, Cressy. This is what is.

This was Jason, whom Garrett and I both loved to the point of agony, each in our own way, whom his sisters loved with simplicity and joy that humbled their parents, whatever agony they also may have felt. By the age of fifteen months he could with great effort point to a part of my face if I held him up over my head and let gravity help the movement. "Where's my nose,

Jason?" I would ask, and the fingers, smaller and lighter than feathers, would move down, winged by the air, down slowly, lightly, to touch my nose, and then he would laugh. I found him dead one morning a year later, in this house, in Cal's room where we had placed the crib so that he would sleep better, away from all human noises, with only the lapping of the sea's own infant—the little cove—to accompany his rest.

"Why was Cal so impossible?" says Helen. "Why didn't he act like other people?"

"He didn't allow himself to admit that he *felt* like other people," says Mark. "That was his tragedy."

"The Press didn't allow him to act like other people," says Luke, "and that was the other side of the coin. It was a two-way thing: They created him and they destroyed him. You're right, Mark. In a way Calvin Linley was only a projection, distorted and magnified by the media out of all proportion to life."

"Destroyed him? He was never destroyed," I say. "He just closed up and refused to listen. He was too stubborn."

"And too alone," Helen added. "Except for Alicia."

As if on cue, the door opens, and Alicia enters with Felix in her arms. She is smiling; he seems intact.

"Well, he's just absolutely fine!" She says, beaming. "Everything seems to be perfectly all right."

In the room I can feel deep breaths drawing, muscles relaxing, bodies shifting. Then Mark again asks Alicia about visiting her on Tuesday, with his friends.

"That would be lovely, dear," says our mother as she hangs up her coat.

"Will you be here still?" Mark looks over at me and Helen. She shakes her head no.

"It's Melissa. I have to go get this all straightened out." Next he looks at Luke, who declines also, regretfully.

"Flight out tomorrow night," he says. "Sorry."

"Where to?" Matt asks. "I'm heading home myself." They compare flights while Mark looks over at me.

"Yes, I guess so," I say finally. "For another day or two. If Helen—Helen, can you take the girls home? They have school on Monday and actually they're supposed to have dinner with Garrett tomorrow night. Will you be home by seven? That's when he's picking them up."

"Absolutely. I have to get back tomorrow night for Michael, myself. He went skiing with his friend Patrick's family—they get home around six P.M."

"Then can you be here Wednesday?" Matthew asks me, out of Alicia's earshot. I say I will.

"Nicky and me," I say. "We'll be here. We'll be here on Tuesday, for sure," I say to Mark, who brightens. I know how he feels. I don't want them all to leave, either.

"Great," says Mark. "There's a couple of people I'd like you both to meet. Matt has met them already." Matt bows his head in acknowledgment.

"Always a troublemaker," he says enigmatically. "Our little Mark," and produces the thin grin once again.

Mark is looking eager, as if the secret is almost out, but not quite. It is the end of the day, teatime is over, and soon there will be children and dinner and Mark and Matthew's train. But as long as we sit here together in this room, we have all the time in the world.

# Chapter

# 10

I WAKE abruptly, sometime in the night, in tears. I have had a vision of Jason's crib, the one in which he died in this house five years ago. But in the crib this time, curled up on the sheet like a baby in the womb, pale and still and lovely as an empty whorled shell on a white beach, is my mother. She wears a flannel nightgown covered with red rosebuds, exactly the rosebud pattern of the wallpaper in the living room of Megan's and Sarah's dollhouse, which was mine before it was theirs, and before mine Helen's, and long before that, when it was new, it belonged to Violet and Alicia. In the dream my mother lies quietly at the bottom of all our family's layers of dolls and dreams and memories, on the sea floor of all our lives, dreaming and remembering nothing, still as my dead son.

The image is too strong to banish by simply waking up, so I lie with it for a while until it weakens and fades, as I have learned that all dreams, no matter how vivid, eventually will do. In the darkness of waking I am glad to hear the night sounds again: Nicky's even breathing right next to my own, and outside the room the black branches and the wind.

As my eyes grow accustomed to the darkness I can not only hear but see Nicholas near me—my second, living, healthy son, deep in sleep. He is tousled and pouting. His head butts up against my neck; his feet sprawl across the pillow on his side of the double bed. He likes to get very close, crowding me in his sleep, so I often find myself at the outer edge of my pillow with my cushioned head hanging out over empty space. Still, I choose to sleep this way, protected by the smell and feel and even the very push of Nicholas, whenever I visit Alicia. It is the only way I have been able to sleep in this house again at all. Sooner or later, I suppose, we will have to give up this arrangement and find him a bed of his own here. For the time being we sleep together, and I don't know which of us draws more comfort from it.

As I let the Alicia dream dissolve away, another comes to take its place, unbidden. It is really just the memory of an image, not a dream. But it could as easily have been a dream, because it dates from a time of dreams and nightmares in my life. Still, it appeared in my waking, troubled mind early in the period of adjustment to Jason's brain-damage diagnosis, after the encephalitis had taken hold of him at five months and kept Garrett and me in hospitals and up late at night all one summer, haggard witnesses to our baby's pain. I was so tired from night vigils that the milk dried up in my breasts. Then I could no longer nurse Jason, hold him to me, willing my own strength into the child, climbing into the spiderweb of wires that attached him to various machines in the intensive care ward of the hospital, as I had done at the beginning of his time there when I was sure that his illness would be short and that my milk would pull him through it. Not being able to feed him was my first defeat.

The diagnosis at the end of that summer, from the best children's hospital we could find, went something like this: "Diffuse cortical atrophy, with dilation of the ventricals. No, we can't predict the impact. Yes, there will be impact, certainly. There will be . . . deficits. Will he ever walk? We don't know, we can't say. Or talk? We can't predict anything at all . . . Will he be able to feed himself? Care for himself at all? Will he be 'retarded'? Mildly? Or severely? We don't know. And actually, we don't use that term any more, Mrs. Trainor. It has become, well, unnecessary, and unkind to the children, we feel. We say 'developmentally delayed' now. I'm sorry that there is no real way to answer your questions, because there are no real answers in a case like this. The future is too uncertain. All we can do is simply wait, and work with him—therapy, exercises, loving care—and see how he develops. We know what *has* happened, in other words, but knowing that does not tell us what *will* happen. We have no way of predicting the nature or the degree of the consequence to your son in the future. I know how difficult it must be to hear this . . ."

It was clear that the specialist who was talking to us was telling the truth. She had spoken to other parents, just like Garrett and me, many times before. She wore their reactions in her intelligent, thoughtful face, with its deeply lined kindness and its sad wisdom.

The days following diagnosis had for me the hideous suspended quality of nightmare, and soon these days became weeks, and the weeks had stretched out into many, many months before finally the world began to come back into perspective. Not knowing the future became just another condition of life. (Who knows the future, anyway? Garrett and I asked each other several months later, in our newfound, hard-won, still-precarious courage.)

Then, unexpected as any blessing, the child himself began to take over our lives with his eagerness and his laughter and his unmistakable affection for his family and for everyone else who was part of his world—doctors, nurses, physical therapists, occupational therapists, preschool teachers for "children with problems." He loved them all, and why not? Jason was no longer ill, only "damaged"—not in pain, only "diagnosed"—and the words were irrelevant, of course. What did he care? He was just a baby who had experienced, along with illness and pain, a tremendous amount of loving physical attention during his short life, and was guaranteed to get a great deal more. He was a year old, pale and thin, but with the blond and blue-eyed good looks of babies in diaper commercials, and an eager, merry smile for all who came near him. He was a baby feeling well again, a baby who spent most of his time in somebody's arms, and enjoyed it. By a year, seven months after the illness began, Jason's character began to shine out over his diagnosis, and his disabilities began to dim. This was true even though he could never walk or talk or feed himself or roll over or even suck his thumb. He never in his life became able to bring a hand close enough to his mouth to do that. It just wouldn't obey him; he had too little muscle control. Instead his arm would stand out stiffly, shaking with effort but immobile. "Intention spasticity," a health-care worker said casually, and I shrank back from her words and prayed it would change with therapy and time. To me, the notion of a baby hurt so badly as to be unable to suck his own thumb for comfort was heartbreakingly unfair.

I was afraid, as parents of children with handicaps are always afraid, in the beginning, that people would stare too long in restaurants, or turn away if he did something odd, or make unwittingly cruel remarks, but it never happened. Maybe we just didn't have time for it to happen—I don't know. But people seemed drawn to him; they always wanted to pick him up and carry him; they ignored the spasms and listened to him laugh, instead, when they made silly faces and whirled him around. Garrett explained it this way: "He's beautiful, he's completely helpless, and without saying a word to you he makes you think you're the greatest thing on earth. What could be more appealing?"

What I recall as I lie here is the image that I lived with during the months after that first ambiguous diagnosis, and I lie awake with it, in Alicia's house, with Nicky next to me in the bed: Having a child diagnosed with brain damage, I thought at the time, is like flying over a beloved city for the first time after it has been bombed. At first, in the shock of your new knowledge, you observe from the air that the place doesn't look so very different. The relief is so overwhelming that you think maybe the early report was incomplete—the city was bombed, yes, but the bombs all fell harmlessly in the river. (He may be a little awkward; it may take him time to catch up with kids who haven't been sick; but he'll be *fine,* eventually.) You circle down, dipping a wing, and as you get closer, you notice that there are one or two things missing from the familiar view—a road here, a factory there—but these are things that can be rebuilt, you think, undiscouraged. (I will teach him to bring his thumb to his mouth; he will learn to turn his head when he hears a sound.) Then finally you are much closer, down at treetop height, so near that you begin to smell the smoke. Now you are forced into a more realistic perspective. You see that the great cathedral, though standing, looks charred, and is smouldering ominously. (Why doesn't he laugh? Why doesn't he wave, the way he should?) You are looking for a place to land, and are passing over the far end of the city, very low. It looks as if the university has been hit. What is gone? The

football field? The science labs? The library? (Dear God, his
body, yes, but not his mind! Oh please, please, not his mind!)

Jason, Alicia, Nicholas, and the wind. Dream image, and
sound, memory and presence all with me in this bed. I start to
cry again, and Nicky shifts and sighs, and then I find myself
smiling. What a grumpy little sigh! (Don't trouble me with
your sadness, Mom. I am the center and the prince of your
world now. Be still, be *my* mother. Let me sleep.)

Finally, after an hour or more, I can see the branches outside the window quite clearly, and the chair where I left Nicky's
clothes and mine in a heap last night. The darkness has lifted a
little bit, and before long I can read my watch. It is fifteen
minutes before six.

Can I safely get up? I know I won't sleep anymore, and I've
lain here long enough. I wedge my pillow lengthwise alongside
my sleeping son, as a surrogate, and carefully climb out of bed,
taking my clothes with me into the bathroom where I put them
on in a hurry. I'll leave the girls a note—on the mirror, not in
the room, to avoid rousing the lamb—and just go outside for a
little walk to clear my head of dreams.

I go downstairs in stocking feet, quietly open the door of
the coat closet, and slip into my jacket and boots. I am stealthy
and soundless, and proud of it, until a fusillade of sharp little
yaps invades the quiet. How could I have forgotten about Felix?
He is barking at me from behind the closed door between the
living room and the hallway leading to the kitchen and Alicia's
room.

Immediately, desperately, I open that door with one hand
and make a frenzied fumble into my jacket pocket with the
other. I know I had some food for Nicholas there yesterday, a
bag of—yes!—Saltines! Mashed and crumbling, but still entic-
ing enough to attract the attention of the dog, who is now
frisking around my boots as only a dog who didn't expect a
walk for hours can frisk. My heart sinks, but softens. I know

that the Saltines, however pleasant, will not make up for the disappointment Felix will suffer if I don't bring him along. I write another note, leave it on the table by the door where Alicia will find it, then reach for the leash draped over the closet doorknob. The dog and I emerge together into the chilly March air.

It is colder than I had expected. When I am at home in Vermont I think of Alicia as living in a southern climate, warm and even sultry compared to our bleak northern farm weather at this time of year. But as I step out now a cloud of frosty breath precedes me, and Felix shakes himself briskly in preparation for the elements. We walk quickly to the main road where it is growing light, but still only one or two cars pass us. Sunday morning churchgoers, maybe.

We pass Martha's driveway as we head again toward the little inlet. I wonder where the wild geese spent the night, and feel grateful that Felix is trotting along in well-behaved happiness beside me at the end of his leash. He still can't believe his luck.

Soon I hear the steady light thump of running shoes behind us, and turn to see Martha, in sweatpants and a sweatshirt and earmuffs, all red. She slows down as she reaches us, stops and breathes heavily for a minute, then laughs.

"God, I hate this! I wasn't meant for jogging. I'm indolent by nature."

"Then why do it?" I ask, smiling. Felix is clearly delighted to see Martha. What a morning! Saltines, fresh air, exercise, the company of women . . .

"It's my clothes," she explains sadly, "I don't know how it happened, but I can't get into them anymore. And I'm too cheap to buy new ones, so here you see me. Exercise. I hate it." She makes a face.

"Well, I guess then there's no alternative," I say sympathetically. "Although I've been hearing lately that running isn't as good for you as walking, actually. Why don't you hang out with Felix and me? We won't tell anybody you weren't jogging."

"You've persuaded me," says Martha, taking off her earmuffs. She reaches down to pat Felix. "My, my! Such a gentleman! I guess your lady friend must have left town in the night. How did he persuade you to take him out this early?"

"It was the other way around, really. I couldn't sleep so I thought I'd take a walk, and he heard me. Simple."

Martha looked at me curiously. "Couldn't sleep? That doesn't sound so simple, not that it's any of my business."

We are walking along companionably enough, and I am very fond of Martha, but I am embarrassed to tell her much of what has been going through my head, so I hesitate. Soon she speaks instead.

"It can't be easy, this business with your mother right now. Especially here, after Jason."

Straight into the heart of things. A bright and red arrow on a chilly morning, bull's-eye! It seems almost uncanny, until I remember that she is Alicia's confidante.

"I don't know," I start to say, "I really don't know why it worries me that she forgets things—have you noticed it a lot?" I turn to look at Martha and see her nod before I even finish the question.

This makes me feel better. I press on.

"I suppose what I feel is loss, but that seems unfair. She's still here, and she's still wonderful, and her memory is really her business. I mean, Helen's right—I should leave her alone, make sure everything is safe and practical, let her be comfortable, and not fret. I wish I didn't have this urge to hover over her like a mother hen, or tweak at her sleeve and remind her I'm here, like a little kid. I feel as if I were saying, 'Stay with me! Don't go away! Don't forget! Don't leave!' I guess it's loss, or something. But she's not lost. Why do I feel loss?"

"Loss is loss," says Martha. "If you feel it, that's what you feel. I can sympathize, but I can't feel what you do. For me your mother is somebody I've *found*, even though I haven't known her for too long. There's no loss for me. I'm crazy about her just the way she is."

I feel chided, and taken aback.

"I'm crazy about her too! It's just—"

"No, let me finish." says Martha. "My own mother is in a nursing home in Maine, and there isn't a thing wrong with her as far as her memory goes. But she has this chronic muscle disease that affects her brain in a whole different way. She's unbelievable, really. She outlived my father—talk about an exhausted man!—and I think she'll outlive the nursing staff too. They've written me twice already to ask us to remove her, because she's been abusive to the aides. She can't help it—she has these spells where she hurts everybody who gets near her. Then it gets better, and she calms down, and they let her stay. The amazing thing is that this is a woman who can hardly function, physically. She has very little use of her limbs. But don't get close to that wheelchair!" She makes a noise that sounds like a laugh, but can't be.

"What happens?" I ask.

"Mostly she pinches. Once in a while she bites. Anybody who comes near her—hard. Oh, not every day," Martha assures me. I must have my mouth hanging open. "Just once in a while. I think that's why they haven't actually kicked her out yet. I suppose she's very angry, and I guess if I were in her place I'd be angry too."

"Oh, Martha, I never knew . . . How long has this been going on?"

"The disease? It was discovered when I was about six, I think. She's been like this for as long as I can remember. Why do you think I went to Europe?" She really is laughing now. How can she laugh?

"Good God!" I shake my head. "And here I am whimpering at you about feeling lost."

She looks surprised. "That's not why I'm telling you—don't be silly. It's not that terrible. After all, I've had almost my whole life to get used to it. It's no worse than any of the things you've had to deal with in your life, or Helen in hers, or your mother in hers. I just wanted you to know why Alicia isn't in the category of 'loss' for me. I don't think she could be. She's something wonderful that I've found. And Noah, too. It's really good for him to have her nearby. It makes up for a lot *he's* lost. I just thought it might help if you saw her the way we do."

She waits while I think about this. Then she speaks again, looking anxious. "Is that okay? Did I say too much?"

"No. I like it." I begin to smile. "Lost and Found. I like thinking that way."

We walk along together until we get to the inlet where there are no geese in sight this time. Martha looks at her watch.

"Oops! Better run back before Noah's awake. The kid gets mad if I'm not there when he wakes up—not that he ever will, since it's Sunday. He usually comes down about noon, well rested, but really grouchy. I hope Helen doesn't mind grouchy teenagers at breakfast."

"Helen? I don't think she'll still be here at noon. Anyway, she *eats* grouchy teenagers for breakfast," I say with sisterly braggadocio.

"Great! Me too!" She bends and stretches a few more times. "Now I suppose I have to jog back home again. Damn. Well, it was fun talking."

"I'm glad you came." I wave at her as she turns and jogs determinedly back the way we came. Felix and I follow at a more sedate pace, and the morning brightens into sunshine as we make our way back toward Alicia's house.

It is almost seven o'clock when we return. I think I can hear stirrings and rustlings from Alicia's room when I let Felix back through the door to that part of the house, and retrieve my note from the hall table. Upstairs, all is just as I left it, with Nicky sleeping across most of the big bed in one room, and the girls, the lamb, and Melissa still soundless across the hall in the room Aunt Violet had the night before. I remove the note on the bathroom mirror and prepare to take a shower. As I finish and am towelling myself off, I think I can hear one of the girls outside the door.

It is Helen, about to go into the girls' room.

"Hi Cress! What are you doing up so early? Martha said she met you on the road about six!"

"Couldn't sleep," I confess. "Too much thinking . . . you know."

"Yes," she said, "I guess I do. Poor Cress. Well, I hate to leave you here alone with your thoughts, but I really think we should leave early. I'm hoping to stop at the school and do a little more talking—God help me—to Melissa's English teacher. She says this teacher understands the kids' point of view best of all. I figure Melissa and the girls can walk around campus—or if the school objects, I'll leave them at McDonald's, or even in the car. Is that okay with you?"

"Sure," I say with some caution. "I'm not sure about the lamb, though."

"Oh, nuts. I forgot. Well, then in the car."

"No, wait," I say. "That's crazy. Megan's going to school tomorrow anyway, and Joe will have more than enough on his hands. I'll keep the lamb here with Nicky. We'll take care of it."

Helen laughs. "Whatever you say. I don't mind, though. Actually, if you keep the lamb things may be a little easier for Mark tomorrow. Animals are great that way."

"What do you mean?" I forget to whisper. "What's going on? Did Mark *tell* you something?" Already, my feelings are hurt again. He probably told Luke and Matthew too. But not me. The little sister is the last to know. Why is sibling rivalry something we never outgrow, when it is surely one of the least admirable and most useless of family feelings? I stand glum, wet, and dripping in the hallway.

Helen moves forward and gives me a strong, long hug, right on top of the damp towel.

"It's okay, Cress," she says. "Don't look like that. He only told me because I'm leaving so early. And he made me promise not to tell, so I can't. It's a surprise. But I swear you'll love it, and so will Nicky. It's just . . . odd. It will be hard to get used to. I can't imagine how Alicia—I'm already talking too much. Do you mind if I wake up the girls? I'd really like to leave soon." She is breathless, her eyes twinkling, happy to be in a hurry.

"Be my guest," I say. "But back me up on the lamb, okay? Say you're allergic to live wool or something. That's why it has to stay with me." She laughs, and we open the door to-gether. For a moment we stand silent, looking in.

There they are. Three lumps under three sets of bedcovers. (Melissa has slept on the floor, on a mattress removed from a roll-away cot in the guest-room closet.) We see quantities of long hair spilling over onto each pillow, two blond heads and one brown—skeins of silk, treasure enough to tempt Marco Polo. The lumps themselves slumber on as Helen and I watch them. Perhaps she is remembering, as I am, all the earlier lumps of these very same sleeping girls: the tiny tight pink-blanketed lump the nurse brings you that first day in the hospital, as soon as both you and the baby have been cleaned up after the mess and turmoil of birth. How it was to see those little-girl buntings, Sarah and Megan, barely named, all warmly wrapped in readi-ness for my arms and for the world. And a few months later the lumps were looser and more personal in their pajama sleepers, settled in their own cribs at home with their blankets and their bottles and their bottoms up in the air. The five-year-old lumps clutched stuffed animals; the eight-year-old lumps often had a tooth under the pillow. (How tough it was for the tooth fairy when one of the lumps was sleeping on her stomach with the pillow, and the tooth, held tightly to her chest!) Ten-year-old lumps might still be afraid of the dark, with a plug-in night-light "in case I have to go to the bathroom or anything." And now these sleeping princesses whose lumps are crowned with silk.

I look at my two sleeping daughters and realize that I don't want to be without them. I don't want them to drive north today with anybody but me, not even Helen. I want to wake them up myself, snuggling my face into that tangled hair, and nuzzling at the rose-colored sleepy slackness of their cheeks, just the way I did ten years ago. I want to hold them, my almost-grown-up daughters, right now in a passionate mother hug, while they are stretching themselves elegantly awake. I want to grab and hold my girl children, and never let go. How they would hate it! I will have to get a better grip on *myself,* that's what I have to do.

"You can tell they're all the same species, can't you?" Helen murmurs to me.

"Ah, yes," I reply. "With so many species-specific behaviors. Groans, snores, wiggles . . . They seem so comfortable there. I don't envy the person who tries to wake them. Gee, Helen, I think I'll let you do it! I just got out of the shower, and I think I can hear Nicky in the other room."

"Chicken!" says Helen, as I make my retreat across the hall. The lamb begins to bleat from its box by Megan's bed.

"I'll be right back!" I call. "Have fun!"

In my own room Nicholas rolls over, half awake, to look at me. He is pink and rumpled, the collar of his pajama rucked up near one ear.

"Wet," he accuses me sleepily, staring at my hair.

"That's right, my bunny. Wet hair. It'll dry soon. It looks funny when it's wet, doesn't it?"

He eyes me all over, still suspicious. I may not get to hug this one for a while today either, I guess, unless I use skillful strategy.

"It will be all dry soon, Nicky—I promise."

I pull my clothes on quickly while he watches, noncommittal, sucking his thumb. Then I towel my hair as dry as I can and brush it rapidly into a recognizable form.

"There!" I say. "And now, Mr. Nicholas the bunny..." I am advancing on him with a meaningful tone in my voice. He giggles, recognizing it from other foolish moments, and pulls the blanket closer. "I...want...a...KISS!"

"KISS," he repeats, his laughter muffled by the sheet he has pulled up over his face. He is wiggling all over, under the covers, like an apprehensive puppy.

"KISS," I threaten happily, my hands on the bedcovers. More wiggles, more giggles, very high pitched. This is getting noisy—I hope Alicia is already awake.

"KISS!" The girls are at the bedside, all three of them, huge in their nightgowns, descending upon Nicholas as I do.

"Good grief!" I can hear Helen somewhere in the background. "Nicky, run for it! All is lost!"

But he is in hysterical glee, rolling and giggling on the bed as his mother and his sisters and his cousin tickle and kiss him, all at the same time. Finally he wiggles out of our clutches and lands on the floor, barefoot and shrieking, his hair sticking out in tufts in all directions. He is at bay in the midst of five women, but grinning at us all, secure in his own invincible self.

Half the size of Megan, who is the smallest among us, Nicholas now brings one hand to his mouth, and plants in the palm of it the loudest, wettest, most grotesquely lip-smacking kiss I have ever heard. A giant in a fairy tale should produce a kiss like that, but nobody smaller. Then he waves his hand at us all, sending that sticky salute floating off toward us with a magnificent, all-inclusive flourish, an emperor's greeting to his public.

"KISS!" shouts Nicholas, and marches alone to the stairs. From just below him, clear and free and lighthearted as any girl's, we can hear the sound of his grandmother's laughter.

# Chapter

# 11

LATER on Sunday Alicia's house seems much too quiet with the bulk of our family gone from it again. Luke and Matthew must be well on the way to the airport by now, heading for their flights west. Matthew will fly with the comfortable knowledge that Gwen is waiting for him at home, but Luke is going back to an empty house, and it will be cold and dark when he walks inside. I imagine him tramping from his car to the front door, wearing the big sheepskin coat he had on when he left Alicia's house Saturday evening, a coat of Cal's that Luke has worn every winter since Alicia gave it to him after our father's death because they were the same size. He will be carrying the army duffel that he uses when he travels, the one he and Emma and their kids always took on camping trips. Most likely his cowboy boots will leave a trail of pointed footprints in the snow that has accumulated on the front path during the time he was gone, with nobody around to shovel it. Early spring in Montana is no warmer than it is in Vermont.

Helen and the three girls drove off mid-morning, with scarcely a backwards glance. Only Megan lingered in my embrace at the door, and only in order to be sure I remembered everything she had told me about the lamb's eating and sleeping arrangements.

"You can't just put the box down somewhere and forget about her," she says to me. "She needs to know you're there. I always put my hand on her back if I wake up at night, just lightly, so she can tell she's not all by herself. Oh!—and if you're feeding her with leftover milk from the refrigerator, you can warm the bottle right up by just running hot water over it —really! The water at Alicia's is much hotter than at home. It's easy. Do you think you'll remember? She doesn't like it if it's cold."

I reassured Megan, kissed her again, and thought how much she reminded me of myself on the telephone with her father last night. (He called this house to confirm the Sunday dinner date with the girls, then offered to keep them overnight, too, and drive them to school in the morning.) "Sarah has to be sure to get to the library tomorrow—there's a book on reserve for her history paper. And Megan needs to remember her toe shoes for ballet class Monday. Tell her she'll get blood blisters all over again if she doesn't put the lambswool in her ballet bag— no, not from my barn, silly—it's a special ballet kind that you buy to put around your toes, in toe shoes. What? . . . I don't know why, maybe Baryshnikov blessed it, or something. Anyway it's a lot cleaner and a lot less smelly than what is in the barn. But you have to keep telling her to take it with her so she uses it. Those blisters are horrible; they take forever to heal."

The teenagers leave in a cloud of scented cleanliness—all three sets of their shampoos and conditioners mingling fragrances in Alicia's doorway as Helen waves the girls on with laughing impatience after her own quick hug and kiss for Alicia and for me. The girls kiss us too, and finally they have all departed. I stand on the steps and watch Helen's car turn out of Alicia's driveway, and I listen to it go down the road until it is out of earshot. Then I go in and close the door behind me, and go looking for my mother and my son.

They are together on the floor of the living room, sitting with an overturned hassock, laughing. The hassock, the shape of a half-moon when righted, has been set on its curved side so that it will rock, like a rocking horse, and Nicky has obviously been rocking on it, and has fallen over. It looks as if Alicia has been rocking on it too. She is dishevelled, twinkling, and in the process of tying her shoelace.

"You are a menace, young man!"

He tugs at her arm. "Again!"

"Nicky!" I protest at the scene, "Your poor Ganna . . ."

"Yes, but first I have to finish tying my shoe," she says to him. Neither of them pays any attention to me.

Again she climbs on the hassock, bending and placing a hand on it to help herself. I observe with shock that one knuckle is lumpy with arthritis—swollen to the size of one of the horse chestnuts in her pocket—and her back has much more of a curve to it than I remember. She climbs on the hassock with effort, and in the effort she frowns, seeking balance. A million wrinkles net the beautiful face: eyes, forehead, down the cheeks, around the chin, as she concentrates. Then she's got it. Alicia is limber and light as ever. She has had no trouble establishing herself on this horse, after all. When she begins to rock, she smiles at Nicky. Such a smile! Such mischief and invitation in it, such merriment! She starts to sing, in a high, quavery, grandmother's Mother Goose voice. "Ride a cock-horse! To Banbury Cross! To see a fine lady upon a white horse!"

"Horse!" Nicky scrambles up to get on it with her, and upsets the balance. This must be exactly what happened before I came in. I see them start to tip over. Why isn't Alicia more careful? I rush at her with a shriek. Broken bones, nursing homes.

". . . and bells on her toes. She shall have music wherever —Oops! Oh dear!" They have gone down, but I am there before they hit the ground. One of my arms is under Nicky's shoulder, and Alicia has landed bonily in my lap, elbows digging into my ribs.

"Oh, my God! Are you all right?" I gasp.

"Yes, I'm perfectly all right." She remains with me for an instant, then gets up with care, first removing her body from mine with some fastidiousness, then straightening her clothes.

"Cress," she says when she catches her breath, "you worry too much. I don't think he really can come to much harm."

"No, I know he can't. I just . . ."

She studies me with penetrating kindness. She was with me when Jason died. But I wasn't thinking about Jason this time, Alicia. I really wasn't, for once.

"And I am equal to my life, Cressy. Can you understand that?"

I remain halfway down on my haunches, in a kind of collapsed catcher's position. Or a frog's. I feel like a frog. Slimy, out of water, not in my element.

"I guess I do. I guess I'm the one who isn't, maybe." I sit all the way down on the floor to stretch out my legs. One of them has developed a cramp.

My mother shakes her head.

"No, that isn't true, dear. You also are equal to your life. Whether you believe it or not."

She turns toward Nicholas while I sit here, basking in this beloved, lifelong sunshine of her praise. It is a physical feeling, like a blush, that comes over me when Alicia says something complimentary. I am sure that everybody who knows her has felt this at one time or another, a suffusion of self-awareness and satisfaction: She has looked directly at me and inside me; she has noticed; she commends.

I am equal to my life. She is right. I feel it. I have equalled the fires of my past and I will equal the fires of my future, whatever they may be. I am equal to everything. I am Alicia's child.

I look gratefully in her direction. Again she is bending over Nicky and the hassock. Again I see how curved her spine has become, and at once I lose the glow. How do I become equal to *your* life, Alicia, at this period? What am I supposed to do about you? You and Cal were the ones who knew everything. Tell me what to do.

Alicia picks up the hassock and sets it straight for Nicky so that he can have a turn rocking by himself. They play this way for fifteen minutes, as I watch, until Alicia says she has to rest. This is the first rest of her day, though there are others. She spends more time resting now than I have ever known her to do, something else new.

All Sunday and Monday we are a family of three: Alicia, Nicholas, and I. We are an unrehearsed trio, and I spend most of my time trying to find jobs for myself in my mother's household, where I no longer have a working role. Nonetheless, I do what I can. In fact I do the things she does when she visits *my* household: I straighten up the living room, wash dishes, pick Nicky's toys up off the floor, and answer the phone when it rings. (Once it was Aunt Violet, to thank her sister for the lovely visit, once Matthew to say he had gotten home safely. We called Luke and Helen Sunday evening ourselves. Everyone's safe arrival is now established.)

We go for walks in the morning and the late afternoon, down to the inlet and back. Otherwise, I tend to wander the house, thinking. Once, while Alicia is resting in her room again and Nicky is playing with a scattering of blocks on the floor in front of the now-cold living room fireplace, I stand in front of the window, watching the birds at the bird feeder and the squirrels on the flagstone terrace outside.

I am thinking now about Alicia and Cal as a couple living perpetually with the sense of being watched, of guarding against watchers. We children lived with it, too, although it was never ours as much as it was theirs. There were serious legitimate concerns about watchers, of course. There are always crazy people, poor things, who are drawn to celebrity, and others who exploit it. But there was also something else, I think. In some ways Cal and Alicia were like the birds and the squirrels here before me, who might also claim that they are not intentionally on display even if they do come, over and over again, into full view of this window. They are simply going about their own private lives. And I can believe that claim. I can believe them all: parents, birds, and squirrels. I think they mean it. Yet there is, I think, an eventual relationship that establishes itself between observers and observed, some symbiosis that develops over time, of birdseed and feeder and window, of diary and museum and book and letter, of public and private life. There arise expectations and understandings on both sides.

Alicia sometimes quotes Cal saying sadly, "Nobody ever forgets us!" He meant, I suppose, that the usual fading of interest between casual acquaintances never occurred with the Linleys. Anyone who met them remembered and wanted to perpetuate the contact. And his complaint was that this was unusual in human relationships, an aberration caused by that other aberration—celebrity. He may have been right. However, Cal and Alicia themselves were unusual, in their own sharing of their lives with people they did not know through their written work. And to be fair to these "others"—these readers of books and these visitors to museums—this may have given them an idea that there was a relationship to be claimed.

There was so much written, and so much saved, and it all must have been directed at somebody out in the world beyond our life in the old stone house, because that's where it all went —out. It went out into the world, even when Cal and Alicia didn't. Both of our parents wrote volumes about themselves for publication, even during periods when they were refusing all media contact and most social invitations. They kept extensive diaries, filed all their correspondence, and in those days before photocopying they made and saved carbon copies of all their letters, presumably for posterity. For a while Cal even tried to bribe me, at a dollar apiece, to save and return to him any letters from himself or Alicia that I had in my possession. I refused, furious. He already had the carbons! There was no way I was going to let him recycle my personal mail into some dusty archive. I would save my letters or lose them, treasure them or send them up in flames, exactly as I pleased. (Not only that, but Helen and I had previously decided that if we ever wanted to, we could run away from home by selling Cal and Alicia's letters to collectors, at a much better price! I did not actually tell Cal of this plan, nor did we ever carry it out.) I have no idea where the letters are today, and yet I think—yes, I am sure—that I still stand by my decision to keep them.

What I am saying, I suppose, is that our parents on the one hand struggled to keep their lives unusually private, and on the other must have considered their lives to be of such public significance that they saved every scrap of evidence that would reveal, eventually, all that they tried to keep secret. They saved letters written and letters received, they saved bills, manuscripts, memos, receipts, requests, unsolicited gifts, and other material I cannot begin to imagine. Literally hundreds of boxes of accumulated personal and household papers have gone to the universities and museums housing Linley collections. Several are still being shipped off from Alicia's house every year. There are rooms full, vaults full of the stuff. One researcher even showed me one of my own poems, a doggerel ABC verse written in honor of Cal's birthday the year I was sixteen ("*M* is for Minnesota Funeral Dirge . . .") filed right along with a bill from Bergdorf Goodman and an appeal from Easter seals. I was touched that the verse had been saved, but baffled about the filing system. It was like being in a friend's kitchen and trying to understand both where and why she keeps things: the spatula goes in the drawer with the steak knives? How odd. What on earth are all these little corks for? She has saved every net bag that ever came into the house containing onions. What will she do with them?

I can remember another archival basement, not dusty but jam-packed with memorabilia of midwestern history and its heroes, including Cal. I stood there with my mother, with Cal's publisher and close friend, and several museum officials, a year after my father had died. We were there, among other reasons, to examine the contents of a trunk Cal had assigned to the museum at some time in the forties or fifties. And so we all stood over it, this neatly packed footlocker, looking at shirts and socks and other items of clothing, very much the kind of thing one sends with one's children to summer camp. Then the publisher picked up a can that looked as if it might contain shoe polish, and slowly, gingerly, pried the lid off. We all jumped back—a two-foot worm on a cloth-covered coil had sprung out at us, right there in the basement of the historical society. Cal had packed it there fifty years earlier, possibly in anticipation of this very moment. Who knows?

"What do you think it means?" someone quietly asked, and it was not until then that I started laughing.

Clearly there was a relationship between my parents and

the people who watched them, and it is just as clear that we children were not included in that relationship. This was true partly because Cal and Alicia had worked so hard to keep our lives free but also because, frankly, celebrities' children are generally not very interesting. We are always trying too hard either to get *in* the way of the attention flowing to and from our parents, in which case we are obnoxious, or *out* of the way, which makes us invisible. And we have no firm status. We are neither watchers nor watched, but something else, someone ambiguously in the middle (unless we become celebrities ourselves, which is a different story entirely). We hear about the watchers from our parents, who have trained us to be allies, and we learn about our parents from the watchers, who see us as intermediaries. Our position is an odd one, forcing us to look at our lives from opposite perspectives, occasionally both at the same time.

This is not all bad. I loved, for instance, the elderly photographer who described to me his joy upon learning of Cal's success in crossing the ocean so long ago. "I was going out to feed my granddad's chickens, you know, but just then the news came in on the radio, and I was so excited I threw the whole bucket down and chased those chickens all over the yard!" I was pleased that my nearest neighbor in Vermont, who had daydreamed as a girl of being invited to ride with Calvin Linley in his airplane, was invited to fly with him when she was in her seventies, one beautiful fall day when he was visiting us, and wanted to rent an airplane and see the autumn foliage from the air. And I have been amused lately by the enthusiastic absurdity of a pilot friend who called up to tell me in mystical tones that the date of my marriage to Joe matched—number for number —the call letters on my father's first airplane. I was most of all warmed and grateful to find Cal's boyhood home after he died. I had never been to the museum during his lifetime; it was not the kind of thing he encouraged his family to do. But it was wonderful afterwards to see the actual books and dishes and tools and toys of his youth. What a remarkable thing for a daughter to be able to do while grieving for her father.

Then there are the strange times: the crazy phone calls from people who learn who my famous relative was and just want to hear my voice so that they can tell their friends. There are the people, only once in a great while now, who seek out our house and drive down the road to gawk. There are letters like the one from the woman who wrote within a week of Cal's death to ask that I send her something he'd touched: "Just anything," she wrote. "A piece of cloth from his shirt, or a button, or even a shoelace." A fingernail? I thought viciously. How about a lock of hair from the corpse, would that be nice? What is it you think I can give you? What do you think we have to do with each other? Even to the people I like, whose stories I enjoy hearing, I sometimes want to say: Thank you for sharing your scrapbook with me. I enjoyed the pictures. But please don't bring it to me as if it were my scrapbook. These are your memories, and I respect them. But they are not mine. When you say, "See this young couple next to the airplane? I got this photograph when I was twelve. See this newspaper clipping? It's about your brother—my aunt gave it to me. See? This is your family." I want to say, "No. This is not my family, and this is not my scrapbook. This is your scrapbook. There are pictures here that you value, and I'll look at them for your sake. But me? I have never seen these people, these colorless, frozen people in the photograph, before in my life."

Worst of all for me are the times when I see my parents in particularly vulnerable moments of their personal history, on film. I have seen these moments played over and over again on the television screen, and feel helpless every time. The most painful are the film clips of Cal and Alicia standing together during the time they had lost their child, but before they knew he was lost. She comes out of some house bareheaded, with her eyes darting nervously this way and that, just the way Sarah's do when she is nervous. She looks remarkably like Sarah, in fact. He is locked in his most formal, grim-Cal mode, stiff and staring in his pinstriped suit. But he is shifting from foot to foot in a way I recognize like a stab in my stomach as completely his own, and he is also holding his mouth just exactly the way Helen's son Michael does today when he is very unhappy but doesn't want anyone to know it. My parents are telling the reporters what their child eats for breakfast, in case somebody finds him. They are younger by far than I am now. I have never met this young couple, but I can almost feel his flesh and smell her perfume, I know them so well. And yet they are forever inside the projected image and I am forever outside of it. I may see this scene a hundred times, but I will never be able to go in there and put my arms around my family. I watch these films with a kind of scream inside.

Certainly there was a sinister, extra apprehension about watchers, especially at night, because of the lost child. Alicia still carefully draws all the curtains of her bedroom close together before going to bed. She has always done this, and if I am visiting I help her. In that case she will sometimes refer to the too-strong light of early morning, pretending that she draws the curtains against the dawn, rather than the darkness. We pulled them closed last night, thick blue curtains like Mary's mantle, around the wooden Madonna statue on her windowsill (a partner to St. Francis in the other room). We pulled them past the little basket of dried flowers with a tiny china doll sitting in it wearing a red kerchief and matching skirt—a gift from one of the grandchildren. We carefully, slowly pulled them behind the rather precarious standing lamp that leans over her "letter desk" with its collection of pigeonholes and well-stained blotters and notes and correspondence. She pulls the curtain and finally the job is done. All is warm and light on this side of the curtains, and the dark is now beyond.

Detail by detail—wooden statue, little basket, china doll, lamp—we divide our lives from darkness, and survive. Cal survived by detail too: the mathematics of engine and airfoil, the pressure in the tire of a car, the smell of a kerosene lamp or a wood fire, the tap of a manual typewriter, the rhythm of a crosscut saw. For me it was Jason's cheek, his fingers, the fine warm heft of him in his blue snowsuit, the wisp of fair hair on my chin—these overruled the spasms and the fears; these were what we really lived by. (But then there were his socks clinging to the innards of the dryer and only appearing weeks after he died. There was the pair of size 2T overalls in the back of the hall, forgotten under a pile of magazines, that I found the following spring: We perish by detail too.)

I don't know how many watchers there are left, or how many watchers there ever were. Millions at one time, perhaps, and maybe still millions, in a more distant way. I don't know about watchers, or about fame, or about celebrity firsthand. But I was part of a family, and I have helped to create another family, and so I know about families. I know that for the family I was born into, among other truths, there is the truth that we have been living for more than half a century under the tremendous strain and distortion of watching ourselves.

We watch ourselves; we hide and protect ourselves; and we hide and protect our parents, as they taught us to do without wanting or realizing it, while they protected us. That's what I'm doing right now, here at this house, where the squirrels ignore me outside and my son plays on the floor and Alicia sleeps. It's a sad thing to do, sometimes. It has its rules and its rewards, always, and of course I will always do it. I wonder sometimes if it is the only thing I have really learned to do well in my life, the one job I can recognize.

I pluck withered leaves off the branch in the Chinese vase. I know every object and piece of furniture of this room by heart, so that if the house burned to the ground and I were the angel of its resurrection I could recreate it—every stone, every table, sometimes I think every book on the shelves. I could easily find the perfect branch for the Chinese vase in this window. I could tell the birds and the squirrels where to feed on the flagstones: right there, where the crumbs of Alicia's toast were crumbled so carefully by her own hand this very morning. And I could recreate—oh so lovingly, without a single forgotten arthritic bump or familiar freckle—I could recreate the hand.

Alicia has been very quiet for an hour now. I am wavering between going to check on her and staying here with Nicky, who now wants me to play with him and the blocks. Characteristically, I can't decide whether to be my mother's daughter or my son's mother. Alicia would tell me there is no difference between the two.

Later Nicky and I and Alicia walk with Felix to the inlet, trailing sticks, looking at the undersides of leaves, picking cattails and tickling each other with them, watching for geese. (We do not see any.) We walk back again with our cheeks flushed and our moods light. We take off our outdoor clothes quietly when we come inside, and go to feed the lamb.

We feed the lamb together, all three of us. Nicky hears the bleating before I do, and comes to me with great excitement. "Lamb!" he says, "Wake up!"

"Time for the bottle," I say. "We'll go get it and bring it upstairs."

We have taken the lamb downstairs for a feeding only once or twice during this time at Alicia's, and only when Felix is outside. With the family gone the dog has abandoned his company behavior and reverted to his original indignation at having a barnyard presence in his home. Felix has to be kept shut in Alicia's room if the lamb is nearby, and he barks constantly until the lamb is upstairs again behind closed doors itself. Having the lamb downstairs without Megan to watch it is not too successful anyway. In the kitchen Numie slips and falls and gets under everyone's feet, and in the living room she clatters into things that fall over (lamps, tables). She is stronger and hungrier now too, and therefore requires a good deal of cleaning up after, with paper towels, following each feeding. Since Megan's departure, instructions notwithstanding, Numantia has spent most of her time in our bedroom.

"That little lamb is hungry *again?*" Alicia speaks with the amusement and pride one feels about all healthy, hungry babies. "Is there anything I can do? Do you need more water?" She comes out of her room and follows us into her kitchen, eager to help.

She is elegantly dressed, as she and her sister always seem to be at all times of day, by instinct. (Helen and I each have the feeling that we did not inherit this instinct, but hope our daughters will remember us with the same awe for *some* quality.) Alicia wears a pair of black trousers, a ribbed black turtleneck sweater with a gold circle pin at the neck, and she is also wearing her pink bedroom slippers. I can smell her perfume and hear the light scuffing of the slippers behind me, along with Nicky's chatter.

Assistance is really not necessary because all we have to do is mix the milk-replacer powder with warm water. However, since Sarah and Megan left, Alicia has insisted upon heating the water on the stove for the lamb.

Alicia and Nicholas watch approvingly as I mix the heated water with the powder in a Pyrex measuring cup, pour the mixture into the lamb's bottle, and fit the coarse black nipple over the top. Lamb nipples look very utilitarian, almost unhealthy, compared to the ones offered to babies.

"Don't you need a funnel for that?" Alicia asks me. I have spilled some of the formula not only down the neck of the bottle, but also on the counter. She moves toward the sink.

"I think it's just clumsiness. I never could pour anything.

Don't worry—I can clean it up." But she has the sponge already in hand and is wiping up after me. Nicky is practically jumping out of his shoes, impatient to the point of frenzy with both of us.

"Lamb's *hungry!*" Indeed the bleating is more and more insistent from upstairs. It's surprising how much noise a baby of any species can make, even at this age. Rhythmic, aggrieved, never ending: a noise designed to make parents do whatever will make it stop.

"We'll go ahead, shall we?" says Alicia to Nicholas. Hand in hand, they go through the living room and up the stairs, with me following closely behind them.

Upstairs, wrapping her in the towel, I gather the lamb from her cardboard box. She is restless with hunger, moving back and forth on the layers of newspaper, peering over the edge of the box, wagging her lamb's tail wildly in anticipation of the feeding, too anxious even to know what to do when the food actually arrives. She kicks and makes sucking movements and turns her head in all directions, but I hold her tightly in the towel and put the nipple in her mouth.

At last! She guzzles eagerly while Alicia and Nicky watch us. I feel all powerful as I feed. It is wonderful to be at the providing end of a nipple. I look over at my mother, who knows the feeling too.

"You do it," I say, and she is surprised, but pleased. She sits right down in the little armchair by the guest-room window and holds out her arms. She takes the lamb and its towel with the gentle awkwardness one always feels when holding someone else's baby for the first time, but once the bottle is firmly in the lamb's mouth again after the anxious moment of transition, she is completely at ease.

"Goodness! What an appetite!" Numie strains and sucks and wiggles and kicks off the towel with all four of her legs moving at once. Alicia is losing her grip, but laughing. I move in.

"Gosh! I guess she may be too big to feed that way now. Maybe we should just let her stand on the floor."

Together we put the lamb down on the floor and arrange its wriggling body so that the head is right between Alicia's legs and she can grip the bottle between her knees if the eager animal tugs too hard. The lamb's feet are now planted firmly on the carpet, and the towel lies in a heap beside them. Nicky is crouched next to the lamb, patting it in rhythm with the sucking.

"Infants have no moderation," I say, watching the scene.

"Why should they?" Alicia responds. Her attention to her task is very focused, and she does not look up. "This is life! The milk is life itself. There's no need for moderation."

"You do it," Nicky says, meaning himself. He wants to feed the lamb now. He stands beside the armchair, leaning against his grandmother's arm.

"Yes," she says, "but hold tightly. He's very strong."

He puts his hands where hers are, and she moves her own hands off the bottle, but still holds it between her knees. The lamb now cannot possibly pull it from Nicky's grasp, though Nicky is tickled by its attempts to do so. Every time the lamb tugs and guzzles at the bottle Nicholas is overcome by giggles, but hangs on. Alicia hugs him, the lamb drains the bottle, and then it sneezes. We all laugh, and the feeding is over.

"Babies are timeless!" sighs Alicia. I agree, though I suppose in a way it is a contradictory statement, as babies also require such limitless quantities of one's time.

When we feed the lamb late on Monday afternoon, Alicia disappears from me, in her way, losing herself in the view outside the window as the sky over the inlet turns a deep, bleeding rose color, and the trees darken into silhouettes. The feeding is over, but my mother has not noticed this. The lamb is sucking air, not milk, from the black nipple, but Alicia is looking out the window, not paying attention to the lamb at all. She is sitting very still. She blinks once, then twice, and I reach over and remove the bottle from her hands. The lamb sputters, licks its lips, totters, and collapses with satisfaction back down into the cardboard box.

"It's very beautiful," I say, as quietly as I can, and let my gaze follow Alicia's toward the black branches, the red sky. We are alone together this time. Nicky is in the living room, having fallen asleep there on the sofa about half an hour earlier.

Alicia does not answer me.

"It is very beautiful," I repeat, a little bit louder, and all at once Alicia wakes up, or comes back, or whatever it is that she does.

"Yes," she says, "it is very beautiful. It always was." She gets up, a little stiffly, this time, and we go downstairs together. I turn on the light at the top of the landing so that both of us can see our way.

# Chapter

## 12

ALICIA and I and Nicky go shopping on Tuesday morning, in preparation for an international tea party. Mark will be coming later in the day with his associates, whoever they are. We don't know how many people he is bringing, but at breakfast Alicia and I recall that the environmental research team includes scientists from all parts of the world. What should we serve with the tea?

"Pastry?" hazards Alicia thoughtfully as she drinks her coffee. "Croissants and brioche? Or am I feeling too breakfastish? Fruit tarts, like the ones we had in Switzerland?"

If that's what you're looking for, there's a great French bakery on the way to Norwalk," Martha suggests. She has stopped in on her way to school to offer her help with any necessary preparations for this afternoon, and Alicia instantly begs her to join us.

"We need your linguistic ability!" Alicia says. "We really do!" Martha gets up to leave, laughing.

"It would be wonderful if you came, but don't feel you have to," I say as I walk along with Martha, or rather run with her, to her car. She is trying to give me directions to the French bakery without making herself late for school. "Your day must be pretty hectic already."

"Second stoplight, at the gray church, take the rotary. I'd love to come if I can help at all, and anyway I'm dying of curiosity about Mark, so I'd come even if I couldn't. Remember, it's the second stoplight. Don't turn at the first one or you'll end up in all kinds of construction. I don't know what they're building, but they've been at it ever since I moved here. I can't figure out how anything could possibly take so long."

If I don't ask her now it will be too late. "Martha, would you ever consider working for Alicia? Part-time?"

"What?" Martha has opened her car door, but does not get in. Her son is already inside, tautly silent with the fear of being late for the bell.

"Would you consider working for Alicia? Helen said you and she had discussed something like it together." Helen and I talked on the telephone for a long time late last night, and we agreed that I would approach Martha today, and she would follow up with a phone call tonight. Martha seems the perfect solution. She loves Alicia, and besides that she needs the money, according to Helen. She has been thinking about trying to find a part-time job to supplement her teaching, which is in itself a part-time job. Best of all, Martha is already here, a friend who lives next door and comes in and out of the house daily anyway, to visit or to bring food or to share a walk or a book or a meal. She is not an interloper in the household. This will be critical to Alicia. For half a century she has valued her privacy, independence, and solitude above all other things. And she will never stop drawing her curtains against watchers.

"Helen said we discussed a part-time job? For me? With Alicia?" Martha looks completely taken by surprise.

"Helen said you talked about Alicia maybe needing someone who could keep her life going the way she likes it."

"Yes, but not me! I have no training."

"Training for what?"

"I don't know . . . a secretary? A nurse of some kind, if it gets really hard for her?"

"But there's no need for a nurse or even a secretary, is there? We thought it should just be a person, someone who could come in for a while every day and kind of pull the ends together, remind her how she normally runs her life, if she forgets. You do the kind of thing I'm talking about already, without even thinking about it. But what if it turned into a real job? For money?"

I hope Martha will not be insulted. Thank God Alicia *has* money. I don't want to think about all the Alicias who do not, women just as independent, just as sensitive, who have no choice but change, disruption, dependency, lack of privacy, and the death of one's own chosen life, which is the only life that counts for most of us. When we lose it we lose ourselves.

"Oh." Martha realizes what I am saying. "I see. I was thinking of someone more professional."

"But that's just it! Alicia would hate the idea of "someone more professional," no matter how well qualified. She'd resent it and it wouldn't be fair to the person, let alone Alicia. Do you see what I mean? She wouldn't want someone professional in her home unless she very clearly *needed* that person in a professional way. I suppose that may come, someday. But now is too soon. She would think there was something wrong with her, and she'd . . ."—I search for the word I want—"she'd wilt, I think."

"Yes, she would. Because she's not sick," says Martha slowly. "I see."

"Exactly. Helen called her doctor yesterday morning. She was afraid he wouldn't talk to her without Alicia's permission, but he said he was very glad to talk. He also said there's really nothing wrong with Alicia."

"No, nothing wrong," Martha says. "That's not it."

"But it's been different lately—we know that. She knows it too, I'm sure she does. The doctor said she was aware of differences in herself, but he said that whatever they are they can't be detected with tests. He did a bunch of tests with her last checkup. Nothing on the CT scan, nothing on the sonograms, no cardiac problem, nothing in the urinalysis. Nothing wrong."

Martha nods her head, as if this all makes sense to her, and I go on.

"The funny thing, as a matter of fact, is that it was Alicia herself who insisted upon the tests. That's why the doctor told Helen she's aware. He personally would not have recommended so many of them, because she always does so well, and he doesn't like to get older people involved in testing where it isn't absolutely necessary. It's stressful and expensive, and frankly there's no point. But she talked him into it, so he went ahead. And they didn't come up with a thing."

"Nothing at all," says Martha. "I see. She wanted to know what was going on."

"And they couldn't tell her," I finish. "So she still doesn't know."

"She knows," says Martha.

"Yes. Even if the doctor doesn't have a name for it, or there isn't a name for it. But he did say to Helen that he recommended Alicia have someone with her for increasing amounts of time each day. And later on, probably all of the time."

"He told Helen that? Did he tell *her* that?" Martha is angry, as I was.

"Well," I say, with a sigh, and there are tears behind the sigh but I find I am able to keep them there, "I guess he did. That's why he was glad Helen called. He's been worried, too—he was afraid she might not do anything about it."

"Aha."

"Aha. He was right, of course. She didn't do anything about it."

"No." We are both still, then I begin again.

"That's why we thought of you. You're already here. She doesn't have to do anything about it if it's you. You're a friend, almost family, in fact. Alicia knows you need another job. You've mentioned that to her, right?"

"Yes. Once or twice, not too seriously, but I did. She was sympathetic. In fact she said she'd try to think of something," Martha recalls, smiling.

"Maybe she has. Maybe this is all her idea. ESP," I say, returning the smile.

Martha remains half-standing in her car doorway, for long enough so that I can tell that she is taken with the idea of the job. I can also see that Noah is now really frantic, tapping a fast drumbeat on his knees with all ten fingers.

"Think it over. Wouldn't it make sense?"

"Maybe it would." Martha finally gets in the car, and for Noah's benefit, I close the door as soon as she sits down in the driver's seat. For a second she stares at the windshield, but Noah hisses something to her, and she sits up abruptly and starts the car. She rolls down the window before putting it in gear, though.

"Wait, Cress. Have you asked your mother about this?"

"Not yet. We will. We thought we should try you first. We're pretty sure she'll love the idea." Even to myself I sound tentative.

"Maybe," Martha says. "But talk to her. Then ask me again. And you should also figure out what the job *is,* so I know what I'm thinking about. Hours, specific tasks, stuff like that."

I shrug. "I don't know what's to figure, really. You and Alicia can probably work it out best."

"You could be right," she says. She speeds out of the driveway, scattering gravel in a way that should make Noah feel a lot better.

The French bakery is easy to find, not too far off Post Road, which does have a great deal more traffic than I remember, and a multitude of new stores, all very different from what I knew when I grew up in Fairfield County. We had five-and-dime stores with thousands of tiny toys in bins, heavy-duty hardware stores that still carried some farming supplies, some sedate 1950s clothing boutiques, and a few sports stores that really sold sports equipment—fishing rods and rifles, maybe a hunter's vest or two—but certainly did not have racquetball equipment or hundred-dollar sneakers in their windows. Life was never this upscale when I lived here, I am thinking, reminding myself of my brother Luke.

Alicia and I park at an angle in front of the bakery window. Our view of its interior is obscured by red-checked and ruffled café curtains and a collection of little white signs advertising the wares in French: *tartes aux framboises, baguettes* in architect's printing. The signs also advertise soups du jour and pâteés de this and that, as well as breads and tarts and croissants and several varieties of Brie and Havarti and Danish blue cheese. One sign even says FONDUE!, which makes me expect a restaurant, but inside the shop it is a real bakery. Long, fragrant, freshly baked loaves of bread of all thicknesses fill baskets and bins everywhere I look. I see everything from brittle sticks as thin as Nicky's wrist to fat loaves the size of my lower thigh, just coming out of the oven. I want to break the ends off these and stuff the soft bread steaming into my mouth. I could eat French bread like angel cake, myself, and the loaves are as delightfully mysterious as so many stalagmites to Nicky, who runs from one part of the store to the other, sniffing at the bread loudly, probably because the first thing I did when I stepped into the shop was to take a deep, satisfied breath myself.

"The smell of France," Alicia says. I am glad to believe this, but before I can pursue this line of thinking we are approached by a well-scrubbed and charming young woman in a red-checked apron, a girl about Sarah's age with very dark hair and very red cheeks. She wraps up our pastries and breads and cheeses and slips Nicky a little piece of warm bread, broken off a long loaf on the counter. He nibbles it like cotton candy at a fair, and stares at her, smitten.

Back in the car again we run into our first snag of the day. I am about to turn around, looking for a highway entrance that will take us away from all the traffic accumulating at the stop-lights along Post Road, when Alicia speaks to me.

"Actually it's a little further up, I think," she says pleasantly. "Near the old Howard Johnson's."

My heart sinks. She is thinking of the Howard Johnson in Darien, surrounded by exits and entrances to the thruway. We are five miles north of it. She has forgotten where we are. Well, I will simply take over, gently but firmly.

"You know, Alicia, I really have the feeling that if we make a U-turn and go back toward Norwalk a little way, we'll find a highway entrance," I say.

"Yes, but you don't have to. You can go to the one just past the Howard Johnson's. It will be easier to go in that direction."

Gentleness, firmness. "We're almost in Norwalk, Alicia. I don't want to go all the way back to Darien to find a highway entrance."

She nods, but she is looking out the window now and does not respond further.

It turns out to be impossible to make a U-turn from the bakery parking area into the traffic, so reluctantly I head along Post Road again, the way Alicia suggested. It will be miles of stop-and-go driving before we get to the Howard Johnson in Darien. I am frustrated and irritated, until we pass a veterinary clinic that looks faintly familiar. I see, just ahead of it, a Lums restaurant, which I recognize as the painted-over haunt of my childhood—Howard Johnson. We used to go there on the way back from our doctor's office in Stamford. And then the building was sold to the Lums chain when I was in junior high school, I remember now. A little way beyond the restaurant is the highway entrance Alicia was referring to. I had forgotten it even existed. I hardly ever drive here anymore. But here it is, just where she said it would be.

I am so embarrassed that it is hard to apologize.

"I've been gone too long, Alicia. I forgot about the old Howard Johnson's—how dumb of me. I should have listened to you."

She turns to me, gracious. "Heavens, dear! How could you be expected to keep track of all these changes. It's just that I come this way so often with Felix. To the vet's, you see."

To the vet's. Of course she does. I even know that, that the vet was in Norwalk, just off the highway. Alicia told me this last week when we were talking about the first Japanese interview. She was chiding herself for not having taken Felix to the vet while the camera crew was here. The veterinarian's office was very convenient, just off the highway.

We pass big trucks on the highway, roaring between New York and New Haven, and Nicky points and exclaims. He doesn't see traffic like this at home. We look down on the tops of trees lining roads that pass under us, far beneath our interstate height. Once we see a graveyard that is set, unfortunately, between factories. I look at it quickly, then away. Graveyards we don't need. But soon after we pass it Alicia asks me, with a laugh still lingering in her voice, "Do you remember this?" She breaks into song, quavering, high pitched, and impeccably in tune:

> *And when I die,*
> *Don't bury me at all*
> *Just pickle my bones*
> *In al-kee-hol!*

It is one of Cal's old songs, the ones he used to hum on the way up the stairs, another Minnesota Funeral Dirge. To hear it again now in Alicia's well-bred eastern aristocrat's voice is too much for me. I start to laugh, and then she does too, and pretty soon neither of us can stop. In the back seat Nicky tries to join us, but he gives up long before we do, lapsing into a pleased but puzzled silence. We continue to laugh, and to laugh and to laugh, sitting side by side in the car while the smell of French bread surrounds us and the tears stream down our faces.

The water is hot and the tea things are laid out in the living room by four-thirty on a tea tray on the long table. The tray is laden with primrose-patterned china teacups and saucers. (Since we don't know how many guests there will be, we have set out eight of each, hoping that will be enough.) I remember the primrose pattern from my grandmother's, Alicia's mother's, tea table, and the little teapot too, and the silver sugar tongs and matching teaspoons, all in their gleaming lightness. Each time I see these things I remember being six years old, grouped with my siblings and our cousins, twelve of us altogether, around a very small, white-haired, formal grandmother who believed in teaching children manners at meals. (And in our

family, tea is a meal.) We sat quietly while she made and
poured the tea, then offered us sugar lumps and slices of lemon
to go with it. I liked the lemon slices best. There were dozens
of them: wafer thin and evenly sliced, as tempting to me as
golden coins in their little dish. I never dared take one when it
was offered, though. I didn't know what to do with it.

I was one of the younger cousins, honored to be included
in the ritual but wary of the tea, though what was poured in
my cup was thinned with hot water from a second pot, and
always very weak, hardly more than colored water. I was even
more wary of my grandmother herself, with her silver teaspoons and her china cups and her enormous house, where the
rooms were full of furniture and draperies and bookshelves that
reached from the floor to the ceiling. And the ceilings were so
high, and the voices were as soft as the carpets underfoot, and
everything was polished—the floors, the windows, the high
foreheads of the people who brought the tea things in and out
of the room.

Then one day my grandmother leaned over as I sat next to
her, and whispered to me. She said that if I let two lumps of
sugar dissolve in the hot water, and then put in two slices of
lemon, and pressed the lemon slices *hard* with my spoon, I
would like my tea much better. Here—she would show me.
And she then took up the sugar tongs with her hand, and took
with them not two but three sugar lumps, and as many golden
slices of lemon, and she put all this in my cup and pressed the
lemon and smiled right at me. Go ahead! Try it! So I did, very
carefully, with the tip of my tongue at first. Then she watched
me to be sure I discovered she was right, and when I nodded,
shyly, she looked at me with such a message of enjoyment that
I could not miss it: You see? Life is not as fearsome as you
think. You simply have to put the right things in it. Don't
forget, now! And that look of my grandmother's told me who
she was and who I was at the same time, and from then on I

loved her. She died when I was nine years old, but to this day, anytime I can get it, I still take extra sugar *and* extra lemon, both. It's the only way to go.

Punctually at five o'clock, a car I have never seen before pulls into Alicia's driveway. Martha and I are in the kitchen, warming the teapot by pouring a little hot water in it and then emptying the water out again and filling the warmed pot entirely the second time, as Alicia has taught us to do. Alicia and Nicky are with Felix in the living room, and I am thinking about the lamb's next feeding time, which will come inconveniently soon.

Three people get out of the car. The first is a child. He looks a little older than Nicky—maybe four? But a woman has gotten out just after him, and bends over, hiding him from view as she does something at his level—zipping up his jacket, I'd bet; it is cold at this time of day. Finally, from the driver's side of the car, my brother Mark emerges. He straightens himself, then looks up at the house. Foolishly I wave at him from the window, eager and inane. Martha, who has been staring as I have at the three, now laughs at me.

"Who on earth—?" I say, and she shakes her head, shrugging.

"I guess we're about to find out."

We open the kitchen door and greet them much too loudly as they come up the walk. "Hi! Nice to see you!" I call out.

The three visitors stop dead in their tracks, then Mark lifts his hand once, like a cop directing traffic, and grins at us. A shy cop, but friendly.

The woman is very dark, with shoulder-length straight hair and a broad, peaceful face. She smiles slowly at the two of us. The child shrinks back under her arm, and her hand rests on his head. He has her coloring, but with a thick head of curls, like Nicky's. His body looks nervous, like Mark's today. Only the woman seems at ease.

"Come in, come in!" I babble and beckon.

"Alicia is in the living room," Martha calls. We are hanging out of the door like twin idiots, and I start to giggle. She does too.

"Stop it!" I say, with an effort. "We *have* to stop it. Oh God. Think of how they must feel."

"Yes, I know. I'm sorry." It takes a second or two, but we are composed when the visitors come through the door.

"Hello!" I say brightly to the woman and the little boy, who is still glued to his mother, and looking at the floor.

She smooths his hair and says to me, "Hello, Cress. I am so glad to be meeting you."

The smile is warm, kind. I can understand the comfort the boy must feel under her hand. Her accent is so foreign that I wonder if she speaks any other English at all, or only these ten words of greeting, rehearsed for this occasion.

"Cress. This is Francesca." Mark looks at me with a sibling's meaningful smile now. Trust me, help me out a little here. "My wife."

Years of habit make me react without a pause. "Hello, Francesca! I am so glad to be meeting you, too!" I almost extend my hand to shake hers, but then instead I stand on tiptoe, and reaching over the child's head without touching him, I put my hands on her shoulders lightly and kiss her first on one cheek and then the other.

"Welcome," I say. "Welcome to the family."

"Yes," she says. That's all.

"And this is our son," Mark continues, with the same look. "Carlo."

He now squats down in front of the little boy and murmurs something in another language. The little boy shakes his head, vehemently. Mark speaks again, then the woman interrupts him, low voiced, shaking her head. Mark stands up again, smiles, and raises his eyebrows at her and then at me, apologetically.

"Shy," he says to me. "Sorry!"

"Don't be silly!" I say, smiling at the mother—a pale northern imitation of her smile, I am sure. "It's fine! My kids never even used to . . ."

"But I don't understand," says a voice from just behind me. I turn to see Alicia, with Nicky behind her. "I just . . ." Her voice is small and odd, and I am afraid, suddenly, for all of us. She is looking at Carlo in great bewilderment, and then she says to me, standing closest to her, "Is this the lost child?"

Martha hears and understands her words, and Mark and I do, but not the others. I look at Martha before answering, and I take it as slowly as possible.

"No. This is Mark's son. His name is Carlo."

"Carol?" She looks at the little boy again. He has not spoken or looked at any of us. "But, is this the lost child?"

"This is the *found* child, Alicia," I say again, now thinking I am crazy and yet saying it again. "This is the *found* child, not the lost child. This is Mark's son. His name is Carlo, not Carol. He's Mark's little boy. Carlo."

"Carlo," Mark repeats, louder. "His mother is Italian. Carlo. Like Carl, or Cal."

Alicia's face clears all at once. "Oh, I see," she says. "Of course. Mark, how happy I am. How wonderful that you should have a child. My dear," she says to Francesca, "I am so touched that you should come with your family. I am so pleased that you have come to see me. Thank you."

"Yes," says Francesca, without haste, "it is a good idea. I am saying this to Mark. Many times."

"I *was* saying this," he corrects her automatically. "I'm sorry, Mother. It was difficult . . . there were reasons." He calls her "Mother," now, I notice. Not Alicia.

"Never mind," she says. "I am so glad you are all here."

Reasons, I think? What reasons could there be? A wife and a child that nobody knows about? And the child is four years old? It crosses my mind that Carlo must have been born about the time that Jason died. That was the reason for Mark's absence at the funeral, but it can't be the reason for keeping the child's existence a secret afterwards. Not to tell us at all? I don't understand, but later I learn, as I watch this new family over the tea things. There was a complicated divorce settlement, I am told. There were questions about the child's protection— they were not married until recently, when everything was finally clear. I am soothed, later, most of all, by the mother's low voice and her constant awareness of the child, by her arms around him as he sits in her lap and clings to her, by her letting him push her arms aside and climb out of her lap to come across the room when Nicky and I bring the lamb downstairs, but also not changing position at all when he leaves, arms ready in case he should change his mind and run back to her. And I am soothed by the way Mark looks at these two, his wife and son in his mother's house, and by the knowledge that this is Mark's family, and he has brought them here to be part of ours.

But now Alicia is alert again, and says to me, "That was a lovely thought, Cress. The 'found child.' Lovely. I hope you still have a little time in your life for writing."

She walks over to this grandson she is meeting for the first time. Leaning down, she takes his hand. He does not look up at her, but he does not resist, either. His mother speaks to him quietly, smoothing his hair, and when she stops speaking he stands, as Nicky does sometimes, on tiptoe, and kisses Alicia's cheek. Then he draws back, except for one hand, which he has allowed her to keep in hers.

"Kiss!" crows Nicky, running into the scene headlong, and grabbing proprietarily at Alicia's leg. As she staggers Mark and I both move forward, but Francesca is quicker. She shoots out an arm to steady Alicia, then the instant Alicia is steadied she lets go.

"Oh! Thank you!" She smiles quickly at her new daughter-in-law, a little surprised. Francesca nods and murmurs something. I wonder if she knows the words, "You're welcome."

Mark and I are standing back a little from this scene, and the two boys are looking at each other from either side of their grandmother's body with mutual interest, but no speech. She looks down at each of them in turn, and extends her other hand to Nicky.

"Come with us, Nicholas," Alicia says to him. And then to Carlo, on her other side, she says, "I expect you must be very tired and hungry. You've come a long, long way."

# Chapter

# 13

I WATCH my son and Mark's son playing together on Alicia's living room floor, and it occurs to me that much of what is said about "language barriers" between people is probably nonsense. We do not have to learn each other's language literally before we can communicate, any more than these two children do. We only have to acknowledge the common language we already share, of eating and sleeping and working and playing and living with others, the language of the human family. Words of any language may be much less important than we think.

During our tea party there is a lot of effort spent on words, at first. Alicia talks a good deal to the two children right away, introducing Carlo to the dog and pointing out the view and offering both boys cookies, which they are grateful to accept and then put immediately into their mouths, thus avoiding the social task of responding to all that she has said. They sit next to her on the sofa for a little while, chewing, big-eyed, until Carlo notices the blocks piled up in a corner of the room. He points at them, with an excited word to his mother. She starts to shake her head, then looks at Alicia, who nods and smiles, and the two boys slip like little seals off the sofa and onto the floor, where they quickly become immersed in play, oblivious to the adults who talk around them.

Martha starts a conversation in Italian with Francesca, but it is a quiet one and does not last long. Francesca occasionally addresses a remark to her husband or her son. Mark talks to me and Alicia and Martha for a while about his child, while Francesca watches him and seems to be listening intently to her husband's description, in rapid, enthusiastic English, of Carlo's shyness, Carlo's intelligence, his habits, his toilet training, the details of his birth. "Francesca was amazing! So *strong!* More than twenty hours in labor. I never really understood before the courage of women"—a foreign construction to his sentences now, as if he doesn't speak English often—"the sheer guts it takes to bear a child." He leans forward to offer us all, the women in the room, the prize of male admiration and respect. We smile and accept it, and Francesca and I find our eyes meeting in a little glance of amusement. What do they expect, anyway?

Alicia focuses her attention almost exclusively on her grandchildren. She turns and smiles at her son and his wife when they speak, though, and my sense is that they feel not neglected but embraced by her concentration upon the child. They watch as she watches, lean forward when she leans forward.

It is very intense, and at one point a little odd, the way she is staring at the children, without turning her head, for minutes at a time.

I say to Alicia, following her line of sight, "It's so much fun to see the boys together—Carlo and Nicky—and Felix," I add brightly. The dog has curled up beside the two boys on the rug.

She pulls back her gaze briefly and stares at me with the blank look I am coming to know, then she asks, on a blink, "And which one is Nicky? Is that your little dog?"

"That's my little *boy*," I say without a pause. I'm getting better at this. Her face clears.

"Such a nice little boy!" she agrees at once. Then we continue watching. Mark and Francesca, in conversation with one another, have not heard this exchange.

The time passes quickly. We have to feed the lamb twice—a delight to Carlo and a trial to Felix, who is again ejected from the room—and it is almost seven o'clock by the time Francesca murmurs to Mark again, and he stands.

"We should leave," he says regretfully. "I hate to say it."

"Why don't you come back tomorrow?" Alicia asks. "The boys enjoy each other so much."

Mark looks nervous. "Don't you have an interview tomorrow" he asks, "with the Japanese TV people? Is that still on?"

"It's at eleven. They said it would only take an hour—no cameras." I say quickly. "Why don't you come earlier? You could even leave Carlo here during the interview and take a walk, show Francesca where you grew up. I bet she'd love that."

"Yes, I think that would be very nice," says Alicia. I suspect she means that it would be nice to have the children with her during the interview.

Mark speaks to Francesca, who looks very pleased indeed.

"Thank you, Cress," she says as she zips Carlo's jacket again at the kitchen door. I give her a hug. I don't know why I am so touched when I hear this new sister-in-law say my name. But as we wave the three visitors down the walk again, this time a quick-stepping, buoyant group, with Carlo on Mark's shoulders and the mother and father holding hands, I remember that we may be losing Emma, Luke's wife, at this very same time, and I think how strangely the tides of family life can ebb and flow, bringing close to us and then taking away with them again children, sisters, cousins, friends, and then, astonishingly, bringing these people back to us again.

The following morning's flow brings a thick-set Japanese man in a long black limousine. He seems to be in his sixties, wears a gray silk suit, and is accompanied by a trim, pretty young woman wearing a pumpkin-colored turtleneck tunic of a dress over leggings the same color. She tells us she will serve as his translator, and as she speaks I realize that she is the company representative in New York, the same woman I have spoken with on the phone. We greet each other with the pleasure of mutual relief. This meeting is finally taking place after all.

These visitors also sit with Alicia in the living room, but they do not take refreshment. Instead they have brought gifts, which Alicia opens while the two boys stand near her, watching her reveal from underneath layers of light tissue paper the outlines of a fan, first, then a little black lacquered box with a tall bird painted on it—a crane, I think—and finally an old photograph in a new silver frame. The photograph is again that sepia color I associate with horse-and-buggy days, but the frame could have been picked up at Tiffany this morning, and winks and gleams in Alicia's hand.

We all look at these things in a hush of good manners. I bless Carlo for his shyness and his silence. Nicky, too, has chosen to imitate his cousin's silence generally, perceiving it perhaps as a sign of maturity. Big boys don't speak.

The two boys lean over the photograph together, trying to see what it is. Alicia too seems puzzled, and studies it carefully. The man speaks to the woman, and she explains.

"He is the executive producer for our film, Mrs. Linley. He lives in Kyoto."

The man looks at the young woman and becomes animated, and to my great surprise chuckles and pats her on the shoulder and then on the knee. This is hardly the strict Japanese behavioral code one hears about. The young woman appears confused for a moment inside her elegant New York pumpkin shell, then she looks at us with the first sign of discomfort I've seen, and seems younger because of it.

"He wants me to tell you that he is my uncle," she says.

"Ah!" says Alicia, smiling brilliantly at the man. He nods many times, both at her and at the niece, who continues to speak only when he has finished nodding.

"He never leaves Japan. This time he did, because years ago, when he was a little boy like these," she indicates Carlo and Nicky, who watch her solemnly and also watch her uncle, smiling and nodding at Alicia as the words come out, "you came to see him. It is shown here."

"I came . . . ?" Alicia stares harder at the photograph, and her face gets pink. Her hand goes to her throat.

I walk over to her and sit down beside her on the sofa. There is that young woman in the photograph I've seen so often, puffy in her flying suit, and there is the slim, much taller young man with her. My parents, yes, in this man's scrapbook. But in Alicia's arms is a little Japanese boy, not more than two years old—younger than these two, certainly—and he is frowning at the camera, round-faced.

"Show-bee!" says the man suddenly to Alicia, pointing at the child in the photograph, beaming. She looks at me. I don't have a clue. She smiles back at him, still very pink.

"What does he say?" I ask the young woman, quietly.

The translator clears her throat. "It is English. He says: chubby." She smiles too, a little hesitant. Chubby. A joke. We all smile.

"That is good." Alicia says to him. "Chubby babies are good."

The woman translates, the man laughs. "Show-bee!" he says again, pointing to himself.

"Still chubby," murmurs the translator, "he says."

Now the man, still gazing at Alicia, speaks very fast in Japanese, and the woman pauses for a moment after he has finished speaking before she translates again.

"He says you came to see him, as you see in the photograph. And you held him up, like this. And you gave him, you know," she is perhaps a little embarrassed, "a kiss." The last word is a little louder than the others. Loud enough for Nicky.

"Kiss!" he shrieks, and launches himself at Alicia. She catches him with one arm as he kisses her the old noisy way, his urge to be silent having vanished.

"Kiss!" repeats Carlo, and more decorously salutes her cheek from his own side.

"Well!" laughs Alicia. "I don't know! All these kisses! Grandchildren," she says through her blushes to the man who claims she has kissed him, too, "are the love affair of old age."

The woman translates, the man laughs and speaks again.

"He has three grandchildren, also," says the woman.

"Good," says Alicia.

"Good. Yes," says the man. He gets up now, bends over her, and kisses her hand. Then he looks at the grandsons on either side of Alicia.

"Kiss," he says. From him it is a verb, a grandfather's bit of advice. While still standing, he speaks again to his niece.

"He has something for you," she tells Alicia. Alicia makes ladylike, demurring gestures with her hands.

"But he has given me so many gifts already!" She waves at

the fan and the box in its wrappings. The man, meanwhile, is reaching into the breast pocket of his suit. From it he takes a white handkerchief, not new but very clean, and evidently there is something inside. Without unwrapping it he starts talking to Alicia, a continuous stream of words that fall now in the cadences of a story. His niece translates as fast as she can.

"He was with his mother—she was a worker at the hospital near where you landed—and there was no one to greet you, but she saw you arrive, and she came with him in her arms to greet you herself. She was the first one. And you had to unload the airplane, no—" The woman stops, puzzled. The man speaks again.

"Ah. The airplane was not an airplane merely, it was . . ."

"It was the seaplane," Alicia tells her, looking directly at her, and then straight up at the uncle. "And your mother came, with you in her arms. She wore blue, I remember. She wore a lovely blue wrapper."

I look at the translator, who is speaking rapidly to the uncle. A blue wrapper? But he nods his head, and grins, and nods again.

"She was beautiful! So young!" My mother says, and once again the man nods, and for an instant he wears the wistful expression of a man who was once a little boy with a beautiful mother, and remembers. "And we had landed in the water, and there was no one to help unload the supplies. So she was going to run back to get the other people, but she had the baby—she had you in her arms." The man nods with delight as the translator conveys this, faster and faster. "And so I took the baby while she ran back—I held you," she finishes with laughter, in triumph holding up the photograph to get a better light.

He keeps on talking, and unwraps the handkerchief to take out something.

"I became . . . fussy, when my mother left me . . ."(I am wondering what "fussy" translates from—a tantrum? Yells, screams, kicks?) "And you gave me this tissue—no, this hand-kerchief." The niece draws out the syllables with precision: "Hand-ker-chief"—probably she normally says "Kleenex," just the way the rest of us do. "And your husband gave me this, to play with, and then the people came, and someone took the picture, and then there were more people and they took you away before I could give it back to you. And now I have brought it with me, for you."

He holds it out to her in the palm of his hand, an army compass, dull green, the glass polished to a shine, the needle fluttering like an eyelash inside, pointing true north.

It does not look like an unusual compass. Cal had several of these, Joe has at least two, and you can buy them in any army-surplus store today. But Alicia looks at this compass as if it were the only one in the world.

"I cannot tell you how much it means to me to have this again," she says, reaching up and taking it into her own hand, handkerchief and all. "It's exactly what I need. Thank you."

When uncle and niece leave the house later, in a multitude of nods and smiles on all sides, Alicia waves at the limousine from the time it begins backing down the driveway until it disappears out on the main road.

"Now that," she says when she closes the front door at last, "is a gentleman of the old school. And he had such a lovely mother!"

I will drive back to Vermont on Thursday morning with Nicky and the lamb. Mark and his family will come to Vermont in the summer, they promise. Martha will work for Alicia, start-ing this week. They have both accepted the proposal, each with her own kind of grace. To bolster it, Helen confided to Alicia on the telephone in the evening before I left that Martha was looking for a part-time job, and I asked the next morning if it might not be a good idea for Alicia to hire her to do whatever she might need done, on an informal basis.

"Secretary? Chauffeur? Cook? Tutor in romance languages? Think what a bargain! And you used to always have a little extra help around here, it wouldn't hurt to have it again, would it?"

"No, dear, it certainly wouldn't," my mother said over the rim of her coffee cup.

"And it would be a kindness, I think . . ."

"Yes, it certainly would be a kindness . . ." Alicia smiled at me. I looked hard at her and she looked right back at me, still smiling, and patted my hand. "It would, Cress. I'm not really teasing you. Don't worry."

"I do need the extra money," says Martha to Alicia later. We are all together, in the kitchen, just before I leave. "But I don't want to get in your way. If there's anything you don't like, just fire me. Right away, if you think it's a bad idea!"

Alicia laughs. "But I think it's a lovely idea," and after that there is really no more to be said.

I love to drive north. I am heading toward my own home, my own adult place, my own life, and I feel freer with every mile. I also love the driving itself, just driving. I always have. I like being a part of the moving arterial busy-ness and hum of the world of roads, of city and country, highway and back street, suburb and farm. For a while I travel right under the V of a group of wild geese who have joined me near Bridgeport. They are heading north as I am, this season, flying into an ambiguous but inevitable spring of their own. We move along together and I remember someone telling me that flocks of birds only *seem* to have one leader when they are flying in this formation, but the truth is that they have many. The lead bird will drop back when it is tired and let another one take over, then another one will take that one's place when the time comes, and so on. Each bird takes its turn, and in that way the group maintains both strength and direction. This flock will fly north over the landscape I see from the highway, covering with its many wings the mountains and the rivers and the roads and the little towns and farms of New England, as their kind have done for generations. If they have their own names for the mountains, they're not telling, or maybe they just write them in the air.